Praise for Meg Allison's *Secrets and Shadows*

4.5 Flags! "Secrets and Shadows by Meg Allison is a refreshing read. I really enjoyed this story. The story has quality to it that I found very nostalgic. ...The plot and secrecy of things that occur within the story were skillfully written and quite engrossing.... The story also has a sensual edge to it. In today's day and time, more and more romance stories have become overly erotic with the usage of vulgar words. But Meg Allison's love scene shines through without the use of such words and is just as equally appealing...." ~ Chantay, Euro Reviews

4 cups! "Fraught with lushly written twists and turns, this story is a fantastic read. The author has created two characters with strength and vulnerabilities that endear, and the danger that lurks around every corner leaves you guessing right up to the very end. The smoldering sexual tensions that grow page by page are the crowning touch." ~ Charissa, Coffee Time Romance

Four Angels! "... *Secrets and Shadows* has it all, action, thrills and chills, suspense, and the best of all, a kick butt romance. Jason is a hero to drool over and Sabrina is a very strong independent woman that hides her feelings. *Secrets and Shadows* is a fabulous read and Ms. Allison is an author to watch for and the books to come...." ~ Sonya, Fallen Angels Reviews

Secrets and Shadows

Meg Allison

A Samhain Publishing, Ltd. publication.

Samhain Publishing, Ltd.
2932 Ross Clark Circle, #384
Dothan, AL 36301
www.samhainpublishing.com

Editing by Sara Reinke
Cover by Vanessa Hawthorne

First Samhain Publishing, Ltd. electronic publication: August 2006
First Samhain Publishing, Ltd. print publication: November 2006

Dedication

So many people have helped with this book over the course of its incarnations, that I couldn't possibly list everyone. Please know that you all have my heartfelt thanks.

This story is specially dedicated to those who have gone the extra mile:

My editor, Sara Reinke, for loving the story as much as I do despite any 'cheesy' dialog she may have found

Laura Hamby, critique partner and reformed English teacher, for being my last line of defense

June Frederick, my mom and best friend, for making sure I didn't give up on the dream

My children, for letting mom on the computer now and then

And to Steve, my very own hero, for being my biggest fan.

Chapter One

Sabrina jerked awake and blinked as a shrill ring pierced the darkness.

The phone trilled again, jangling across her taut nerves and wrenching her mind from the soft shadows of sleep to sharp focus. It was him. It had to be.

She glanced at the instrument on her bedside table and sat up. Her gaze darted anxiously around the room as she searched the shadows, but the room was empty.

The emptiness of the small, dark apartment settled like a fog around her. Suffocating. Isolating. She swallowed hard, reaching a shaking hand out as the phone rang for the third time. She had to answer. She couldn't spend her life afraid to pick up the telephone. Her heart thudded as she took a deep breath and forced her fingers around the receiver. Her throat tightened.

"Hello?"

The subtle breathing on the other end made her shudder. She closed her eyes. After a moment of complete silence came the voice she'd begun to dread.

"Never fear, my love." The deep, muffled timbre sent a chill down her spine. It struck some chord of her memory. "No one will harm you again, Sabrina-fair. I watch over you. Forever."

A click and the line went dead. She stared at the silver-gray shadows that poured across the floor and splashed against the wall. She frowned, straining to remember why the voice somehow seemed familiar, like a blurred image in an old photograph. Her hand trembled as she hung up.

He had called before.

The first few times, her stomach hadn't dipped and churned with fear. It had simply been a distorted voice she couldn't place. A faceless shadow falling across her life.

Sabrina hadn't been afraid of the dark since she was six years old. Now she saw monsters lurking in every corner. She wanted to hide, wishing the whole thing would go away or, better yet, pretend it wasn't happening. But this goblin was real. She hadn't met it face-to-face, but somehow she knew that would be the next step.

The phone rang again and she bolted off the bed toward the other side of the room. Her heart pounded so hard she thought it would burst. Her gaze fixed on the telephone as she fumbled for her robe hanging behind the closet door.

She wanted to dive beneath the covers and pull them over her head, like she had as a child. Back then, angry voices in the house had echoed down the corridor, confusing her and making her insides shake like jelly. But she was a grown woman now—alone, on her own. There was no situation she couldn't handle and no quilt thick enough to protect her from her fears, real or imagined.

She flicked on the lights and inched toward the nightstand. Drawing in a deep breath, she picked up the receiver and waited.

"Hello?" Her eyes flew wide at the sound of the familiar voice—a voice straight out of the past. But it couldn't be him…could it? "Sabrina?"

The tension in her shoulders melted a little, even as she struggled to focus her racing thoughts. "Y-yes?"

"Sabrina, it's Jason…Jason Sinclair."

"Yes…yes, I know," she replied, hoping her voice didn't shake like the rest of her. "I recognized your voice. It's been a long time."

"Ten years," he said, then cleared his throat. "I'm sorry to call like this, but I thought you should hear it from me instead of the morning paper."

"What?" Tension gripped her again, her muscles going rigid. The soft glow of lamplight did little to dispel the shadows that still lingered in the corners of the shabby little room.

"Your father had an accident." Her stomach tightened. "His car went off the mountainside earlier this evening. I'm sorry, Sabrina. They said he died instantly."

The image of her father's face flashed before her: clear blue eyes, straight nose; handsome, angry, demanding that she leave and never come back. The knife twisted in her heart. Hate. How she wanted to hate the man, to shrug away the news of his death like it didn't matter. Her heart fractured despite the fact that she'd spent the last six years convincing herself she didn't care.

Daddy.

"Oh, no...no." She swayed on her feet. "Th-that's not possible. He...he was a good driver."

"Sabrina, I don't know what to say. I wish..."

The hand holding the receiver dropped to her side as she sank down onto the firm mattress. Jason's voice faded. She stared at the mirror across the room. A bit of her father's features gazed back at her, the same dimpled chin, a frown line etched between full brows. She looked like her mother, but had always somehow been her father's image as well, their main difference being he'd never laughed. Not with her.

"Sabrina?" Jason's urgent call reached up to her. She lifted the receiver.

"I'm sorry. What did you say?"

"I said I wish there was an easier way to tell you..." His voice trailed off and she wondered what else she had missed. "The funeral will be Wednesday at the family cemetery."

"Yes, of course." She took a deep breath. "I'll be there."

Silence stretched between them, pulling at her already taut nerves. Jason sighed. "Sabrina, are you sure you want to do this? No one would blame you for not coming home."

"Yes, yes, I do. I owe him that much."

"Okay, then I'll meet you at the airport. Just call as soon as know what flight you'll be taking."

"No!" The thought of seeing Jason made her insides churn. She had to put off the inevitable, if only for a while. "I'll take a cab. There's no reason for you to go out of your way."

"There's every reason in the world," he said. "We were friends once. Maybe it's the least I owe you."

She didn't know what to say. Silence seemed the safest reply.

"Sabrina, are you there?"

"Yes, I'm here. I'm fine."

Jason sighed. "I am sorry…for everything. Call me."

She hung up, her head spinning with a montage of surreal images. Dead. Her father was dead. Sinking back into the pillows, she curled her body into a small ball and thought of the other phone call. The one from her creepy admirer. It couldn't be related. *No, that's insane.*

She squeezed her eyes shut to block out a sudden wave of nausea and pain. It couldn't be connected. It was an accident. Only an accident.

* * *

The flying tin can that passed as a charter plane jumped and jerked down the short runway as the pilot announced their arrival at Pocono Mountains Municipal Airport. Dark gray clouds that had followed the flight since La Guardia now hovered above, leaking in a steady drizzle that resembled a depressed crying jag not unlike the one Sabrina had suffered on the night she'd heard of her father's death. The mountaintop airport seemed an afterthought among the tall trees and for a moment upon landing, Sabrina's mind had created a picture of the bouncing airplane crashing into the thick brush.

She sighed and unfolded herself from the hard seat, promptly bumping her temple on the overhead baggage compartment when she stood. Pain shot through her skull. Her legs ached in protest, whether to her sleepless nights, the damp weather or her confined flight, she couldn't be sure. But this was no way to arrive home after six long years. Then again, she never thought she'd ever come there again. Life had a funny way of throwing curves when least expected.

"Can I help you, Miss Layne?" the flight attendant asked brightly. Sabrina cringed at the saccharine sweetness in the women's voice and smile. In her present state of mind, it was like rubbing salt in a wound. How could anyone, anywhere be *that* happy?

"No, thanks," she replied as she swung her overnight case down with a thump. "I've got it."

"Is there someone meeting you?" the attendant continued, insistent on making herself of use for some reason. Sabrina knew her father's death had been front-page news and had received the benefit of many helpful Samaritans during the weekend. Sad thing was, she'd never know if it was true concern or merely dollar signs that flashed in each stranger's smile.

"No, I'll just phone for a taxi," she said.

Sabrina's cool manner and short replies seemed to squelch the woman's compassion. With a somewhat icy smile, she nodded and turned back toward the cockpit. As Sabrina bumped down the aisle in the attendant's wake, the events of the past two days floated through her mind. For a young woman who had lived most of her life on the fringes of her multi-millionaire father's spotlight, she still found it difficult to deal with the scrutiny—especially when the television and newspaper reporters saw fit to broadcast a list of David Anthony Layne's most recent and sordid indiscretions along with his obituary.

A blast of cold, wet wind sprayed through the portal as Sabrina stepped out of the plane. With careful, sideways steps, she descended the metal stairs with one hand clutching the rail while she fought to keep the overnight bag firmly on one shoulder with the other. She grimaced as the breeze blew her hair about and her black skirt plastered itself against her legs. There wouldn't be time to change before the funeral so she'd worn sedate black from head to toe. Now she wished she'd worn jeans and a turtle-neck.

The walk to the terminal took less than a minute, but her clothes were damp by the time she reached the doors. Stepping inside, Sabrina was surprised by how little anything had changed since she'd last went through the airport six years ago on her way back to New York. But then, it seemed very few things changed in the mountains of Pennsylvania—especially not where her father had been concerned.

Sabrina moved through the small terminal and passed beneath the metal detector without incident. After collecting her suitcase from the baggage claim area, she moved toward the front entrance where she hoped to find a cab waiting outside. It was then that she saw him, the sight making her heart race like a rabbit running from a wolf. Jason Sinclair's eyes bore into her across the threshold of the airport doorway. Then he nodded, a small smile curling his lips for a moment before disappearing.

She hadn't called as he'd instructed. She hadn't wanted to see him at her most vulnerable moment, but there he stood, a black chauffeur's cap in hand as the block-long limousine rumbled gently behind him at the curb.

"What are you doing here?" she demanded, hating that she couldn't see his eyes behind the dark lenses he wore. Too late to play it cool, she let her temper run free.

"You didn't call."

"No, I didn't. I can get a cab."

"You don't need a cab. I'm here."

"But—"

"It's my job."

A bucket of ice water in her face would've been more subtle. Of course it was just a job; that's all she'd ever been to the man. A job. An obligation. The geeky kid that no one wanted and who couldn't make any real friends. The memories still made her stomach twist painfully.

Sabrina hated feeling exposed in front of him, knowing every emotion showed clearly on her face. "Fine, you're here now, so I guess that's that. Can you stow my bag?"

"Yes, ma'am. Get in."

His formal address felt like a jab from a knife, but she ignored the feeling and climbed into back of the black car without another word. The partition between them remained closed as he got in front and drove out of the parking lot, down the mountain road toward the cemetery. She had enough to think about, to sort out, and her depressing past with the former chauffeur's son was not a topic she wished to contemplate at the moment. Jason would see her emotions as weakness; her adoration of him had been unwanted, detested.

She would not let herself care about him again. If Sabrina had learned one thing in the past six years, it was that showing weakness attracted the vultures, the ones that preyed on the lost and weary. Right now she had too many ghosts to deal with—foremost among them being that of her shattered relationship with her father.

Twenty minutes later, Sabrina stood apart from the crowd at the foot of her father's freshly dug grave. The rain coated her skin; its dampness seeped into her bones and deepened her already gloomy mood.

Her eyes burned with grit from sleepless nights and the early morning flight. The old priest raised his voice, his hollow words of the rote prayer resonated through her body, echoing the emptiness of her life and the desolation of her homecoming. Icy loneliness closed around her, yet she couldn't cry. Not even in regret.

The cleric waved his hand up and down, back and forth. Some of the mourners shifted on their feet, black umbrellas thumping together as they moved. A woman cried. It didn't seem fair that a stranger should be so overcome while she was unable to shed a tear. She glanced around in search of the sobbing woman. Her irritation grew as she realized she didn't recognize anyone but the lawyer at her side.

Who are these people? she thought.

Less than twenty men and women stood around her, most of them showing respect but very little remorse. Obviously her father's popularity hadn't improved since she'd left. Six years…it didn't seem like it had been that long. Yet, in some ways, it seemed much longer.

Her gaze rested on Jason, who stood several feet away, dressed in black from head to foot, his head bent as rain beaded on the silky black strands of his hair. How disconcerting to discover his presence still had the most peculiar effect on her. His take-charge methods and easy assurance rankled every independent nerve, even as his innate strength drew some deep part of her. The lost part that longed to trust. The lonely young girl who yearned to be in his arms.

"Are you all right, Sabrina?" The lawyer, Marcus Talbridge, moved the umbrella. But nothing could shield her from the numbing cold.

"Yes, I'm fine."

The priest cleared his throat, glancing at the two who had dared to whisper at the foot of the open grave. Sabrina turned her attention to the mound of dirt beside the slick, black casket. The scent of spring rain, fresh earth and lilies filled her senses. The prayers continued.

No, she was not all right. How could she be? How could she go from this day to the next wondering what had happened to make the man in that casket dislike her so intensely? Frustration gripped her by the throat, choking her when she realized how her father could still cause pain. Why did she long for his love after having spent most of her life telling herself she was better off without him and his millions?

Money. God, how she hated the money. The smell of it, the power behind it, the way it changed people.

People lied for money and the chance to be near the kind of wealth the Layne family commanded. When motives and friendship were suspect, trust became impossible. Being alone was easier than facing another lie and disappointment. Sabrina had learned that lesson the hard way time after heartbreaking time.

Memories flashed across her mind like a reel of home movies, but not the kind with smiling kids and parents at the Grand Canyon or backyard barbecues. In hers, there were countless arguments, weeks alone with the servants for company, her mother's funeral, her father's string of mistresses, her eviction from both his house and heart when she refused to follow his dreams.

She shrugged off the ancient images and focused on the flowers. Lilies…so many lilies. He hated them. Didn't his friends know that?

David Layne, wealthy financier and antiques dealer, dead at fifty-six. Money, power, women…but what good had it done him in the end? He still died alone. Just the way he had lived.

A tingle spread across her skin, the hair on the back of her neck lifted as she sensed Jason's gaze upon her. She looked up. His vivid blue eyes seemed to be the only source of color in the shades of gray surrounding them. He gave her a small smile. Sabrina frowned, her fingers digging into the black leather of her handbag.

After all that fuss about getting his MBA so young, it seemed strange that Jason would still be in Castle's Grove driving for her father. *He should be out running a major corporation or making millions on the Internet,* she thought.

She took a deep, ragged breath as she fought to ignore the way he could twist her inside-out with just one look. Sabrina tried to concentrate, reaching for a logical explanation for his presence. If anyone understood how dreams and plans could die, it was her.

Seeing him again shouldn't have hurt so much. But it did. He'd been the first man she'd ever loved, the first she'd dreamed of in the quiet lonely nights. The chauffeur's son had been the star of her erotic fantasies, the desire of her young heart. Her body had never ached for any man the way it had for him.

She shook her head in self-disgust. Here they were, burying the man she once called *Daddy* and one look from Jason's blue eyes sent her rocketing right back into puberty. Guilt wrapped around her as she tried to keep her attention on the funeral. But he made it so hard to stay centered. The tension in her shoulders ebbed when he looked away.

He was still beautiful. More so. The sight of him took her breath away like a cool drink on a hot, humid summer day. A thin, white scar on his jaw was the sole imperfection, the one reminder of the reckless boy he'd once been. Long, angular lines had filled out into a tightly honed physique that was emphasized by the cut of his dark suit. He looked strong and solid, despite the slight limp she'd noticed at the airport.

But it didn't matter how handsome he'd become. Jason had lied, like everyone else. Their friendship had meant nothing to him. She'd meant nothing.

The others began moving, pulling Sabrina from her thoughts as they murmured inadequate words of condolence. Many looked at her with more than a little curiosity. Had they come to grieve or get a good look at the disinherited debutante? No doubt she'd been the subject of much gossip in the small, mountain community.

She sighed. It wouldn't do any good to wallow in self-pity. Her father was gone and nothing could change that. Any chance they might have had to be a family died right along with him. Not that he had wanted one. No. Family had never been a priority on David Layne's agenda.

She felt a hand on hers and looked up at the lawyer. Such a nice man, about the same age as her father had been, but Talbridge appeared much older with his white hair and deeply etched worry lines.

"What do I do now?" Sabrina asked.

He smiled sadly. "You just let me take care of things. A small reception has been arranged for later this evening and then the will has to be taken care of before I leave for Pittsburgh."

"Oh, no. That has nothing to do with me, Marcus. I know he wrote me out when I…when I married Sam." Saying her ex-husband's name still left the malignant taste of betrayal in her mouth. "I really don't want to sit there and listen to how he's divided things up between his pet charities and his mistresses."

The lawyer's eyes grew wide in surprise and shock before narrowing again beneath a frown. "Young lady, you shouldn't talk about your father like that. As far as you being disinherited, well, that's just plain nonsense."

"But…but when I told him I was getting married, he said…"

"I don't know what he said," Talbridge interrupted. "I do know what he did and didn't do where legal matters are concerned. He never had you taken out of his will. But this is neither the time nor the place to discuss the details."

She didn't want the details. She didn't want the money and all the baggage that came with it—the lies, the games. Even from the grave, her father's legacy seemed determined to cast a shadow across her life.

Talbridge took gentle hold of her elbow and steered her around the headstones of white, gray and pink marble toward the road that wound through the graveyard. "Where's your car?"

She shook her head, her mind still reeling from the revelation that her father, a man of his word, had not cut her off without a dime as he had threatened.

"Jason picked me up at the airport."

"Well, maybe you should come with me now."

"What?" she asked, somewhat distracted as she mulled over the implications of what the will might contain.

They reached the narrow paved road and skirted around cars parked end to end. Rumbling sounds of engines being brought back to life seemed to mock the somber atmosphere of moments before. Ashes to ashes…and life went on.

Jason stood sentinel at the long, black limousine parked first in line. No one could leave until it did, unless they wanted to drive across the graves. He pulled the door open as they neared.

"Would you like me to drive you home?" Talbridge asked, his brisk pace slowing.

Home? Where on earth would that be? She wasn't sure she had a real home anymore. "Oh, no, thank you. I'll be fine."

"Miss Layne," Jason murmured with a polite nod. His eyes sparkled for a brief moment, calling to mind a tenderness she'd experienced so many years ago. But then it was gone.

"Well, then…" the lawyer hesitated. He wrinkled his nose and gave the younger man a look most people reserved for mud smeared on their shoe. "I'll see you later at the mansion. Do drive carefully, Jason. You've got precious cargo on board."

Jason's jaw tightened, the vein at his temple jumped. "Yes, sir."

Sabrina watched Talbridge walk toward the other cars, the umbrella bobbing above his head like a buoy on the ocean. It seemed incredible to her that the man would still condemn Jason for things that had happened a lifetime ago, even after he had been cleared of all blame.

"Are you coming?" Jason asked.

She frowned at the defensive inflection in his tone. "Of course. Why wouldn't I?"

He shrugged. Sabrina took a small step forward, hesitating when his warmth reached out and buffeted against the cold shroud that had settled over her skin. It was strange how his nearness revived the butterflies in her stomach and yet she still felt comforted by his strength.

She swallowed back the confusion and tried to smile. "I trust your driving."

"Do you?"

"Yes. I do." She turned and tucked herself into the spacious back seat.

* * *

Jason couldn't believe she was more beautiful than ever. How he wished she had stayed in New York, out of danger and far from the mess he had yet to get under control. Eight years working deep undercover with David Layne, posing as the millionaire's chauffeur, had taught him how dangerous the world could be.

Jason maneuvered the long car down the narrow lane to the graveyard gates. The small, private cemetery dated back to the Layne family's beginnings in the Pocono Mountains. They had been among the first to settle the rocky region. They had also been the first to cash in on what became that region's greatest tourist attraction—skiing. It was rumored that Sabrina's great-grandfather had garnered over three million dollars selling a portion of his mountains. The Layne men, generation after generation, had known how to spot a good investment when they'd seen it. Her father had been no exception.

After a brief pause at the entrance, Jason flicked a nervous glance at the rearview mirror. The tinted partition behind the driver's seat blocked his view.

It had been ten years since he'd last seen Sabrina. Ten long years of guilt over the way he'd hurt her and ruined their friendship. Leaving her and running off like a hunted man had been the stupidest move of his life, the one thing he still regretted. Four years later, he had heard she was getting married. By then, he'd been so deep in his new life with the CIA, he'd been too busy to give the event much more than a passing thought.

He should have stopped her. From what her father told him about the intended groom, Jason had felt she was making a big mistake—felt it to the bone. But instead, he had gone about his business and let her father handle the situation. The man had handled it all right. He'd practically pushed the girl into the gold digger's arms. Jason shook his head in disgust.

Why the hell did she have to come back now? He wasn't sure she'd return for the funeral...had hoped she wouldn't. Not until he knew who was responsible for her father's death. How was he going to keep her safe when he still wasn't sure who had rigged David's car to crash and burn?

This was why he hadn't gotten involved with anyone since joining the agency. It was bad enough when innocent strangers got hurt in the crossfire. But someone he knew? Cared about? He couldn't allow that to happen. He'd heard of the numerous marriages that died slow deaths from neglect. He'd seen what had been left of one poor slob's girlfriend who had been targeted when the man screwed up.

He would never involve a woman he loved or children of his own in that kind of danger, as David had. Jason chose his way of life for the excitement and the sense of making a difference in the world; of having a purpose beyond filling a back account and marking time until called to the grave. If it meant his life would remain a solitary one, so be it.

19

He could handle solitude. What he could not deal with was the kind of guilt that could rip you from the inside out. He understood it all too well. He'd dealt with it before and had lost a piece of himself that would never heal.

One choice that had gone horribly wrong. Homecoming night, his senior year in high school…he'd insisted his sweetheart drive because he and his buddies had too many beers down by the lake. Unable to handle the wheel on the backcountry roads, she'd lost control and wound up dead in a ditch. The all-consuming pain of it had almost killed him. If he hadn't been drinking like a fish, she might still be alive.

He swung the limousine out onto the winding mountain road, his hands guiding the vehicle as he remembered the time after the accident. A time when young Sabrina had helped and encouraged him to mend his broken body and shattered spirit. She had believed in his innocence when so many others had demanded he be charged with manslaughter.

Mountain hikes and moonlit swims, a special closeness he had shared with no other, fears revealed only to her. Such sweet passion and such soul-rending pain. He'd seen it all in her large, dark eyes the last time he'd turned away and walked out of her life. He'd lost his best friend that day.

But it wasn't entirely his fault. She'd wanted love—something that he could never offer. Sabrina had been like a little sister. A friend. With his life headed in an exciting and dangerous new direction, he'd known he could never expose her to whatever the future held. Even if he had wanted to.

Jason's thoughts jerked back to the present as a white-tail buck broke through the trees and landed on the road about twenty-five feet ahead. Pressing on the brakes, he watched the animal twitch its ears at the sound of the squealing tires. He pumped the pedal, steering into the skid and praying that the buck would move before the car fishtailed off the narrow road.

As if the spectacle of the long black car careening toward it finally registered, the animal hunched back on its powerful hind legs and sprang off into the woods on the other side of the road. It disappeared with a flick of its tail.

The car screeched to a halt on the damp pavement, lurching violently. Jason sat still, breathing hard and staring out the windshield. His knuckles were white from the iron grip he had on the wheel. He leaned back and sighed just as the partition slid down behind his head.

"What's going on?" Sabrina demanded as she peered through the opening.

He glanced back. To his relief, she seemed unharmed, though the flash of fire in her eyes told him she was more than a little angry.

"Sorry about that." His gaze rested on the curve of her cheek, the way her skin flushed a warm, rosy pink. "A buck jumped into the road. I had nowhere to go, but he decided this wasn't his day to die."

She sat up straight, peering into the dense growth. "Was he big?"

Jason smiled. "Just a two pointer, I'd say, but he'd better get some common sense if he wants to live longer."

Another impatient frown passed over her face. He remembered that frown; it etched a line between her brows every time she was concentrating or aggravated. That had been the expression on her face when he walked out after telling her he just didn't see her *that* way. What a liar. What an absolute jerk he'd been.

Pushing back the festering memories, Jason glanced at Sabrina, who had removed a compact from her bag. She made a great show of repairing her makeup as he resumed their course to the Layne Estate. The partition stayed down and for a moment, he almost closed it again. But he liked looking at her—liked it a bit too much.

Without the barrier there, it became more difficult to concentrate on the road. His gaze drifted back to Sabrina's image in the rearview mirror. There was something different about her. He'd noticed it at the airport earlier that morning but he couldn't quite figure it out.

He did like the way she wore her dark hair now, cut so that it curved under her chin, lightly brushing against her neck. An image passed through his mind—lifting the silky strands with his fingers as his lips caressed the pulse beneath her ear. Jason sat straighter, pushing the fantasy aside. *Where on earth did that come from? It's Sabrina, not a conquest.*

Along the drive, their gazes kept clashing in the mirror. At last, he noticed a hint of irritation in her glance.

"Hadn't you better keep your eyes on the road?" she asked, that familiar frown creasing her brow.

Jason smiled. "It's good to see you, too."

"What are you doing here, anyway?"

"Where should I be?"

She made an impatient sound. "Anywhere but behind the wheel of a limousine. What happened to your MBA and international finance? To the big dreams of fame and the Fortune 500?"

Her anger washed over him. He understood it all too well. She was being defensive, the situation more and more confusing. But it didn't bother him half as much as the physical reaction he seemed to be having to her without any provocation. The fire in her eyes sparked something within the confines of the luxury car. He shifted in his seat. Since when did he react like a randy teenager? Not since that night, ten years ago when he'd almost forgotten who they both were.

He cleared his throat. "Let's just say high finance didn't work out. I discovered I was more suited to other things."

With a little grunt, she turned to stare out the window, her arms folded beneath her chest. His gaze lingered, just for a moment, before switching back to the road ahead.

As he rounded a bend, he applied the brakes. With a quick circle of the steering wheel, he turned the limo off the black top and onto a rough, gravel drive. There was barely enough room to pull the long car off the two-lane before a heavy, iron gate blocked them.

Lowering his window, Jason opened a door to what appeared to be a country mailbox, revealing a small keypad. After punching in his security code, the gates opened, creaking as they moved to allow the limo access to the five-hundred-acre estate. Once the tail of the car slid past the gate, it swung shut with a loud, ringing clang.

Further along the quarter-mile drive, they met another gate. It was much the same as the first, except not as ornamental. He went through the routine, very much aware of Sabrina's gaze following his every move.

A small green light on top of the gate began to blink and then the iron bars slid out of the way, folding into each other like an accordion. Once the long, black car cleared the obstruction, the bars clanged shut.

Sabrina sat back against the leather seat and glanced at Jason in the mirror. "Impressive. I guess some things have changed since I left. But how will the guests get by all that?"

"We have the gates on visual monitors at the house. When the guests are positively identified, the guard on duty will open the gates from his station. They aren't allowed to open both at once and only two or three individuals outside of the household staff are allowed access on a regular basis."

Sabrina nodded, glancing around at the thick growth of trees lining the driveway. "So, if they aren't on the list, they don't get in?"

"Exactly."

She would make his job difficult, but somehow the thought didn't bother him as much as it should. As the car rolled to a stop in front of the house, he looked up to see a flood of emotions pass over her face. He frowned. It bothered him that she looked so nervous. This was her home, the one place where everyone who loved her had gathered to offer support. The one place she should feel at ease, despite the past.

Shaking his head, Jason performed his duty and slid out of the limo first, walking around to open her door. The sweet fragrance of her perfume filled his senses as she stood. For a moment he thought she wavered on her feet and he fought the urge to steady her, blindsided by an intense longing to take her in his arms.

He longed to soothe away the pain he saw in those dark eyes. But he didn't dare touch her. He'd given up that right when he'd destroyed their friendship. Now there were too many secrets and lies between them. The girl he remembered hated lies.

She froze at his side as her gaze fixed on the sprawling three-story Victorian. He saw her hands clutch at the leather bag she held.

"I-I can't do this…" she whispered.

He touched her arm and she turned, looking up into his eyes. So beautiful, so warm and compelling. So very alone.

"Why?" he whispered, confused by her sudden show of nerves and the magnetic pull she seemed to have on him.

"I don't belong here. He made me leave." She bit her lip, her lashes blinking against tears.

"He's gone, Bree. This is your home. You never should have left."

Still, she hesitated and for a moment Jason glimpsed the scared young girl hiding within the grown woman's body. Afraid to go home again but longing to all the same. His chest tightened and he fought the urge to curse the dearly departed.

"You can do anything, Sabrina. You always could and you always have."

Chapter Two

Sabrina longed to wrap her arms around Jason and never let go. His strength drew her like a magnet to steel. But she knew what would happen if she got too close. Disaster. Humiliation. Just like before.

It frightened her that one glance from the man could barrel through her defenses. The last time she'd given in to her desire for Jason Sinclair, she'd wound up with her heart in shattered pieces at his feet and an aching, empty place in her soul.

He wrapped his hand around her arm and gently urged her up the stairs to the wide, black, double doors. Her steps faltered as she gained the top tread, but as she hesitated, he gave a reassuring squeeze. The warmth of his hand did strange things to her insides, shoring up her crumbling defenses like mortar pressed into the cracks of a failing dam. His presence gave her courage; his apparent support offered her strength.

Sabrina had once thought she'd never return to this mausoleum of a house where her childhood and innocence had been deftly killed and buried. It was a house, not a home. Yet it was still the one place she fervently wished to belong.

Jason reached around her to press the doorbell, and his spicy cologne filled her senses. Distinct chimes echoed behind the heavy doors and thick, stone walls. A shadow fluttered on the other side of the frosted, stained-glass window at the left of the door. Sabrina took a deep breath, leaning a little more into Jason's supportive grip as it swung open.

"Sabrina!" Thomas St. John's deep English voice filled with pleasure at the sight of her. "It is so good to see you again." The thin man gazed down at her with twinkling green eyes. He looked much the same except for a bit more gray at the temples.

"Thomas, it's been so long." Sabrina smiled up at the butler even as tears burned her throat. "I wasn't sure if you'd still be here after all these years."

"Of course. I've nowhere else to go." His smile wavered and he ushered them through the threshold. She felt Jason's hand fall away as they entered the foyer. "May I express my deepest sympathies?"

Sabrina turned, tears again filling her eyes. She had missed this man so very much, her dearest friend. Why had she let her father keep her away for so long? On impulse, she hurled herself at Thomas, clinging to him for a moment before taking a step back. He turned away slightly, she thought to hide the tears in his own eyes.

"Sorry…" she murmured. "Just chalk it up to feminine sentimentality. I've missed you."

Thomas cleared his throat and nodded. For a horrifying moment, she thought the man might cry. A startled yelp sounded from behind and she turned in time to see the housekeeper, Martha, bounding toward her, wiping her plump hands on her white apron.

"Welcome home!" the woman exclaimed, grabbing her in a bear hug. After a moment she let go and looked up at Sabrina, her eyes shimmering behind a well of tears. "It's so good to have you back at last. I just wish it happened years ago. We have so much to catch up on."

Sabrina nodded, breathing deeply as she forced a sob back down her throat. Anger mingled with other feelings, tearing at her from the inside out. Damn him! It shouldn't have taken her father's death for her to be allowed back among these people who had been her true family.

But what good was anger directed at a dead man? None. It was the height of futility.

Martha murmured more sympathy and then patted her arm. "Come on, dear girl, let's get you settled in before the riffraff get here. I've got your room all aired out and as cozy as you please." Sabrina let the other woman lead her to the stairs. "You can freshen up and have a bit of a rest. I'll have Jason bring your bags up later."

As they ascended the long, curved staircase, Sabrina felt a tingling sensation slip across her skin. It beckoned to her until she couldn't help looking over her shoulder. She caught sight of Thomas heading off down the hall toward the study. Her gaze skimmed past him to Jason, standing alone as he watched her climb the staircase. He nodded, his eyes locked with hers.

For a moment, it was if she'd stepped back in time. A feeling of déjà vu washed over her, gripping her senses in gentle confusion as her mind reached out to search for the exact moment this one resembled…Jason watching over her from the background with a smile of encouragement.

She could still feel the hopeful butterflies of young love that his touch, his mere glance had once brought to life. While the moment seemed the same, she knew to many things had changed. She had changed. But how she longed for the time she could confide in him.

Was such a thing possible when she found it hard to trust anyone? Maybe not, but perhaps she could find an anchor in this latest storm. Alone for so many years, Sabrina needed that strength more than ever.

She smiled a little, silently offering him a tentative truce. His brow rose in surprise and she jerked back around, her cheeks warming as she tried to concentrate on Martha's gentle prattle.

She shouldn't think about Jason now. There were too many feelings churning inside. If someone was to jostle her, she'd explode like a bottle of pop. She needed time to think about what to say or whether or not she could allow herself to trust him again, even a little. He was the one man that could sneak past all her defenses if she wasn't careful.

Once in the sanctuary of her old bedroom suite, the tensions of the past two days melted away. Martha disappeared into the bathroom. The sound of water running soon drifted out to Sabrina.

"You take your time, dear," the housekeeper said as she walked back into the room. "The reception is set to start at five, but I'll make sure Thomas keeps the wolves at bay until you're good and ready to face them. A long, hot bath is just what the doctor ordered."

Martha wrapped her in a motherly hug. Sabrina savored the warmth and affection as it seeped into her cold skin.

"It'll be all right. It doesn't seem so now, but it will be." Martha pulled away and paused for a moment as if searching for the right words. "I know this is very late coming, but I was so sorry to hear about your divorce. I just wanted you to know that I wish I could have been there for you, Sabrina. It must have been very difficult to deal with so much on your own."

"Thank you." Sabrina bent to place a kiss on the woman's plump cheek. "Some things just aren't meant to be...some men aren't capable of fidelity." Martha's eyes went wide and she made a soft, distressed sound. "It's okay, really. I've been over Sam for quite a while. I just picked the wrong man and rushed into marriage for all the wrong reasons." She sighed. "I can't tell you how much I've missed you."

Martha blushed, waving a hand in dismissal as she turned to leave. "Go on, dear. You relax and get yourself cleaned up a bit. I put in some of that vanilla bubble bath you used to like so much. We'll have time to talk more later. The hired help should be arriving soon and I need to supervise."

She stopped outside the door and turned back, her hand on the doorknob. "Sabrina, why *did* you marry that young man? Seems you jumped into things so quickly."

"I was lonely and I thought he loved me." Sabrina laughed, the sound still bitter after so many years. "Sam is quite a con artist. I..." She looked away from Martha's sympathy and swallowed back the pride sticking in her throat. If she couldn't tell her oldest confidant, who could she tell? "I didn't think he knew who I was...who my father was. But he did. Sam likes money and women. Somehow Dad knew what he was after. But I was too stubborn to listen."

Martha's lips pressed together and she gave a sharp nod. "Later, dear, you and I will have a nice long talk when there's time. It's way past due, I think." The door shut behind her.

Left alone, Sabrina gazed around the room, absorbing every detail. Pale blue walls were decorated with framed photos she had taken so many years ago of her beloved mountains.

She kicked off her heels and padded across the thick, area rugs, her toes sinking into the rich pile. Sabrina stopped for a moment, savoring the vaguely familiar feeling. A studio portrait hanging above the bedside table caught her attention. Her heart struck a new tempo as she moved toward it.

A face smiled back at her from the eight-by-ten frame, almost a mirror image with deep, rich eyes the color of milk chocolate. The woman held a baby in her arms, the sheer joy on her face reaching out of the frame until it squeezed Sabrina's heart like a vice. She turned away from the shadowy memories the image of her mother evoked and concentrated on the rest of the room.

Everything was just as she had left it ten years earlier. Almost as if she'd never gone away, never severed ties with all of those she loved and needed. Being told to leave and never come back…it had ripped away that part of her that had always clung to a shred of hope that someday, somehow, her father would want her. Love her.

She had wandered through her life for days afterward, feeling like a child lost in a big, frightening world with no one to lean on. For that alone, she had hated her father, had wished him to an early grave.

But now he was dead and she longed for one more chance, one more moment with him to say that she was sorry and to admit that he had been right about so many things, even while being wrong about others. One more chance to say, "Daddy, I love you."

Her breath caught in her throat, burning with the tears that welled there. The pain bubbled up from deep within, pushing the trapped air out in a gut-wrenching sob. Sabrina fell across the queen-sized bed and buried her face in the thick comforter. Wave after wave of anguish racked her body.

Sometime later, the sharp crack of knuckles on wood roused her from her waning torment. She sucked in a deep breath and sat up to dry her eyes as the door swung open. Jason stood in the doorway, her bags tucked under both arms. His eyes widened in surprise at the sight of her.

"I'm sorry. When you didn't answer I thought you'd be in the…" His words died and he took a tentative step into the room. "Are you okay?"

Sabrina wiped away the fresh tears and nodded. "I will be, thank you." She sniffed, wishing he'd leave so she could pull herself together without an audience.

"Is that water running?" he asked as he deposited the bags on the floor near her dresser.

"Water? Oh!" Her eyes widened. "Oh, no!" She bolted off the bed and ran into the bathroom, twisting off the faucet just as the tub neared overflow level. "Damn!"

"No harm done." Sabrina spun around at the sound of Jason's voice from the doorway. He gave her a small, crooked smile—the one that had always melted her from the inside out. *Oh, God.* It still did. "It wouldn't be the first time a tub has overflowed in this house. Just open the drain a little."

She lifted one eyebrow. "Thanks, I never would have figured that one out on my own."

"Yeah, I'm sure you could." He shrugged. "I know you too well, Bree. Don't play tough. I'm here if you need me."

Swallowing hard, she wrapped her arms about her middle to keep from reaching for him. How she wanted to throw herself at him, to be nestled against his broad chest with those arms banded around her. Yes, he knew her. Maybe too well.

"I'll remember that. Thanks." She waited, but he didn't seem inclined to leave. "Lock the door on your way out, please. I think I'll take that bath now."

A whisper of flame sparkled in his deep blue eyes and then he turned, making his way across the room. Sabrina heard the door click behind him.

* * *

"Such a shame...he was still so young, so much life left..." Sabrina nodded numbly at the rotund gentleman as he expressed his condolences. The glare of the chandelier off his thick glasses and smooth, bald head distracted her. "If there's anything we can do for you, young lady, please do let us know."

She wanted to ask who he was, but years of lessons in manners and how to be the perfect hostess kept her tongue silent. She realized he had introduced himself, but for the life of her, she couldn't place one face with any of the dozens of names and titles she'd heard in the last two hours.

"Thank you, I'll do that," she murmured, shaking the clammy hand the nameless Samaritan proffered. No doubt he was a local politician or banker.

The moment she'd come downstairs, Sabrina realized the large gathering would be an even greater ordeal than the funeral. She knew no one except Talbridge. She couldn't remember much about the parties held while she'd grown up there. She had often watched from the fringes, envying her father's friends, sizing up his lover *de jour*.

Thomas and Jason stood at the edge of the room, ever the proper servants, while Martha was kept confined to the kitchen. Temporary help, hired just for the reception, mingled discreetly as they served drinks and passed around silver platters of canapés and jumbo shrimp.

Sabrina noted that the guests gobbled up the shrimp faster than it could be replenished. *Must be the rich man's comfort food*, she thought.

As she extracted herself from yet another of her father's close associates, she grabbed a glass of red wine off the tray a waiter carried past. Her eyes wandered around the perimeter of the living room. It hadn't changed a bit. Low bookshelves lined the red-painted walls. Chunky, overstuffed furniture skirted the Oriental rug, giving the room a casual warmth so much of the house lacked.

Sabrina drifted through the crowd to stand at one of the tall, multi-paned windows overlooking the rear gardens. Light from the setting sun glistened off frozen rain that encased pine boughs and the gray branches of nude, quaking aspens and sugar maples.

Her fingers itched for the feel of her camera as the scene unfolding stirred her artist's soul. Such beauty should be captured for the world to see. So many people hurried through life unaware, uncaring of the quiet display of light and color surrounding them. For Sabrina, such images brought solace. It made the ugliness easier to bear.

"Miss Layne…" The light feminine voice caught her attention.

"Yes?" She turned to gaze at the woman who stood at eye-level with her. She seemed familiar. Oh, yes, the one crying at her father's grave. A quick, appraising glance noted the woman's smoothly styled, dark blonde hair and hazel eyes that were red around the rims. She was attractive, in a made-up sort of way, and held a full tumbler of dark liquid in one hand while a cigarette burned in the other. Sabrina also noticed the woman's long, red-painted fingernails.

My, what big claws you have… She grimaced, chastising herself for acting so feline. The woman apparently interpreted the expression for one of grief.

"Oh, dear…now you just cry if you need to," she crooned, moving to slide an arm about her shoulders. The smoke of the tapered cigarette curled around Sabrina's head, threatening to gag her. She moved away, smiling so as not to offend. The woman reeked of whiskey, cigarettes and heavy cologne.

"No…no, I'm fine, thank you."

"Well, I'm not. I've lost the love of my life and I didn't realize it until…until it was too late!"

While one part of Sabrina's brain noted the way the blonde swayed on her two-inch heels, the other sorted through her dramatic speech.

"You knew my father well?"

"Oh, yes, we were very close," she whispered in a voice that would have made any stage director proud. Sabrina cringed.

"I'm sure you were." She glanced to either side to see if anyone might be listening. "He was very fond of attractive women."

"Oh, oh, yes." The woman's pencil-thin eyebrows rose as she took a deep drag of smoke into her lungs. Sabrina thought a flash of irritation sparked in her eyes, but the woman glanced away. "He asked me to marry him but I wasn't sure and then…then the accident…"

Sabrina winced as the woman broke into tears. She grasped a box of tissues from an end table and thrust them at the blonde, whose mascara was beginning to streak.

"Forgive me." She sniffled and dabbed at her eyes. "It still hasn't sunk in, I'm afraid. Your father was such a kind, loving man."

Sabrina choked on her wine, sputtering in a most unladylike fashion as the woman pounded her on the back. A shower of gray ash filled the air around them.

"Yes," she croaked. "I suppose he was. I'm sorry, but I didn't catch your name."

"Oh, you mean he didn't…that is to say, your father hadn't mentioned me?"

Sabrina stared, mouth gaping. How well did this woman know David Layne? Could she have wandered in on the wrong funeral?

"Uh, no, we haven't spoken in…in quite a while."

"Oh?" The woman stared, a small frown puckering her smooth forehead. Sabrina found herself glancing at her hairline for telltale facelift scars. "I'm Vivian James. Your father hired me as his private secretary about three years ago and well…we became rather close."

"Private secretary? Oh, even if we had spoken…" which they hadn't for six years, "…my father never talked to me about his mist…uh, his secretaries."

Oh, dear, almost blew that one. Sabrina decided that she had better lay off the booze before she wound up dancing on the baby grand and telling everyone what a cold, unfeeling jerk the deceased had been. She set her glass down.

Vivian moved closer, glancing around as she stage-whispered near her ear. "It wasn't an accident."

Sabrina blinked as the fumes of the other woman's breath hit her full in the face. "What wasn't?"

"Your father. He was an excellent driver. They say he was drunk and driving too fast. Well, I'm sure it's just not true."

A blaring siren cut through Vivian's chatter, freezing everyone to the spot.

"What the hell?" the woman sputtered, her drink sloshing over the rug beneath their feet.

The shrill sound was joined by a more distant, insistent clanging. Sabrina plastered her hands against her ears, wincing as the noise drove like an ice pick through her eardrums. It was then she caught sight of movement and turned in time to see Jason and Thomas darting through the foyer and out the front door. Some seconds later, the alarms stopped. Everyone breathed sighs of relief and glanced around. Excited speculations were being tossed about when Jason reappeared. He strolled back into the room and smiled.

"Sorry, folks. It seems a deer jumped a fence in the eastern quadrant and set off the alarms. I'm afraid we'll have to reset all the systems and that means the reception will have to be cut short. I apologize, but I'm sure you are all aware of the delicacy of these security systems."

There was some murmuring, but everyone seemed more than willing to comply. Sabrina nodded as a few of the guests returned and repeated some form or other of the same tired speeches she'd already heard. Within half an hour, the last was out the door and, she assumed, being monitored as they drove back down the long drive to the curving mountain road.

She wandered into the hall, watching Jason as he shut the front door and punched several numbers into a keypad recessed into the wood molding.

"A deer?"

He whirled around and Sabrina suppressed a smile. She had always enjoyed making him squirm when they were younger. What an unlikely pair they had made—the chauffeur's teenage son and the millionaire's scrawny, preteen daughter.

"Yes, a deer," he replied.

"Let's see." Sabrina glanced at the ceiling, tapping one finger on her chin. "The eastern quadrant is surrounded by a ten-foot-tall, three-foot-thick stone wall." Her eyebrows arched. "A deer jumped that?"

Jason flushed a little, but didn't flinch. "Yes."

"That's your story and you're sticking to it?"

His gaze narrowed. "What is that supposed to mean?"

"Oh, nothing… nothing at all. Now, I suggest you get someone to help Ms. James to a guestroom. She passed out on the settee as you were shuffling the rest out the door."

Sabrina turned and began to climb the stairs. "Oh." She stopped and looked back at Jason. He hadn't moved. "I'd like to take a car out in an hour. Will you have all your little gizmos fixed by then?"

"Yes, but you're not going out alone."

Her eyebrows lifted with irritation. How dare he order her about? "Oh, yes I am, Mr. Sinclair. Or are you worried another buck will jump me?"

"No, you're not, Miss Layne," he growled, ignoring her double-edged barb about the high-vaulting deer. "Talbridge is waiting in your father's study. He wants to go ahead with the reading of the will tonight…something about having an appointment in Pittsburgh tomorrow."

Looking around the grand entry, she felt all the old feelings surface. She could suffocate under the memories of loneliness. Now she had no one to blame them on. Her father was dead. Why hadn't the pain died with him? Resentment washed over her. No matter how much she thought she'd moved on, her father still had the power to make her soul bleed.

She turned the frustrating anger on the only man available. "Fine. I'll listen to the will if that's what has to be done but then I'm going for drive." Her gaze caught Jason's, challenging him to try and stop her.

His jaw clenched, but he didn't say a word as he turned and walked down the hall toward the study. Sabrina hesitated a moment on the steps before following. Jason opened the door, standing to one side of the opening so that she had to brush past him. His warmth and the scent of his spicy cologne reached out to her, lifting her senses to high alert.

Talbridge sat in the leather executive's chair behind a massive walnut desk. He rose as she entered, a smile brightening his somber face. "Good, I'm glad Jason was able to catch you before you turned in for the night, Sabrina."

She tried to smile but her heart wasn't in it. Memories jostled against her frayed nerves as her gaze darted about the room. How many times had she sneaked in here as a child, only to be chased away by her father's angry rebuff?

Yet, there had been other times...before her mother died. Small moments when he had smiled and lifted her into his lap, calling her his little secretary as he let her scribble with his favorite fountain pen. The memory sent a jagged pain ripping through her heart. Hate and love mingled together with incessant longing...a desire for something that was now beyond reach.

"Sabrina?"

Blinking back the scalding tears, she took a seat opposite Talbridge's. "Yes, I'm ready. Go ahead, Marcus."

He nodded, then glanced at Jason standing at the study door. "That will be all for the moment."

Sabrina cringed at the icy dismissal, her gaze moving to Jason's face. He seemed frozen, unfeeling. The subtle jump at his temple betrayed the anger held in check. The injustice of it all struck her full force. So many years had passed and yet he was still fighting the stigma that came from one reckless night. One bad choice.

She spoke, interrupting the rigid silence that had settled over the room. "If it's all right with both of you..." The men looked at her and she swallowed. "I would like Jason to stay."

She didn't look at him. Didn't dare. He might read all sorts of innuendo into her request, but it was as simple as stated. He was the closest thing she had to a friend and somehow she was sure his presence would make this ordeal easier.

Talbridge set his jaw but nodded as he resumed his seat behind the intimidating desk. After a second's hesitation, Jason closed the door and stepped forward, standing at the side of her chair like a sentinel at ease.

Sabrina dared a sideways glance and relaxed a little when she realized he was staring over the lawyer's head at a painting of a lighthouse on the opposite wall. The image seemed familiar, but before she could decipher why, the lawyer cleared his throat to gain her attention.

The whisper of papers being shuffled filled the air. Talbridge examined the document over the top of his reading glasses. "Now, I'm assuming you won't mind if we skip over this first part about being of sound mind and what not?" She shook her head, her last nerve on the verge of snapping.

"Good, then here's the important part." He cleared his throat once more. "'… I hereby bequeath all my worldly possessions, including cash, stocks, bonds, controlling shares of Layne Antiques, all properties, furniture, works of art and automobiles to my daughter, Sabrina Saunders Layne. I also leave all personal items to Sabrina with the provision that she dispose of any and all clothing and/or jewelry as she sees fit…'"

Sabrina stared. A hard ball of heat settled in her belly. Her mouth was as dry as chalk. "H-how…" The creaking sound that was her voice set her teeth on edge. She swallowed. "What does this mean…monetarily speaking?"

Marcus shrugged as he scanned the last pages of the thick document. "According to the audit and insurance review conducted when the new security system was installed, your father's estate was appointed a net worth of approximately twenty million dollars. Give or take a million or two."

Oh. God.

"Of course, he also held a ten-million dollar life insurance policy. But that has been divided to his specifications between several members of the household staff and trusted employees, both past and present." He flicked a glance up at Jason's face. "It includes bequests to Jason and his parents as well as Thomas and Martha."

She couldn't speak, couldn't think of anything to say in the aftermath of the bomb he'd just dropped in her lap. To say that she had no idea her father controlled such wealth was an understatement. Four million, she had thought; five, tops. But twenty and counting?

Talbridge slid the document back into its leather binder, pages rattling as small tremors shook his hands. "Sabrina, I know this has been a very trying ordeal. I want you to understand that I will be more than glad to continue in the service of your family, handling all aspects of both the business and personal financial affairs. It cannot be an easy role for a young woman such as yourself to be thrust into on such short notice."

She shook her head, still too stunned to let his Old World ideas irritate her. "No, you're right. I wouldn't have a clue how to begin...where to begin with so much."

He smiled, glancing at his watch as he stood and gathered his things. "Rest assured, I will be more than happy to take care of it all for you, Sabrina. But we can discuss things in more detail once the shock has worn off. As it is, I need to get to the airport so that I don't miss my flight."

She sat, motionless, her mind drifting in a haze of shock as Talbridge murmured his apologies and made a beeline for the door. Thoughts churning, she barely noticed as Jason laid a hand on her shoulder.

"Are you all right?" His quiet voice drew her gaze upward. She blinked at the sympathy in his eyes, wondering at the brief glimpse of tenderness there.

"I...I'm not sure."

He studied her face for a moment and seemed to reach a decision. "Go and change into something warm and we'll go for a drive, like we used to do. I think we both need a breather."

She stared, wishing she could find enough steely resolve to keep the man at arm's length. But it seemed her strength had vanished beneath the megaton jolt she'd just absorbed. Like it or not, she could use some of his support just about now.

Sabrina nodded. "Okay. I'll just be a minute."

Chapter Three

She stared out the window of the low, black Mercedes as countless trees rushed by in the outer beam of the headlights.

Everything…everything…everything…

The word echoed through her mind like a mantra. What could one person do with so much wealth?

"Sabrina?" Jason's quiet voice stole through the fog in her brain. She turned her head to look at him.

His long, lean hands smoothly turned the steering wheel, guiding the thousand-pound piece of luxurious steel along the winding mountain road. There were no streetlights to guide them, only the soft white beams of the car, the red aura of taillights glowing behind as they curved ever higher up the sloping road.

"You still with me?" His gaze remained intent on their destination.

Sabrina nodded. "Yes, I think so. It's just that I didn't expect this." Her voice trailed off as he swung the car around a sharp bend. She knew if she could see far beyond her window, the view of the downhill side of the mountain might make her sick.

Sabrina had always had an unreasonable fear of falling. In her mind she could see, almost feel, the ground give way as she tumbled into blackness. The knowledge that this was how her father had died—his car plunging down the placid, tree-covered mountain—had given her very vivid nightmares.

"You mean the money?"

"Yes." Sabrina turned her body toward him, the seatbelt biting into her neck. "When I told him that I was getting married, he said I wouldn't get a dime from him. You know my father—he never made a threat he didn't intend to keep. Now here I am, his sole heir, and I haven't a clue why. Why did he do that, Jason? Did he ever say anything to you about me or the will or…?" She reached out, laying her hand on Jason's arm. His muscle jumped beneath her fingertips as if her touch shocked him. Sabrina lost all train of thought.

It happened every time she touched him…electric, sizzling heat and awareness. Ten years hadn't dimmed the flame. Did he feel it as well? She dropped her hand, clasping it with the other in her lap as she gazed at his profile in the green-tinted light from the dash.

Jason cleared his throat. "I wasn't privy to his financial decisions and he sure didn't confide in me where his estate was concerned. After all, I am just the chauffeur."

Sabrina frowned. "Why are you still working for my dad? And what was that business earlier about a deer scaling a ten-foot wall and that it wasn't safe for me to drive alone? You want to tell me what's going on?"

He glanced at her. The tightening of his jaw spoke volumes. Jason was trying to figure out how much to tell her.

"What are you hiding?" she asked. Then, like a light clicking on, it all came together—Vivian's comments, Jason's reticence. "It wasn't an accident."

She thought Jason's shoulders tensed beneath the dark fabric of his suit.

"No." The word was spoken so softly that for a moment Sabrina thought she'd imagined it.

"What happened?"

"He hadn't been drinking, even though they did find an empty scotch bottle in his car, and I know the difference between brake-lines that have been cut versus the damage that can be done in a wreck. There was also some internal damage in the steering column that seemed very unusual."

"How do you know all that?"

"You remember Bill Wright? He's been the Chief of Police here for a little over six years. We've been friends forever and I talked him into letting me look at the car. What was left of it."

She stared at him a moment as his last words sunk in. Her stomach rolled at the image that came to mind—twisted, smoldering metal. "What does the chief think about all of this?"

Jason sighed. "He's investigating, but thinks I'm overreacting. Besides, he's got the town council breathing down his neck, stressing how much the upcoming Spring Carnival needs good public relations. They don't want it getting out that we might have a murder on our hands."

"Why is the carnival so much more important than my father's life?"

"It's not that…it's because this is a major source of income for Castle's Grove," he told her. Sabrina clutched the door handle as they gunned through a rather sharp curve. "Besides, on the surface it does look like an accident. They'd much rather accept the facts at face value—a rich man drank too much and took his 'Vette for a spin off the mountain."

She swallowed hard, trying to keep her mind on their conversation and away from thoughts of cars falling off the mountainside.

"My father had a lot of enemies. His personality alone would account for that. But I have a hard time believing some well-heeled antiques collector got mad enough to have him murdered. Are you sure about all this?"

Sabrina watched him, waiting for an answer. Then she realized he hadn't been listening. Jason's gaze darted back and forth between the area illuminated by the headlights to the rearview mirror. He frowned, his jaw tense.

"Jason?"

"Quiet!" He glanced in the mirror again as they rounded a bend, then turned his head to the side mirror at his left.

"What's wrong?" Sabrina asked as she looked over her shoulder. They came upon a straight stretch of road. She noticed a car about two hundred yards behind them and closing in fast. Sabrina glanced at the narrow road ahead. There was little leeway for passing. Another idiot tourist trying to get

41

someone killed? Or something worse? Her heart pounded as her mouth went dry.

"Maybe you should pull over and let them by."

Jason shook his head. "I don't think passing is what they have in mind."

All the while he spoke, Jason's gaze switched between the road and the rearview mirror. Sabrina turned to watch, a cold lump of fear settling in her stomach. The other vehicle was three car lengths away. Jason pressed down on the gas, giving the powerful engine its head as he smoothly maneuvered down the two-lane road, straddling the centerline around the curves.

"Jason…?" His name left her on a whisper of fear, her fingers digging into the seat and door handle.

"Hold on," he murmured.

She heard a loud popping sound and the Mercedes' rear window splintered. The other car's headlights illuminated the glass and Sabrina blinked at it in shock. The design created looked like a bluish, crystalline spider web. "What was—?"

"Get down!" He took a hand off the wheel and pushed her head down into the seat. Sabrina lay there for a moment as icy terror wrapped around her like a serpent. She could feel the pressure of his hip against the top of her head. The rich aroma of leather mingled with the scent of Jason's cologne.

Someone was shooting at them. It couldn't be real. That kind of thing happened on TV or the movies, not in the Poconos. People skied the mountain slopes. They honeymooned and bathed in heart-shaped tubs. They came to drink and listen to comedians. They did not shoot at the residents.

Another shot, and more glass shattered. She felt Jason's body jerk, heard a series of sharp cracks and then Jason's deep voice cursing above her.

"Are you hurt?" She tried to raise her head but another shot zinged by, fracturing the windshield. She heard a scream, realizing a moment later that it was she who'd made the sound.

"I'm fine—stay down," he said in clipped tones. "I've got an idea." Her body slid into him as the Mercedes glided around another curve. The squeal of tires—theirs or the other car's, she wasn't sure—made her stomach lurch. "When I count to three, hold on to something and don't let go. You got that?"

Sabrina nodded, then realizing he couldn't see her added, "Yes."

For what seemed an eternity, she listened to the powerful roar of the engine and the squawl of rubber on asphalt. Sabrina felt the road curve under her as the car moved, then they seemed to be on a straightaway. Her body tensed. Her fingers dug into the creamy leather.

"Here we go," Jason said. "One... two..."

Sabrina filled her lungs, wondering if it would be the last breath she ever took.

Don't fall off the mountain...don't fall off the mountain...

"Three!"

The world tilted and spun. Her scream mingled with the sound of shrieking tires. The spin pushed her back against the seat as she clung to the leather for dear life. A grinding forward lurch and the car jerked to a bone-jarring stop.

* * *

Jason heard a sickening thud, and then another and another. Silence laced a steady pounding that wouldn't subside. It took him a moment to realize it was his own heartbeat.

He lay back against the seat, squeezing his eyes shut to block out the pain and flickering lights that had exploded in his head when he hit the steering wheel. Fine time to discover the airbags in the car weren't worth a damn.

"Jason?" Sabrina whispered. Cold fingers touched his cheek. She sounded so scared. He opened his eyes and found himself staring into the dark depths of her beautiful gaze. He'd never forgotten the color or the warmth of those eyes.

"Oh... I thought..." She started shaking.

His arm went around her, pulling her close as he rubbed her back and glanced out into the still night. The other car was gone; he was sure they had sailed over the edge just as he had hoped.

When they'd reached the straightaway, he had taken a chance that the other driver wasn't familiar with the road. He wouldn't know about the narrow area off the opposite side for runaway trucks. Jason had done a one-eighty and somehow managed to steer the speeding Mercedes into the rough, gravel incline.

It had been a risk, but with the assassins hot on their tail and with Sabrina in danger, it was all he could come up with. Their luck in the chase wouldn't have held out forever. The other driver had apparently tried to match Jason's maneuver but wasn't so lucky. There had been several crashing thuds as the dark sedan had turned end over end down the mountainside.

Jason noted that Sabrina had stopped shaking and lay against his chest. He sighed. His arm tightened around her. It surprised him how good she felt against him.

"They were shooting at us!" She lifted her head and looked into his eyes. The fear and confusion there made him want to gather her even closer, just like when he'd caught her crying in her room earlier. But he knew he still didn't have that right, despite her gesture of trust when she'd asked him to stay for the reading of the will. He had to keep his distance.

"Jase, why were they shooting at us?"

He swallowed, fighting back the urge to tell her the truth, all of it. He knew she'd be safer if she didn't know. He had to get her out of this somehow. He had to get her back to New York where she'd be out of harm's way.

"I don't know what's going on, sweetheart." He felt a twinge of guilt, yet he hadn't lied. Not really. "Come on, let's get you home." As she sat up, she laid a hand against his left shoulder. He flinched.

"Oh!" She reached behind and touched his shoulder, where a fiery pain began to surface. "You've been shot! Why didn't you say something?"

He smiled and shook his head. He could feel the hot, sticky warmth spread over his skin. "In all the excitement I didn't realize it. I thought a piece of glass nicked me."

"We've got to get you to a hospital."

"I'll be fine. I'm sure it's just superficial."

"But you're bleeding!" Sabrina snapped. He knew she was as stubborn as her father when she got mad. She leaned across his lap to flick on the interior lights.

The sudden rush of warmth her nearness evoked caught Jason off guard. Just like the innocent touch earlier, he felt an awakening flame respond as she moved closer, her hands searching the torn fabric of his coat.

"I think the bullet just grazed you," she said, confirming his suspicions. "But we'd better get indoors where I can look at it."

He glanced out the cracked windshield, forcing his thoughts away from her warmth and the sweet fragrance that enveloped her. When had little Bree gained the power to spark a fire in his blood?

Jason swallowed hard. "Yeah, the sooner the better. It's supposed to snow tonight and these roads will ice up in record time."

He reached toward the key, grimacing as a knife of pain shot down his arm. After a couple of futile attempts to restart the stalled engine, he realized more than one bullet might have hit its mark.

"What's wrong?" Sabrina asked.

"I'm not sure, but I think we're going to have to walk."

"Wait, what about the cell phone? We could call someone." She glanced around. "I think it fell off the seat…" Sabrina undid her seatbelt and leaned over, groping around the floor. "Ah… here it is." She sat up, cracking her head against the dashboard.

Jason cringed, one hand reaching out. He dropped it without touching her as he shoved away the instinct to take her into his arms again. The feelings she evoked were intense and a little startling. "You okay, Bree?"

She held the phone out to him, one hand pressed to her head. "Oh, yeah. Just dandy."

Flipping the instrument open, he put it to his ear. Nothing. He glanced down at the display and squinted at it in the dim light. "Damn. I think we're out of range or the battery's dead."

"Great. What do we do now?"

"I guess we walk after all."

"Walk? Where? Oh…did Dad keep the cabin?"

Jason glanced out the window, calculating the distance to David Layne's summer hideaway. A few small snowflakes began to fall, clinging to the windshield for moment before melting.

"Yeah, he kept it and I think we're about five miles away…but it may be only two if we hike up over the hill instead of taking the road."

Sabrina sighed. "Good thing I changed. Okay, we'd better get going before it gets any worse out there."

Jason nodded, not sure why he found her bossiness amusing. It used to aggravate the hell out of him. Sabrina got out and walked around the car, opening his door before he had the chance. Clenching his jaw, he slid his legs out. A flash of pain fired through his shoulder as he pushed himself up and out of the car. She stepped closer, reaching a tentative hand out to steady him.

"I'm fine." He shrugged off her touch, irritated at how much her nearness affected him. This was Sabrina. His friend, the girl who had cheered him up and helped him through a long, grueling year of physical and emotional healing. She was not one of his women. Sabrina was a sweet, innocent, forever-after type of girl. Like Jeanine had been. His gut twisted but he pushed the guilt away with an ease that came from years of practice.

"Good." She moved away, stuffing both hands into her coat pockets. She glanced around at the dark woods. "Do you have a flashlight in the car?"

"Yeah, in the trunk. We should put out flares, too. No one travels this stretch much at night, but you never know." He walked around the car, bending to examine the wheels embedded in the heavy gravel. "Damn! Both rear tires are blown out. This just isn't our night."

Jason opened the trunk with his key. "We've got flashlights…some trail mix…a canteen of water and rain ponchos."

"It's not raining."

"No, but when the snow starts melting on your wool coat, you'll be soaked to the skin. They'll help insulate us."

Sabrina grunted. "Are you always such a Boy Scout?"

Jason looked at her. The red glow of the taillights made her seem mysterious, ethereal. He pulled his gaze away.

"I try to be prepared," he replied. "It makes the bumps easier to deal with."

By the time they'd retrieved two flashlights and set the flares blazing around the car, it had started snowing in earnest. Fat white flakes fell from the black sky, blanketing the cold damp ground with amazing speed.

She stomped her feet in turn, pushing both arms through the ungainly sleeves of the plastic poncho. "So, I guess we go up?"

Jason followed the direction of her gaze. "Yeah, up and over." He looked at her. "It'll be steep in places. Can you handle it?"

Sabrina's shoulders stiffened as she looked him in the eye. "Is that a challenge, Jase?"

He felt the smile tugging at his lips but fought it back. He knew the best way to keep her going, to fuel her determination. "If you want it to be."

Her eyes narrowed and she turned away from him, long strides following her flashlight's beam toward the tree line beside the road. She stopped and looked back. "Are you coming or do you need something to lean on?"

Jason smiled. Sassy, bossy… he had missed her.

* * *

This had to be one of the worst nights of her life. It ranked in the top ten. Sabrina groaned as her foot caught on yet another root protruding from the ground. She didn't fall. This time.

"You okay?" Jason called from his position ahead.

She glanced up as a beam of light skimmed over her body toward her face. "Yes," she snapped. "Fine. Don't worry. I'll scream if I need you."

She thought she heard a deep chuckle but chose to ignore it. He could just go ahead and laugh. It wasn't her fault the trees seemed to come to life, grasping at her shoes and clothes with giant, claw-like hands. She shivered. She needed to stop reading thrillers.

"Are we…any closer?" she panted, not caring if she sounded like a petulant child.

Jason's light stilled, his shadowy figure seeming to become part of the trees surrounding them. It was incredibly dark. Everything beyond the soft white glow of their flashlights loomed as black, forbidding shadows against the gray sky. She gripped her light as tightly as her frozen fingers would allow.

"Yeah, we're close. The ground is starting to level out."

She grunted. "Since when?"

Jason kept walking. "Just a few more hundred yards and it'll dip down. By then, you should be able to see the cabin."

Sabrina tried to sigh, but couldn't get enough air into her lungs. "Great."

The night hung around them, still, silent. It was too quiet for conversation. Not that she had enough breath in her lungs to hold one. After three hours of hiking, the snow had stopped, but the temperature continued to plummet. Clouds began drifting, slits of sky showing through as the full moon peeped out, bathing the land in an eerie, silver light.

Watching her feet as she skirted another root, Sabrina ran smack into Jason's broad back. "Oh!"

He turned and steadied her, his fingers firm on her arms. "We're here."

She looked up, her gaze skipping over his shadowed face to the view some forty yards below them where the land dipped. Under the full light of the moon, she could distinguish the outline of the Layne summer cabin, nestled among the pines in the secluded ravine.

Relief and apprehension washed over her in close succession. Warmth and shelter waited, but so did painful memories. She pulled away from Jason's touch and straightened her shoulders.

"Great. Let's hope someone left a key under the mat."

With that, she struck out ahead of him, not needing to look back to know that he followed.

Several long minutes later, they crossed the threshold into the one-and-a-half story log cabin. Jason fired up the gas-powered generator and Sabrina breathed a sigh of relief as she touched a switch by the door and lights flickered on without hesitation. She wasn't sure she could steel her emotions in the romantic setting if all they had to go by was candlelight.

Her boots clopped across the polished wood floors as she maneuvered around a pine futon that sat parallel with the large, stone fireplace. She glanced around, the sights and odors bringing a flash of memory, a distant longing that made her ache inside.

Stripped, honey-colored logs that gleamed in the lamplight spanned the fifteen-foot ceiling. Her breath made clouds of frost in the frigid air. She moved further away from Jason, who was discarding his poncho and coat. It was a vain hope that distance would help clear her head.

Building a fire ought to give her time to recoup. Stooping to open the grate, Sabrina laid several dry logs in a crisscross formation. Long sulfur matches were in a box on the mantle, just as she remembered. Soon a fire crackled in the hearth, the warm glow painting the walls and ceiling gold. The flames grew, leaping over the logs in a devouring dance of heat and flame.

But even the blaze couldn't burn the memories from her mind. So many images jumbled together like a kaleidoscope; past and present in a surreal show of sight and sound. The frightening car chase, shots ringing in the night. A younger Jason, his eyes dark and drugged with alcohol and lust...his lips on hers, his arms around her as they sank to the sofa. Her father's funeral...the vague image of his car plunging off the mountain...metal crunching, flames leaping above the trees. Again, the dark sedan...spinning, screeching tires. Silence. Dead. Cold. Silence.

Oh, my God, it wasn't an accident. It was murder and the killer just tried again.

Sabrina gave her head a hard shake as heat blazed across her cheeks. She glanced over her shoulder at Jason, her breath catching as their gazes met. An echo of the flames danced in his eyes. He remembered.

She turned away, almost running toward the bathroom. "I'd better get some first aid supplies before you bleed to death."

"I think you're being a little dramatic, Bree," he replied as she disappeared. "I'm pretty sure the bleeding's stopped. It's just a flesh wound, otherwise it'd be hurting a hell of a lot more."

* * *

Jason breathed a sigh of relief, berating himself for responding like an oversexed teenager. It was bad enough watching her relive that night ten years ago when he had almost given in to a moment of madness.

There would be more lies before this was over, half-truths and misinformation that he would have to utter. It had to be done. Yet, he knew in the end, it would ruin any chance he might have at gaining back her trust. If she was to ever find out the truth...to discover his secrets, it would kill any tender feelings she might still harbor.

The thought hurt. But he would deal with that guilt and her rejection when it came. He would not let anything happen to her. He would not take a chance with her life.

A light clicked on behind him. There were some rummaging noises and the scraping slide of drawers being opened and shut. He sat and listened. A thud followed by a mild curse made him smile. A bit more shuffling before Sabrina's footsteps returned. When she stepped back around in front of him, Jason noted she had packaged bandages, ointment and a bowl of water.

"Here we go..." She knelt at his feet, setting her bundle onto the floor. Then she looked up with a tentative smile. "I wasn't sure what we'd need. Let's get that jacket and shirt off so I can how much damage has been done."

She rose up on her knees and smoothed the black linen jacket off his good shoulder before tugging it down his injured arm. Jason grimaced, clenching his jaw against the pain.

As she fingered the shoulder of the ruined garment, Sabrina shuddered. Her wide eyes lifted up to him. "Jason, you could have been killed. Why were they shooting at us? Is there something you're not telling me?"

"I'm not sure, but it's too much of a coincidence. It must have something to do with your dad's accident." He lifted his good shoulder and squeezed his eyes shut against a new wave of pain. "Help me with the shirt."

She nodded, then began undoing the buttons. He could feel the heat of her hands through the fabric. Sabrina bit her bottom lip. Jason swallowed back a moan as his body reacted to the innocent gesture. Her fingers shook, dancing across his collarbone and shoulder like butterfly kisses as she opened the bloody shirt and peeled it down one arm and then the other. The fabric pulled away from the blood caked around the wound. He winced.

Her face lowered to her task, and he couldn't see her eyes. "Bree…" She glanced up again and he saw the tears shimmering there. His gut clenched. He never wanted to cause her more pain. "I'll be fine. We're safe here."

A powerful urge washed over him. He wanted nothing more than to pull her into his arms and take up where they'd left off so many years ago, writhing against each other, overwhelmed by a passion he had never expected and over which he'd experienced countless hours of guilt and remorse. At the time, he had thought it was the alcohol singing through his bloodstream that had caused him to respond to her kiss. Now he wasn't so sure.

"You better be right, 'cause I don't feel like sewing you up," she said as she finished pulling the ruined garment away from him. Cool air washed over his back as the heat of the fire and Sabrina's proximity flushed over his chest. "I'm not much of a seamstress. I'd hate for you to wind up with a crooked scar."

Jason laughed. "You still do that, don't you?"

"Do what? Sew bullet wounds up like button holes?"

"No, you still crack jokes when you're nervous." He smiled as she frowned at him. Her annoyance was tangible. Jason swore he could see it seething around her like an aura of red, pulsating light. "And I don't think you're supposed to sew up button holes, by the way. Makes it hard to get a button through."

Sabrina glanced heavenward. "Very funny. I suppose that may be true about the jokes. But didn't your mama ever tell you it's impolite to point out people's weaknesses?"

Jason couldn't answer while her soft, warm hands ran up his forearm, biceps and over his shoulder as she rose to examine the wound. He squeezed his eyes shut when her fingers brushed over the sore flesh. It wasn't pain that caused him to flinch. An intense, erotic shock shot through his body as her fingertips touched the nape of his neck and her sweet breath fanned his cheek.

She glanced at his face again, her eyes filled with concern. "I'm sorry. I'm trying to be careful."

Jason swallowed a bark of laughter. She had no idea how she was affecting him. Sabrina leaned closer, her body between his thighs as she peered at his shoulder. She wore a soft cotton sweater in sunny yellow with long sleeves and a deep, scooped neckline. A pair of faded blue jeans hugged her round hips and long, slender legs. Her clothes clung to every curve, molding her figure in a way he didn't want to notice. But he was sure the image would haunt his dreams.

Friends. They were friends. That was all he could promise and maybe more than he could deliver. He hadn't done so well with that the last time they'd been in this cabin together. How was she turning him inside out without even trying?

Gentle fingers probed the tender flesh around the wound. The touch might have hurt if it wasn't for the adrenaline pumping like mad through his veins.

Sabrina leaned over him to get a better look. "I'll have to wash the blood away, but I think you're right after all. I don't think it's very deep."

Her sigh sounded relieved. All he could think about was burying his face in the warm, dark valley between her breasts. Her fragrance reached out to him, pulled at him until he couldn't think. She smelled like flowers and vanilla.

"Great." His voice was ragged, choked.

Sabrina eyed him, frowning. "You need something for the pain. I forgot to bring a washcloth anyway. Will you be okay for a second?"

Jason nodded. He didn't trust his voice. Eventually, she'd figure out that the overriding sensation radiated about three feet below the bullet wound. He didn't want her to know. There could never be anything more between them.

With her out of range again, Jason breathed deeply, trying to cleanse her intoxicating scent from his senses. He could hear water running, cabinet doors opening and shutting, the sound of a cap being popped off a medicine bottle and the rattle of pills. He listened with eyes closed and head bowed, taking more deep breaths to steady his nerves. Being shot at was one thing. But being so close to Sabrina and experiencing these strong, unexpected desires was sheer hell.

"Here…"

He jumped.

"Sorry," she murmured. "You'd better take these. It should help ease the pain."

Jason looked up into her dark brown eyes and smiled. She held out her hand and he took the pills, glancing at the brown tablets. He rarely took any kind of medication.

"What is it?" he asked.

"Ibuprofen…four tablets are the same as a prescription dose. I figure you need all the help you can get right now."

When he still didn't look convinced, she sighed and shoved a glass of water into his other hand.

"I'm not trying to poison you, Jason. I injured myself during a shoot a few years back and the doctor told me to take them like that since I couldn't afford a prescription. Look, Mr. Healthnut, it's okay as long as you don't make a habit of it."

He narrowed his gaze. "You couldn't afford a prescription? Where did you find the doctor?"

"It's no big deal. Money got tight from time to time in the beginning. I was an adult. I made my choices." She shrugged. "The doctor worked at the neighborhood clinic. He was a real nice guy. I took pictures of his kids and in return he treated my knee when I sprained it."

Jason watched her face as he tossed the pills back into his mouth and took a swig of water. A faint blush crept over her cheeks. Sabrina looked away and she bent to plunge the washcloth in the water on the end table. He watched as she wrung it out. Her hands shook.

He closed his eyes and vowed not to touch her again. He couldn't play with her life and emotions that way. She was too good for that.

But, God, how he'd missed her gentle nature and quick wit. She moved the cloth over his tender skin. He felt a bead of cool water run down his back. She leaned closer, focusing on the task and didn't notice how strongly his body reacted to her nearness. Jason swallowed hard as he searched for some thought that would keep this need to gather her close from overriding common sense.

"So...did you travel a lot with my dad?" she asked, her voice a little breathless. Was she feeling this chemistry, too?

He sighed, rubbing his eyes with one hand. "Yes, actually. He took me everywhere. Said he couldn't always depend on hired drivers in foreign countries. Didn't trust them."

He flinched as the cloth came too close to the open wound. "Oh, I'm sorry!" she gasped.

"It's okay," he said through clenched teeth. "Keep going. I'll bite the bullet."

"I've always wanted to travel," she murmured, her touch lighter. "Guess now I'll have a chance to do that." She wrung out the cloth, the water turning dark with his blood. "Where would you recommend? Any countries I should avoid?"

He shook his head. Memories of his last assignment pushed through the wall he'd erected around them. He had cruised the back allies of a small Argentine city while David rubbed elbows with a rich collector, a man suspected of laundering money for a particularly nasty band of rebels.

While David had attended parties in black tie and drank imported champagne, Jason had discovered a real lead as he downed Tequila shooters in a bug-infested saloon. He'd barely escaped with his life and cover intact that time.

David had been furious. Jason had told him to go to hell. He'd almost quit that day. Almost.

"Depends," he responded. "Are you planning on traveling alone?"

She shrugged, her features hidden from view as she peered over his shoulder. "Probably. Unless I can hire a big, strong bodyguard to take along."

He grinned. "Well, South America is beautiful, but you definitely need an escort to go there. Not the place for a gorgeous American heiress on her own."

"Oh, I don't think I'm that adventurous yet. What about Ireland? Or Scotland?"

"Hmmm, we never made it to Ireland." He dropped his head forward as her gentle ministrations began to relax his taut muscles. "But we flew over it a few times. It's beautiful."

"Then maybe that's where we should start."

We. He liked the sound of that. But it could never be. Once again, the niggling doubt surfaced, the small sense of discontent when he thought of his life for any length of time. It bothered him that spending just a few hours with Sabrina would have him questioning his choices.

Chapter Four

Sabrina rummaged in the kitchen cabinets, her stomach churning from both lack of food and a deluge of emotions. She needed to keep busy. Cooking was a better alternative to succumbing to the deep sadness that reached out to overwhelm her self-control.

"Not much to choose from," she said over her shoulder. The bright note in her voice sounded false. "There's a lot of cocoa and a big bag of popcorn. No popper though."

"There should be a large pot under the sink," Jason told her. "If there's oil left, we can pop it over the fire."

"You really are a Boy Scout, aren't you?" She placed a box of cocoa mix and bag of yellow popcorn kernels on the counter. A big metal pot with a long handle and lid took up most of the space beneath the sink. She lifted it up, the metal clanging against the shining granite.

"Now, if we just have oil and salt, we'll be in business," she murmured. Another cabinet, a small cry of success and Sabrina turned a smile toward Jason. It froze on her lips as she caught his expression, dark and unfathomable, flickering with an emotion that bordered on affection. No that was stupid. Only a fool believed in miracles.

She cleared her throat. "Well, butter would be nice, but I…I guess this will do."

She forced her gaze to remain on his face as she tried to ignore the way firelight lapped at honed muscles of his arms, the chiseled plain of his stomach. The sight of him half-naked made her blood thrum through her veins.

That last night, ten years ago, she had stripped him naked to the waist in this very room. But then he'd opened his eyes and regained his senses.

He'd changed. Time and steel had shaped the young, lean body she remembered. His back still carried scars from the accident that almost took his life. But he could now boast muscles sculpted beneath the press of metal bars.

She slapped the cabinet door shut, silently cursing herself for delving so far into the past as she filled a teakettle with water. Nostalgia could be a powerful aphrodisiac. Lust should be beyond her after the continuous disappointment she'd experienced with her ex-husband. But it lurked in the shadowed recesses of her mind, ever hopeful.

Music lilted through the air with a low, seductive beat, startling her out of her reverie. She glanced at Jason's broad back turned toward her as he browsed through a rack of CDs at the entertainment center. It was compact and hidden discreetly behind gleaming wood doors, but had obviously been updated. All the pieces were state-of-the-art, sleek mirror images of items she'd seen in numerous ads.

"Did Dad spend a lot of time here?" she asked as she walked toward the hearth and set the pot, popcorn and oil on the rug.

He looked over his shoulder, that quirky little smile tugging at his lips. Sabrina's heart skittered. "No, he didn't. But he let Thomas and me use it. It's a great place to unwind for a weekend. He also let a friend of mine crash here after he got out of rehab."

Her eyes went wide as the little piece of information sank in. Her father had helped someone recovering from addiction? It seemed so unlike the man she'd grown up with, the unforgiving individual who had treated her weaknesses with contempt.

"Oh, well…that's nice." What else could she say? The image just didn't gel.

Jason moved toward her and dropped to his knees on the floor near her feet. She took a hasty step backward. Her breath hitched a bit before she realized he was simply getting the popper ready. Heat flushed through her. What an idiot she was being. She only hoped he hadn't noticed.

"Is the music okay with you?" he asked as he dumped the hard kernels into the pan. They rattled and pinged against the metal.

"Yeah, sounds good." She swallowed. "Are the CDs yours?"

Jason scooted to the fire on his knees, pulling the screen out of the way. "Yes, that one is. Your dad has a few and I think Thomas left one or two behind."

Sabrina stepped back, watching as he held the pan over the fire and shook it every few seconds. She retreated to a safer distance from the heat and busied herself getting the cups ready for the hot water.

"You know what you're doing?" she asked.

"Of course. Don't you remember? I'm the best corn-popper east of the Mississippi." His grin widened as she looked in his direction, one brow quirked. "Well, that's the title I can brag about, anyway. The other is too risqué for innocent ears."

She felt heat rise in her face in response to his teasing. At that moment, a familiar song started, breaking open the floodgates to their painful last night together. She remembered his lean, hard body pressed into hers, the rough-woven fabric at her back, the warm male against her breasts. She had felt his hands sliding across her skin as he'd pushed at her strapless dress.

No. Pushed her away. That's what had happened. He had pushed her away, wrenching her arms from about his neck as he'd rolled off her.

Sabrina had wanted to be the one at his side, watching the silver slip through his dark hair and the laugh lines deepen beside his Caribbean-blue eyes. She thought she could make him see her as a woman. But he had felt her desperate love in that clumsy kiss and walked away.

He had never been interested in her that way and Sabrina would not let herself hope for that again. No matter how devastating the attraction. Giving herself a mental shake, she forced her thoughts to other things as she tried to block out the song. He didn't seem to remember it, thank heavens.

"What are you going to do now?" she asked as the teapot began a low whistle. She flicked off the burner.

"Well, I think as soon as the phone is working we should—"

"No," she interrupted with a self-conscious chuckle. "I mean, now that Dad is…is gone. What are you going to do?"

Jason turned his head, but not before she saw the strange flicker of emotion in his eyes. She heard the first ping as kernels began to explode. He shook the pot harder. The play of muscles beneath his skin made her heart skip a beat. She jerked back to face the counter, cocoa mix flying in all directions.

"I hadn't thought that far ahead. I suppose I'll keep working."

A beat of silence followed and he continued in a poorly executed British accent. "Do you need a chauffeur, Miss Layne? I've got years of experience and great references."

She laughed, a weight lifting from her shoulders. It felt good for a change. "As a matter of fact, I will need someone who knows his way around cars."

"That would be me. I do know how to make a delicate engine purr." The look in his eyes said more, but he turned away, focusing his attention on the job at hand. Corn popped at a frantic pace, pushing at the lid until smoke curled up through a small gap. "All right then, I think we're almost done. I'll need a potholder. Can you grab one? I think they're in a drawer by the stove."

"Oh!" She scrambled to find him a hotpad as she grabbed a large bowl she'd noticed in another cupboard. Sabrina sprinted across the room, laying the thick square in his outstretched hand.

"Thank you," he murmured. His biceps flexed as he lifted the pot, still shaking the contents until it rested on the flagstone away from the heat. "I think we did it."

The lid came off, spilling hot, white popcorn on the floor. They laughed together as he tried to tip the heavy pot and dump the rest into the bowl, but about a quarter of it tumbled to the stone.

"Nothing burned, good," he said as he surveyed their feast. "I guess we can throw the dirty ones outside. I'm sure the birds will appreciate it in the morning."

She smiled up at him until a dark look settled across his features. His eyes turned a shade of navy blue she'd only seen one other time in her life—one of the vivid images etched in her mind from their short night of passion. Sabrina sat back on her heels and scrambled to her feet.

"Why don't you grab the cocoa and the salt?" she said, hating the way her voice shook. She made a beeline for the bathroom and leaned heavily against the closed door once inside. The mirror above the vanity told all—her eyes were bright, her cheeks as red as if she'd been sunning on the beach in Mexico. *Damn.* She really had to pull herself together. One humiliation in front of Jason was enough for this lifetime.

They spent the next hour munching popcorn and discussing everything from weather to music and politics until the polite small talk ran out. Sabrina stared into the flames, her thoughts still whirling even as her body began to relax in the warm glow.

"Why would he turn me away and then leave me everything?"

Jason frowned at her sudden leap of conversation. "David was a difficult man to get a handle on. Don't be too hard on yourself. He tended to keep everyone at arm's length."

"Oh, I know. It wasn't me...well, it was, but I don't know what I could have done differently."

He laid his hand over hers, applying gentle pressure with his long fingers. "He did care about you."

"No...no, I don't think so." She shook her head, not able to bear one more half-baked attempt at condolence. Not from him. "Now's not the time for worn out platitudes, Jase. You know what it was like – what *he* was like. He hated me and..."

"Bree!"

"Okay." She fluttered a hand to stop his denials. "Maybe *hate* is too strong a word. But he didn't like me. He certainly didn't approve of the way I chose to live my life."

"I really don't think that's true."

"Do you remember the last time my father told me he loved me?"

"No."

Damn. The tears were back. "Neither do I."

He stood up and stuffed his hands into the pockets of his tailored slacks as he paced across the room. After a moment, his quiet voice stole over the crackling of the fire and the low melody playing from the speakers overhead.

"He followed your career from the beginning."

Sabrina stared, her brain a total blank as she tried to decipher what Jason was telling her. "He what?"

"It's the truth." He turned toward her. The sad look on his face gripped her heart. "I accompanied him to every exhibit you ever entered. The lighthouse painting above his desk...did you see it? Didn't you recognize it?" She shook her head. "He bought your original photo from a gallery and commissioned an artist to do the painting from it. The original is hanging in his bedroom along with all your other photographs he bought over the years."

His words seemed to vibrate down a long tunnel, coming from some distant place. The sounds made no sense; it was like trying to understand a foreign film without subtitles.

"W-wait just a minute." She slid her feet off the low oval table and carefully set down her empty mug. "My father bought my photos? Jason, I'm lost here."

"You are so talented! The old man would mist up every time he saw your work. So did I. I never knew you could do that. You see things through that camera lens that no one else can. You show such insight in those photos—they make people stop and think...make them feel."

She didn't move. Then some neuron sparked and the trance was broken. "I think we'd better check you for a head injury," she quipped, her voice shaky. "You must have gotten something scrambled in that thick skull of yours."

"My brain is functioning quite well." The corners of his mouth turned up into a sad smile. "He should have told you these things himself. But now…he made his choices and I'm not going to let you believe the lies any longer. He loved you. He loved you and bragged about you and he was one of the proudest fathers I've ever known."

"No!" She surged to her feet, her heart thudding in her chest as if she'd run a mile. "I don't want to hear this garbage! Don't you dare stand there and tell me what a loving, devoted father David Layne was. I was there." She jabbed a finger into her chest. "I'm the one who had to hear: 'You're always disappointing me, young lady,' and-and 'Go away, Sabrina, I'm working.'"

Tears filled her eyes, quavered in her voice, but she bore on like a runaway train. "I'm the one he wouldn't talk to when I refused to go back to business school. I'm the one he told to never come back when I married that bastard Sam. I'm the one who could never come home again."

"Bree!" Jason strode forward and took her by the arms, gently shaking her. "Stop it, stop."

Tears poured down her face. "You're wrong," she whispered. "You have to be. Don't you understand? If you're not then…" Her voice broke. "If you're not, then I can't hate him anymore. And I have to hate him. I have to. It hurts too much not to."

Jason pulled her resisting body into his embrace. His arms wrapped around her but she resisted his comfort for a moment. It couldn't be true. It just couldn't. She fought against the breakdown she felt coming, the power of it surging upward like a volcano about to explode.

With a sob, she crumpled against his chest and cried. Unable to hold back the release of years of pain, she felt her body shake with the force of it. It frightened her.

Jason seemed to sense her fear, to understand her pain. He pressed her head to his good shoulder with one hand as the other caressed the curve of her spine. The slow, gentle strokes grounded her, kept some part of her sane as the pain rolled over her like a freight train.

"Sshh…it's all right," he whispered, his breath warm against her hair. "Let it out. It's the only way to heal. I'll take care of you. I'll keep you safe. Just let it go."

So she let go, her very cells seeming to rip and shred with the pain; pain that had always been there, lurking beneath the surface of her false smile and bravado. Some time later, the sobs wilted to small, dejected sniffles. But Jason kept holding her. Sabrina's hands were trapped between them.

"I'm sorry," he murmured. "I didn't plan on this. I should have found a better way to tell you."

She shook her head. "I don't understand."

"Your father…" He shook his head. "I think your father acted that way with you because he was trying to keep you distant."

"Why?" She tilted her head back to look into his eyes.

"To keep you safe. I guess he just didn't know any other way to do it."

"That makes no sense. What was he afraid of?"

"I think he was afraid of losing you…of hurting again like he did when your mom died." Jason shrugged, that crooked smile more sad than anything now. It pricked at her heart. "When you lose someone like that…when you feel like it's your fault somehow, it's a hard thing to get over. Your dad never did."

"But it wasn't his fault mom died."

"Maybe, maybe not. But he felt responsible all the same."

She pushed away, anger slowly filling the cracks in her newly shattered heart. "So he just ignored me? Left me alone and parentless because he couldn't deal with my mom's death?"

Jason sighed as he pushed a hand through his tousled hair. "I never said it was a good response, but I know for a fact that he loved you more than anything in the world. These last six years without you ate away at him. But you were both too damn proud to make the first move."

"No!" She turned away. "I don't want to hear anymore of this." Tension radiated around them, mixing with the heat of the blazing fire and her anger.

"Okay, no more talking. I know this is a lot to take in at once." He sighed. "I think I'd better see if the cell phone battery is charged before it gets much later. If we don't let Thomas know where we are, they'll have the cops searching the mountainside."

It felt as if the cabin had shrunk to miniscule proportions. She needed air and space to think. Sabrina stalked to the door, grabbing her coat and boots along the way.

"What are you doing, Bree?"

She shrugged into her coat. "I need some fresh air. I think better outdoors." He silently watched her stuff her feet into her tall leather boots.

"Haven't we walked enough for one night?"

"No," she snapped.

"Do you want some company?"

"No, I don't." She flicked a glance across his naked chest. "Besides, you're injured and half-dressed. You stay here and check on the phone. I won't go far."

She pulled open the door and stepped outside into the crisp breeze before he could say another word. Taking the steps off the covered porch, Sabrina marched to the driveway and stared up at the night sky. There weren't any stars, just a deep, still blackness. The sudden blast of cold registered, the breeze stinging her cheeks as the snow began falling again. Spring had arrived, but the air still smelled of winter woodsmoke and ice.

She shivered beneath her coat, tugging the sides together as she walked down the gravel drive. It took her several minutes to reach the end of it. Her feet and legs ached from the long trek up the mountain, but she needed to clear her head. Her world had tilted on its axis and still wove out of control.

It didn't seem real, yet it all made sense somehow in view of her chaotic childhood. Before her mother had died, David had been a doting father, praising his little girl, carrying her long after she learned to walk. He had treated her like a princess. Then when her mother died, it was as if she'd lost both parents.

Maybe it hadn't been her fault that he seemed incapable of showing affection. Maybe it had been his way of trying to protect his child from unseen dangers in the world. Or maybe he'd been selfishly protecting his own heart.

"Damn you," she muttered as tears burned her eyes. "You could have said you loved me. What good does it do me now?"

Sabrina kicked the snow-dusted gravel, her fists clenched at her sides. An icy gust of wind snaked through the edge of her coat, burrowing beneath the hem of her sweater. She shivered.

"That was one lousy way to deal with things, Dad."

She felt like shouting and cursing. She wanted to kick something. She needed to hear the satisfying sound of shattering glass or the shotgun echo of a door slamming shut. But she stood, staring at the silent snow. The icy wind numbed her face and hands.

If her father had loved her and had not been just a womanizing jerk, then a lot her perceptions were ill conceived. If Jason told the truth, then David Layne had loved her. Sabrina didn't want it to be true. It made losing her father all the more painful. They might have had a chance at being a real family one day.

If only...

She turned and trudged up and down the drive, her boots crunched the powdery snow. After several trips, her thighs and calves burned from exertion; the cold air stung her lungs. She gave up and walked back to the cabin just as the door swung open. Looking up, she met Jason's troubled gaze. Sabrina glanced down. He had pulled on a black sweater and his shoes.

"I was getting worried," he said. "What took you so long?"

It felt nice to have someone looking out for her. "I had a lot to think about."

He moved sideways so she could enter. "I was just about to come looking for you. The battery is almost ready."

Sabrina felt a whoosh of cold air on her back as Jason closed the door. She pulled off her coat, hanging it on a hook by the door.

"Where did you find the sweater?" she asked as she toed off her boots.

"Your father kept a stash of clothes here."

Sabrina could feel his gaze following her as she sauntered to the fire. The heat of the flames reached out, wrapping her in a soft glow as it thawed her from head to foot. She rubbed her hands together.

"Are there any women's clothes or should I ask Vivian first before I borrow something? I don't suppose she left any flannel pajamas behind? She didn't really seem the flannel type."

"Vivian?"

Sabrina turned to find Jason frowning at her.

"Yes, Vivian…Vivian James?" She sighed, flinging her arms wide in irritation. "She told me all about her relationship with my father. You don't have to play dumb, Jase. It doesn't matter who his latest conquest was."

"Hey, hold it. David didn't care who knew what about his sex life but…" He ran a hand through his dark hair, shaking his head as if trying to make sense of it all. "Vivian works for his import business as a secretary but he never said a word about her on a personal level. She was window dressing as far as I know. I could've sworn he didn't even like her. Your dad didn't have a lot of women friends in the last couple of years. He seemed to be getting tired of the playboy lifestyle. He said there were some changes he needed to make before…"

"Before what?" she prompted.

He looked at her, compassion filling his clear blue eyes. Sabrina wished his arms were wrapped around her again. It hurt too much to think of what might have been. She'd grown up, virtually alone, and had become a very independent woman. Yet, there were times when she longed for someone to take the reins and shelter her from life's storms, just for a while.

"Before he ran out of chances," he admitted. "Before he pushed you so far away that he could never reach you again."

"Why didn't he worry about that years ago?" Her voice caught. She felt the scalding tears form behind her eyes but blinked them away. "Why didn't he try to be a father when I needed one? Like before I married that bastard and spent two years living in hell?"

Jason moved toward her, his expression filled with such tenderness that she couldn't hold back the few tears that slipped down her face.

"I don't know, sweetheart," he whispered as he cupped her cheek. He brushed the tears away with the pad of his thumb. "I think he thought a little 'tough love' would have you toeing the line. He just forgot what a strong-willed woman you turned out to be. I'm not sure he ever knew how to show his love to you."

The knowledge that his death hadn't been an accident, that someone had killed her father, sent a knife-like pain through her heart. A spasm rippled through her body.

"Who did it? Who killed him, Jase? Why would they want to hurt us, too?"

He closed his eyes for a moment and shook his head. When he looked at her again, Sabrina felt that familiar attraction. It came from the inner strength he wrapped around himself like a shield of armor. The complete confidence that fit Jason Sinclair like a well-worn glove. She longed to brace her body against him, to draw on that power he possessed.

Jason sighed. "Someone from the past. Someone wanting revenge…I just don't know. I wish I did, but nothing fits. It doesn't make sense…unless…you were just caught…in the cross fire."

His words softened to a whisper. He stared into her eyes and she couldn't help but wonder what he saw there. His touch set her skin on fire. Sabrina felt her body sway toward him. She stared at his full, firm mouth. Just one kiss and she'd be satisfied.

Who was she trying to kid? One taste of Jason would just leave her wanting more. She still wanted more, despite the heartbreak and ten years of distance.

"Bree…" He whispered her name, his warm breath fanning her face like a sweet summer breeze. "This isn't a good idea."

She shook her head. "No. Not a good idea."

His throat convulsed as he swallowed, his gaze fastened on her mouth. "I don't want to hurt you again."

The magnetic pull intensified, her body pressing into his as little shock waves rippled down her spine. Jason's body responded. She felt the shudder that coursed through him.

"I've missed you," he whispered. "I'm sorry—for everything. I should never have kissed you like that. You were so damn beautiful. I just couldn't keep my hands off of you."

"You were drunk."

He shook his head. "Not that drunk…not enough to take advantage of the sweetest girl I'd ever met."

"It was one kiss, not a seduction. I'm the one who started it." Her words contradicted the pain she felt wash over her. She wanted to understand what had happened. "Walking away…lying to me like all the others. That's what hurt."

Jason went rigid. "I meant what I said that night. We were still friends. I couldn't see you as anything else. I didn't want that to change."

"But things did change." Her voice held a note of betrayal that couldn't be erased. It was indelibly etched on her soul. "You left for D.C. and I never saw or heard from you again. You didn't come back for my graduation."

"I thought it was for the best."

She pushed away from him; her body screamed in protest at the loss of his warmth. "Jason, let's be honest here. I can't stand lies or liars. There have been too many in my life." She thought he flinched as his gaze slipped from hers. "You didn't think about me at all once you left Castle's Grove. I'm sure it didn't take long for you to find someone more experienced... more attractive to take up where that kiss left off."

"Bree—"

"No." She stepped back, shame lighting a blaze in her cheeks even as pride stiffened her spine. "It's okay. Maybe there will always be a little spark between us, but lust doesn't interest me. That kind of attraction leads nowhere. I want more than that from a relationship."

A sad look settled in his eyes, a mixture of longing and regret. "That's all I have to offer. And I'm not even sure that would be a good idea. For either of us."

Tears burned her throat. She had known the truth all along but hearing the words spoken aloud ripped at the ancient wound.

"That's too bad." She turned away and walked toward the sofa. "I think you're selling yourself short. But maybe someday you'll realize that. Maybe the right woman will come along and help you see the truth."

Chapter Five

He watched her perch upon the sofa, stiff and unyielding. He'd seen her so differently before, though he hated to think of it. She had been sensual, earthy. Her untutored kisses had dragged him to the point of no return. Toward possibilities…like falling in love.

He froze. He did not want her love. Not then, not now. He was not prepared to offer his heart. Did he even possess one after these past few years of watching, even encouraging people to betray one another?

He couldn't offer a woman like Sabrina a stable life or even a safe one, let alone the kind of love she deserved. She thrived in a world of light and laughter while he held his own in the deep, dark recesses of humanity's cesspool. One-night stands, bar pick-ups and people that would sell their souls for a few thousand dollars or that next hit of the latest designer drug—that was his world.

Jason knew he'd have to remain alone, lurking in the shadows, as he struggled to remember why he was there in the first place. Sabrina didn't belong and couldn't survive it any more than a vampire could brave the noonday sun. But maybe, for a time, he could enjoy the light reflected in her sweet, sparkling laughter and the smile that danced in her eyes.

He couldn't let himself get too close. It would hurt too much when she left him behind. Just like he'd abandoned her, his best friend.

She sat at the edge of the futon, avoiding his gaze. He kicked himself for humiliating her again. But it couldn't be helped. Better now than later when it would hurt more.

"I don't need protection." Her tone was cool, almost devoid of emotion. "I've been on my own for ten years. I can handle myself."

He sighed as he scrubbed a hand over his face. "Bree, I know you can. But this isn't the same as avoiding muggers in Central Park. We don't know what or who we're up against."

"Maybe I'm not experienced with hired killers. But neither are you. Shouldn't you just let the police chief handle this?"

"Yes, I should, except that he doesn't have the manpower or the evidence to do anything. I told him about the threats David received, but the calls stopped before they could be traced."

She jerked her head around, her eyes wide. "Calls?"

"Yeah." He wondered at her tone and the sudden fear in her eyes. "I thought it might just be a prank—local kids, a disgruntled employee or lover. But nothing came of it after the new alarms and sensors were installed. The calls stopped."

He could see her relax a little, though a ghost of a frown lingered on her brow. "I can't just lock myself in my room and wait for you to get yourself killed," she said.

"That's not going to happen."

"Oh, so, tonight was just a prank, right? Those were blanks that almost took your arm off. Why should I worry?"

Even though she tried to mask her concern with sarcasm, it touched him. It had been a long time since any woman had given a damn about what happened to him beyond the bedroom.

He cleared his throat, pushing the disturbing feelings aside. "Listen, I think we'd both better get a good night's rest. I'll have some detective work to do tomorrow. We have to find out who those clowns were that chased us up the mountain. You take the bed in the loft. I'll camp out on the futon."

She gazed at him a moment and he wondered where the warring thoughts flitting through her eyes would lead them. Sabrina shrugged.

"Didn't you have to call Thomas?"

He looked away, part of him glad for the change of subject and yet feeling disappointment.

"Yeah," he replied. "The phone should work now. I'd better make sure the police know about the accident."

A shadow passed over her face. "Do you think the men in the car survived?"

Jason shook his head. "I don't know. I sure hope so. Maybe they can give us some answers."

Sabrina sighed, stretching her arms overhead and arching her back in one fluid move. His mouth went dry as he stared, unable to wrench his gaze from her soft curves.

She stood. "Well, I think I'm going to take a shower while you're on the phone. I'm starting to ache all over."

He cleared his throat. "Must be from all the hiking."

"Must be." Sabrina turned and walked toward the bathroom. He watched her, mesmerized by the gentle sway of her hips encased in form-fitting jeans. The door closed between them and he let out a frustrated breath. "Hell, I think I'm the one that needs a protector!"

He walked to the kitchen to retrieve the phone. To his relief the display lit up, indicating it was ready. He punched buttons, fighting to concentrate on the numbers instead of the woman in the other room. "Come on Thomas, pick up. Where is…"

"Layne residence, may I help you?" The cool English voice seemed unusually polite for being disturbed after midnight.

"Thomas…"

"Where the hell have you been? Sabrina's gone!"

"Hey, slow down, she's fine, we're together."

"You're together? What do you mean? Jason, you should have told someone before we called the police and turned the entire house upside down!"

"Oh, great." Jason dropped onto the sofa, pushing his free hand through his hair. He sighed. "Thomas, I am sorry, but I didn't think we'd be gone this long. Someone followed us and took a few shots."

"Shots? Are you all right? Was she hurt?" Jason smiled at the concern in the other man's voice. The butler had often shown more caring for the heiress than her father ever had.

"We're both fine, but the guys in the sedan weren't so lucky." He could still hear the echoing crash of the other vehicle tumbling end over end down the mountain. Jason relayed the events of their chase, including where the police could find the wreckage. "We hiked here. My car wouldn't start and both rear tires were blown out."

"Why didn't you call me sooner? I've had the entire security staff combing the grounds for the past three hours."

Jason sighed. "Again, I'm sorry, but I wasn't able to get the phone working until now. Can you have someone swing by for my car in the morning?"

"Would you like me to come around and pick you up now?"

"No, we're both worn out and the roads are probably a sheet of ice. I don't want to risk anyone else having an accident. We can spend the night."

Thomas cleared his throat. "Do you think that's wise, Jason?"

He stiffened. "What is that supposed to mean?"

"Well, it's just that…" The older man sighed. From his years of experience with the Englishman, Jason knew he was struggling with honesty over tact. "Sabrina has been through quite a bit today and she used to have a thing for you. Such proximity might prove a bit uncomfortable overnight. I can be there in an hour and have you two home in no time."

Tact had lost that battle in supreme fashion. Jason couldn't help but grin. "No, thank you, we'll be fine, Tommy old boy." He heard a sharp intake of breath and his grin widened. "But I do have another call to make, so I'll see you in the morning."

"Of course."

"And Thomas?" Conscious of Sabrina's closeness, Jason lowered his voice. "Find out all you can about the sedan passengers. This might be our first break."

"Will do. You sleep well, Jason. I mean that."

A spark of anger flickered at the suggestion in Thomas's voice. "I am not going to take advantage of her. I'm trying to be a friend."

"I didn't say you would, Jason," the butler replied. "It's just that when so many emotions are in play..."

"I know," he interrupted. "Believe me, I'm treading carefully. I don't want to hurt her."

"Of course not. Just be sure you don't get hurt either."

The admonition took him aback. "I won't. Good night, Thomas."

"Good night."

He hung up and stared into the fire a moment before dialing again. As he waited for an answer, he glanced toward the bathroom door and cringed. *Yeah, some friend.* A friend wouldn't have been tempted to take what she offered ten years ago, knowing the pain she was going through. He wouldn't have pushed her away and run like a scared rabbit, leaving her feeling dirty and used. The role of friend had been the last thing on his mind. The fact that he had stopped and walked away gave him the guts to look her in the eye again.

"Hello?"

He sat upright, flicking a glance back to the door and lowering his voice. The less she knew the better.

"It's me. We've got a new development..."

* * *

Sabrina leaned on the bathroom door and tried to hear what Jason said. She supposed she should feel guilty about eavesdropping, but she didn't. Jason seemed to be holding something back from her. Things just didn't feel right.

Every once in a while, she caught that certain look in his eyes—the same one he'd had when they were kids and he tried to lie.

The first call to Thomas seemed strange. She wasn't sure why Jason insisted on investigating something that should be left to the professionals. But this second call had her baffled. He spoke so softly that she wondered how the other party could even hear.

She pressed her ear against the wooden door, cursing the architect for having such thick interior doors installed. All she could make out was the gentle murmur of his deep voice.

Letting her curiosity get the better of her, she twisted the knob and edged the door open a fraction of an inch.

"I don't give a damn what you think I should do…" She flinched at the anger in his voice. "No…no!… Listen! I will not put her in any more danger."

Sabrina peeked through the crack, wishing she could hear what the other person said. Was Jason talking about her? She saw his shoulders stiffen, his body turned slightly toward her.

"Hey, I've gotta go… yeah, yeah, I know… Yes. You know I will… Okay, goodbye."

He slapped the phone closed against his palm and sat staring into the fire. Sabrina bit her lip, trying to decide what she might have just heard. It didn't make much sense. She closed the door, turning the button lock before slipping out her clothes. A long hot shower would do her a world of good.

* * *

She came out of the bathroom almost an hour later, damp and warm from the shower and wearing nothing but a large towel. The living room air felt cool against her skin.

Jason glanced down at the fluffy red bath sheet that encased her body. His eyes darkened. A jolt of awareness sparked through her, but she shoved it aside.

His gaze slid away from her. "We better get to bed."

"Oh?" Her stomach flipped and she grasped for the sarcastic humor like a warrior brandishing a shield. "Is that an order or a proposition?"

He turned his back. "Listen, I'm sorry about what almost happened. It won't again."

She stared at him and nodded. It was what she wanted—distance, safety. He was lying to her, keeping something from her. She couldn't trust her heart to anyone that kept secrets. Never again.

But why did she feel so bereft?

He cleared his throat. "I think we both better keep this...this attraction under control before something happens that we wind up regretting." The emotionless tone tore at her heart even more than the words themselves.

"Regretting?" She cringed at the hurt sound of her own voice. "Yes, I suppose you're right." She turned for the ladder that led to the loft. It would not be a graceful exit, swathed only in a towel, but it couldn't be helped. Sabrina needed to retreat before he saw the pain she was feeling.

"Goodnight, Bree."

She tried to answer but the words stuck in her throat.

* * *

"Thirty-four, thirty-five..." She stared at the vaulted ceiling, squinting at the dim wash of firelight as the numbers whispered past her lips. "Thirty-six...thirty-seven. Thirty-seven knot holes in the wood beams. Yep, I think this is going to be a long, long night."

Her stomach tightened with disgust. How could she do that? How could she let go of her emotions and come so close to his trap?

Jason had plenty of experience ensnaring women. When he'd been sixteen, there had been many girls that couldn't wait to get Castle Grove's bad boy into the back of his van. Bragging rights, she assumed. Or maybe each thought they had what it took to tame the boy with the wicked gleam in his brilliant blue eyes.

Sabrina had known she couldn't compete. She'd never tried. But oh, how she had longed to feel his arms around her. To know what it was like to be kissed senseless by the boy who lived over her father's garage. Her friend. The man she had loved.

She felt a twinge of anger at him for the unnerving way he had dismissed their interlude, even though it was what she'd wanted. It hurt that he hadn't been moved by their closeness.

"He still acts like a cave man—'me protect'!" She stared into the shadows. "Or maybe he's more like Tarzan. Primitive, primal..." The image of Jason in a loincloth sprang to mind, almost making her choke on a breath of air. Sabrina bolted upright on the bed, her borrowed T-shirt riding high up on her thighs.

"Oh, my, don't go there, Bree, you'll be falling down the ladder and jumping him next."

She fought the insane impulse to do just that and flopped back down on her side. After tugging the pillows and blankets into different positions for several minutes, she kicked everything off.

Jason couldn't offer the security she needed. He didn't want the same things from life.

She rubbed her eyes. "Who am I kidding? I don't know what I want, either." After spending most of her life giving her heart to cold, unfeeling men, Sabrina knew she must tread cautiously. She'd trusted Jason before and had wound up bruised and humiliated.

Sabrina squeezed her eyes shut. He wanted a woman with the soul of a seductress, a heart like tempered steel. She could never fit that bill. It wouldn't take much to lose herself in his eyes.

She thought of his broad back and chest glistening like bronzed sculpture in the firelight. Sabrina sighed. He had always possessed the power to turn her insides to jelly, leaving her breathless and self-conscious. Yet, no matter how good it felt in his arms, she never should have admitted how much he'd hurt her before. It would have been better if he kept thinking she had forgotten that night long ago.

Sabrina rolled over. She'd have to find some way to smooth things over and start fresh. She would not let him go on thinking she still longed for him. No matter how close to the truth that might be.

* * *

Downstairs, the object of her churning thoughts tossed and turned on the thin futon mattress. He could hear every squeak of springs in the loft overhead. He thought he heard Sabrina's voice, whispering among the crackling flames of the fire in the hearth.

Jason groaned and turned over again. He shouldn't have touched her. *Damn!* What had happened to his resolve? His determination to find her father's enemy and restore their friendship? He didn't have the right to touch her. He couldn't want her that way; she had always been like a sister to him. A friend when he'd needed one the most.

Too much stood between them, including the truth. She might forgive him many things, but lying was not one of them. He knew that. He understood that. He was in big trouble.

Until he figured out who had rigged David Layne's car to crash and burn, he would keep his hands off the millionaire's daughter. He had to keep a clear head and his eyes open at all times. He couldn't afford to concentrate on these unexpected feelings raging through him. That would be a sure way to get them both killed.

In the stillness of the night, he relived those stolen moments ten years ago. She had been so distraught over being stood up for her senior prom. At that moment, as she confessed her humiliation to him, Jason realized what a burden being wealthy must have on her sensitive spirit. Everyone seemed more than willing to use Sabrina for whatever they could get.

Instead of facing an empty house or the ridicule of her peers, she begged Jason to take her somewhere quiet…just for a few hours. Her father had been out of the country but she didn't want the other servants to know of her shame.

Even while the warning bells clanged in his brain, he agreed. They wound up at the cabin, indulging in the brandy her father had left in the liquor cabinet. They drank and talked, getting a little tipsy as the dark, warm liquid drifted through their veins.

Sabrina started to cry. She looked so fragile, so beautiful in her red satin dress with her dark hair piled high on her head, like a china doll teetering on the edge of a high shelf. As the firelight splashed over her skin, he had taken her into his arms. The embrace stirred very unbrotherly feelings.

He hadn't realized the edginess he'd been feeling around her that night was more than just wanderlust. It was lust, period. Jason had been both ashamed and enticed. At least he'd had enough sense left not to let the passion carry him away.

After pushing apart from her, he promised he wasn't angry. He swore that they would always be friends. Of course, he'd been lying through his teeth. He was sure he'd never see her again. The next morning, Jason had boarded a plane for Washington D.C., fully intending to never look back.

Sabrina had been forgotten. Replaced, just as she had accused, by a busty, experienced redhead who was more than willing to take the new kid under her wing and into her bed.

Jason sighed as the familiar guilt twisted his insides. He turned his back to the dancing flames. He needed sleep, not self-recriminations about things that happened years ago.

He would protect Sabrina as always. This time, she wouldn't need to worry about him taking liberties and causing embarrassment. He had learned his lesson the hard way.

* * *

He jerked awake, his bleary gaze focusing out the tall front windows as the midnight black of the sky began to fade. Washed purple by the faint glow of the sun's first rays, it held the promise of a clear, bright day.

Dreams of chocolate-brown eyes and chestnut hair haunted him. He could almost feel the silken strands caressing his face, tangled around his fingers, brushing over his chest. Jason stretched, arms reaching overhead until a knife of pain shot through him. He winced. The pain soon calmed to a dull ache and he wondered what had pulled him from the seductive dream.

A light knock on the front door had him sitting up, all senses on full alert.

"Jason?"

He expelled the breath in his lungs and ran a hand over his face. "Hang on, Thomas."

The futon's wooden frame creaked in protest as he stood. Pain shot like fiery darts through his limbs and the wooden floorboards felt icy beneath his bare feet.

Opening the door, he moved aside as the butler swept into the house. He carried a large, wicker hamper. The smell of coffee and fresh bread filled the room. Jason inhaled, savoring the rich aroma as it filled his lungs.

"Good morning, Jason," Thomas said as he strode to the kitchen table.

"Good morning. To what do we owe this honor?"

Thomas glanced at him, one eyebrow raised as he began to unpack the hamper. "I've had your car towed into town. One from the garage is waiting in the driveway. You're to use it until the Mercedes can be repaired."

Jason walked to the table, eyeing the large foam boxes and two heavy glass carafes, one of coffee and the other filled with what looked like fresh orange juice. The buttery smell of fluffy scrambled eggs, crisp bacon and the light, sweet scent of fresh fruit joined together. His mouth watered as the succulent odors wafted upward.

"And you brought breakfast? My, my…how efficient."

Thomas moved to the cabinets without response, his knowledge of the cabin showing as he pulled out plates, cups and silverware.

"I trust you and Sabrina slept well?" he asked, his gaze moving past Jason to the rumpled pillows and blankets on the futon. A smile of satisfaction lit the man's face.

"Of course," Jason replied. He would play the game, knowing he had nothing to be ashamed of this time around. But it was somewhat galling how Thomas managed to read his mind while he knew very little of the older man's personal life.

"Good..." the butler murmured. "Then you'll be more than ready to visit Chief Wright and give him a statement."

Jason sighed. "Yeah, I suppose so." His gaze shifted to the loft and back again. "What did they find?"

Thomas followed the direction of his gaze, motioning with one hand as he lowered his voice. "Is she still sleeping?" Jason nodded. "Good. They found a late model sedan about two hundred feet below the road where your car stalled."

"Anyone in it?"

Thomas nodded as he poured two glasses of fresh orange juice. "One body, a man killed on impact according to the preliminary coroner's report. He was thrown through the windshield—didn't have his seatbelt on. But the driver is still missing."

Jason let out a frustrated sigh. "Have they identified the dead man?"

"No, not when I last saw Wright at the scene. He wasn't too keen on my being there, by the way. 'Unauthorized snooping', he called it. Said you should get up at the crack of dawn and do your own dirty work from now on."

Jason grinned. "And what did you say to that?"

"I told him he could bloody well go jump off the nearest cliff." Thomas turned to look at him, his expression placid even as his green eyes twinkled with a momentary spark of mischief. "Jason, I don't much like this turn of events. She could have been killed."

"I know that. It just doesn't make sense. Why come after both of us?"

Thomas sighed. "I think until we find out what's going on, we'll have to make sure Sabrina stays at the mansion where we can keep an eye on things—and her."

Jason chuckled. "Oh, yeah. I can just see it now. Which one of us is going to tell Sabrina that she has to stay under lock and key until we find her father's killer?"

Thomas's eyes went wide. "What have you told her?"

"Everything."

"You what?"

Jason held a hand up to stop the tirade he saw brewing. "Okay, not everything. But I told her about the accident being suspicious and…" He hesitated.

Thomas narrowed his eyes, folding his arms across his chest. "Go on. I'm sure I'm going to love this."

"I told her that, despite evidence to the contrary, David loved her." The silence that fell was so thick he could have cut it with a knife.

"Yes, well, that admission is long overdue. Although I wish it had come from David himself. Are you sure it's wise to tell her about the accident? I think the less she knows…"

"The safer I'll be?" They both turned to see Sabrina standing at the foot of the ladder. "Now the question is, just what didn't he tell me, Thomas?"

* * *

She searched for the truth in their faces. It was akin to deciphering the shapes of inkblots or the dregs in the bottom of a cup of tea.

Catching Jason's gaze, she saw it move downward, sweeping over her body with a mixture of shock and intrigue. Sabrina felt her cheeks flush. She self-consciously tugged at the hem of the large T-shirt, wishing it reached her knees.

Thomas cleared his throat. "I don't believe he forgot anything of importance, Sabrina." His smile softened the anger she'd felt upon hearing them discussing her like a child.

She stared at him as a light sparked between neurons. They were keeping something from her—both of them. The knowledge slammed into her gut like a fist. Of all the people in the world, Thomas was one she had thought beyond reproach. But maybe she'd misjudged someone once again.

"Okay, I'll trust you, Thomas," she said, watching for signs of the guilt she hoped to spark. "You were always good to me when I was a kid. You...you made things easier after Mom died." She didn't look at Jason as she spoke but could sense his gaze upon her. "What do you want me to do? How can I help?"

"You can start by eating the breakfast Martha packed for the two of you. Then you can continue to help by staying at the mansion until the police catch the killer."

"But…"

"No, Sabrina." Thomas moved forward until he stood so close, she had to look up into his eyes. "You could have been died last night. I swore after your mother was killed that I would do everything in my power to protect you. That's why I stayed. I am not going to take a chance with your life."

Tears pricked her eyelids, burned in her throat. She'd always cherished her special bond with Thomas. When her mother had been killed in a car accident and her father retreated from her, Thomas became more than the hired help. Much more. She'd often pretended he was her father.

Sabrina took a deep breath. "Okay, I'll do as you ask, though I don't like the whole idea of being held hostage in my own home." She looked at Jason, her gaze skittering away when she saw the dark, confusing expression there. "Now I'll just make myself decent and we can eat. I'm starved."

Head held high, she made her way to the bathroom where she'd left her clothes the night before. A warm tingle spread over her skin, the hair at her nape lifting in response. As she turned to close the door, her gaze clashed with

Jason's. The sparkle in his eyes threatened to steal her breath away. Gone was the cold, distant look of her protector. Lust glimmered in its place.

Sabrina swallowed and shut the door, leaning against it as her body began to shake. Too much...this whole situation was getting to be too much to handle. It felt as if she'd walked onto a movie set. Nothing had changed since she'd left six years ago, but everything was different. Confusing.

She glanced at her reflection in the vanity mirror. Her hair looked as if it had been tangled in a lover's fingers. Her eyes shone large and dark in contrast to her pale cheeks. She cringed as she saw how the shirt clung to every curve, leaving little to the imagination. No wonder he had looked at her like a hungry wolf eyeing a doe. It was amazing that Thomas had been able to hang onto his cool British reserve.

She groaned deep in her throat, combing both hands through the tangles in her hair. Deep breath. She could do this. If she could just convince her thrumming heart that whatever Jason thought or felt didn't matter. She couldn't long for his kisses or the strength of his arms around her. There would be no heartaches this time—she would make sure of that.

Opening the door a while later, Sabrina straightened her shoulders and stepped out of the bathroom. Her jeans and sweater felt more of a shield against the sensual onslaught of Jason's burning gaze.

She stopped in mid-stride. Thomas was nowhere to be seen. Jason stood at the front window, his back to her as he stared out. She walked up behind him, treading softly as she searched for something to say, some way to deal with the tension between them. Glancing over his shoulder, the beauty of the bright, sunny morning drew her thoughts outward.

The snow had already begun to melt. Icicles hung from the eaves of the cabin, reflecting the morning light. Beads of water formed on the tips, suspended for a moment before they dropped into the thin layer of snow that covered the ground. Yellow morning rays whispered over the snow, catching and reflecting in the miniscule crystals. Everything shimmered and glittered with silver flecks of light.

The mountains were beautiful any time of year, but never as much as when dusted with a fresh coat of new snow. She again regretted not having a camera in her hands. It had been a constant companion in the last six years, particularly after her disastrous marriage had ended. Behind the lens she felt safe, protected. Within the viewfinder, she found beauty and compassion in an otherwise cold, ugly world.

Sabrina drew her gaze from the view, fastening it to Jason's broad back. What had gone so wrong that he felt he had nothing to offer a woman? Her heart squeezed at the thought of his spending the rest of his life alone, moving from one meaningless encounter to another. He deserved so much more. Why couldn't he see that?

She swallowed. "Hi."

"Hi, yourself," he murmured, glancing over his shoulder.

Silence filled the room as she stood twisting her fingers together, her gaze dancing across the room before settling on him once more.

"Did you sleep okay?" he asked.

She nodded. "How about you?"

"No. I couldn't stop thinking about you."

Sabrina gazed at him, her lips parted. "I'm sorry, Jase."

"For what?" His voice slid across her skin like a caress.

"For last night. For crying all over you." She looked away, unable to hold his gaze when she'd acted like such a fool. She wanted to sink into a hole in the ground.

"You don't have to ask my forgiveness. We've been friends much too long." His gaze slipped over her body. She wanted to melt into a puddle right at his feet.

"Where's Thomas?" She glanced around, fighting the urge to back away from the hunger in his eyes like a frightened virgin.

"He had to go. We've had some glitches in the security system and he needed to get back to make sure they get things fixed."

"Does the butler normally fix security glitches?" she asked with a frown.

"Um, in this case, yes. Thomas is a very talented man."

She nodded, not quite understanding but unwilling to delve further at the moment. "Did you eat?"

"Not yet. I was waiting for you." He moved toward the kitchen. She felt her heart lurch as fear mingled with hope that he would take her in his arms again. But he continued past. "We can nuke the eggs; they should be fine. There's juice and coffee. Which would you like?"

She shrugged. "Both. I've got quite an appetite this morning."

He froze, his gaze roving over her face for a moment before he turned away. "Yeah. That makes two of us."

She watched him move around the kitchen, popping containers into the microwave, pouring coffee. All the while his eyes never once met hers. But distance was a good thing. It was safer.

"I'm in the way. I'll go straighten up while you finish."

She moved toward the living room and surveyed the damage. Jason's mother had often complained about his messy tendencies. He hadn't changed much. Shaking her head, Sabrina folded the discarded blanket and twisted sheets. When they were stacked, she tossed the pillows on the floor. One forceful shove pushed the futon back into sitting position.

She stared at it for a moment, remembering how strong and warm his arms felt around her. She sank into the tactile memory of his body pressed to hers. Sabrina sighed, closing her eyes as memories flashed through her mind.

"Hungry?"

She jumped, spinning around to face him, nose to chest.

Jason chuckled. "Scared you good that time!"

Sabrina narrowed her gaze and frowned, fisting her hands on her hips. "You think you're cute, don't you? Aren't you ever going to grow up?"

He laughed and shook his head, mimicking her posture. "Not if I can help it."

"Me, either!" Sabrina grabbed a pillow and swung it in a wide arch. It connected with his head in a resounding slap.

"Can I play, too?"

She shook her head. "Find your own weapons, Jase. The pillows are mine."

"Wanna bet?"

He grinned as she skirted around the sofa when he reached to grab her arm. "Come on, sweetheart. You have to let a guy get even, don't you?"

"Not in my rule book!"

A well-aimed pillow sailed toward her head. Sabrina shrieked and ducked. Jason lunged over the futon, grabbing her by the arm and pulling her over the back. Fighting for balance, he fell. Sabrina grunted as she found herself sandwiched between the big man and the thin cushion.

He sucked air in through his teeth, eyes squeezed shut. A wave of guilt washed over her as she witnessed his pain.

"Jase? I'm so sorry. Are you okay?"

He nodded but didn't say anything. After a moment she felt his body relax. Sabrina became aware of how intimately they were pressed together from chest to knee.

A breathless chuckle washed over her and she looked up into his eyes. They sparkled like sunlight off a deep blue ocean.

"My fault," he said. "I should know better than to start something I can't finish."

Sabrina shoved at his chest. "Up! I can't breathe…"

Jason pushed up on his elbows and she sucked in a deep breath. He didn't move further but gazed down at her. She panicked as the playful glint in his eyes heated.

"What's the matter?" he whispered. "Am I too big for you?"

Heat suffused her cheeks. "Don't you wish."

It was the wrong thing to say. His smile faded, confusion and desire warring in his clear blue eyes. Liquid warmth spread through her limbs, pooling in her belly.

Meg Allison

She touched his shoulder, an inner battle raging between her prudent self and the one that wanted to pull him down into her arms. Sticky warmth under her fingers brought her back to reality.

"You're bleeding again."

"I just tore the wound open a little. I'll be fine." He stared at her mouth. "Bree..." His head bent closer, their lips a breath apart.

A shrill electronic ringing cut through the air. They both jumped. Jason tumbled off her and landed with a thud on the floor.

"The phone..." He struggled to his feet, lines of pain etching the sides of his mouth. Relief flickered in his eyes when he stood and scanned the room for the cell phone. Jason picked it up and turned his back to her. "Hello?" He glanced in her direction, but Sabrina looked away. Her whole body blazed with heat. How could she be friends with this man if every touch set her off like a torch in a keg of fireworks? "Hold on..." he told the caller, then covered the mouthpiece. "Bree, go ahead and get started on the food. I'll be right there. It's just the garage calling about the Mercedes."

"I need to check your shoulder."

He nodded. "Sure, but after breakfast. It's okay."

She shrugged, not daring to look him in the eye again. Straightening her sweater, Sabrina stood. Her legs wobbled beneath her. How far would she have let things go if it hadn't been for the intrusion? She had to stay focused on finding her father's killer, not on Jason's gorgeous blue eyes.

She made her way to the table and sat down, digging into one of the plates he'd prepared, despite the churning in her stomach. Somehow the food filled the void she felt inside, at least for the moment. The eggs were buttery and almost melted in her mouth. The bacon was crisp, just the way she liked it. But no matter how hard she tried not to listen, nothing could block the quiet hum of Jason's conversation across the room.

Leaning back in her chair, she turned to see his brows drawn down into a deep frown as anger sparked like fire in his eyes. He glanced at her. His features relaxed a little as he moved toward the door.

88

"The battery must be getting weak again," he explained. "I have to take it outside to see if the reception is better." With that he stepped onto the porch, pulling the door closed behind him.

Sabrina frowned and stabbed at her eggs. "Weak battery...I'll just bet."

She swallowed even as the food stuck in her throat. It shouldn't bother her so much if Jason lied. Not after all these years. She'd given up on him and moved on with her life.

But it did bother her. A lot.

Chapter Six

"What happened to D.C.?"

Jason glanced at her, then back at the road as he rounded another curve. Sabrina hadn't spoken much since the last phone call. The silence between them was so thick, you could slice it.

"Nothing happened to it." He attempted a light tone. "As far as I know, it's still there."

"Very funny. No, I mean, the last thing I heard, you were headed for some investment banker's job. Didn't you like high finance?"

Great. He'd known this would come up sooner or later. The carefully mapped-out lie lodged in his throat, despite each detail rehearsed with precision over the past eight years. It had almost become his reality. But how could he blithely voice the words to this woman? This genuine, honest person who hated treachery above all things?

"I liked the job just fine," he said, concentrating on the curving road as he avoided her dark, doe eyes. "But there's a lot they don't teach you at graduate school. I didn't have what it takes to make it in the real world."

"What could you possibly lack? You graduated early and at the top of your class. You were smart and charming, any employer's dream."

He sighed. "I wasn't good at dealing with the clients. You have to be able to read people, not just the market. I didn't have what it takes. So when my dad retired, I came back to take over his old job."

"How could you do that to yourself, Jason? How could you just give up like that and settle for this?" She waved a hand, encompassing the car and passing scenery.

His own words came back at him from years before, bragging how he'd make his mark on the world someday and leave the rocks of Castle's Grove far behind him. He'd found a way to make that mark, to make the world a better place. Along the way, he'd discovered that his hometown wasn't such a dead end after all. It had become the one place he felt at ease, where he felt peace after seeing so much of the world in turmoil.

Sabrina didn't know all that and he couldn't tell her. He was used to people believing he had crashed and burned, then given up on his dreams. It never bothered him before because he knew the truth. For some reason, it bothered him now. Especially when he saw disappointment reflected in her eyes.

"I didn't *settle* for anything."

"Oh, right. The big man on campus, one of the youngest to receive his MBA and yet you wound up schlepping an arrogant millionaire around the globe. No, that's not settling."

Jason flinched. Her sarcasm hurt this time. He could deal with sassy and irreverent; he loved her like that. But he couldn't stand the little barbs that hit dead center on his ego.

"There's nothing wrong with making an honest living. My dad was a chauffeur for over thirty years and is one of the finest men I've ever met." He swallowed, hating the bitter taste of anger that stuck in his throat. "Maybe I've just accepted myself. At least I'm being truthful about who I am."

"What is that supposed to mean?"

"You and your lofty pride, slumming it in order to prove you could make it on your own." He soon regretted his words. Her face went white, her dark eyes wide and stark in her pale face. He should shut up now, but he couldn't. He'd been holding back for too many years. "Grow up, Bree. Stop running from your father's money and use it instead. Just think of the advantages you would have. Think of how many people are out there struggling, trying to make a difference, trying to survive. What they wouldn't give to have the kind of advantage you do. You can pursue your dreams without starving yourself or living in seedy neighborhoods and endangering your life."

"I thought you understood," she whispered.

"I do! I understand the baggage that goes with wealth. I have ever since prom night when that jerk dumped you flat because David refused to foot the bill. But I don't agree with how you've handled it.

"Your dad hurt you. He's a lousy parent. But he could be worse. Life could be a hell of a lot worse. You're a smart, talented and sexy lady. Why can't you take gorgeous photos and live in a penthouse instead of a third-floor walk-up?"

"Was," she whispered, staring out the window.

Jason looked at her. "What?"

She turned her head. He caught a glimpse of tears brimming in those dark eyes. "He *was* a lousy parent. He's gone, remember? Dead. No second chances, no way to say 'I'm sorry' or 'I love you.' Now, like it or not, I've got *all* the money to deal with."

"Bree…"

"No." She held up one hand to silence him. "I think we've both said enough for a little while, don't you?"

Jason stared at the road, wanting to kick himself for blowing his cool. But part of him was glad he had the guts to tell her what he thought. He hoped she'd forgive him.

* * *

"Just tell them exactly what happened on the mountain last night," Jason said as he parked the car in front of the Castle's Grove Police Station.

Sabrina wanted to jump out and run from him and the cruel things he'd said. But a little voice in her head mocked her. Where would she go? Wasn't it about time she stopped running from herself?

"Okay, fine." She climbed out as he did, refusing to even glance in his direction. One look into those eyes would make her forget the anger. It was safer to stay mad and keep him at arm's length. When you let people close, you got hurt. When she'd let Jason close before, it had ended in excruciating pain.

He stepped onto the sidewalk, his warmth reaching out to her. The bright spring sun shone down from a clear blue sky, fighting the ice in the cool mountain air as it blew fitfully around her body. Sabrina shivered.

"It'll be all right, Bree," he murmured, apparently convinced it was fear that made her tremble. "This is just routine. There's nothing to worry about."

"I'm not a child anymore, so quit treating me like one!" she snapped.

"I realize you're very much a woman now." He gazed down at her for a moment. Heat spiraled between them, despite the eddy of air whispering through the same space. She wrapped her arms across her middle to ward off the traitorous reactions of her body and to keep the anger intact. Jason cleared his throat. "Come on. This shouldn't take too long. He's waiting for us."

Sabrina let him guide her up the cement steps, his hand like a weight at the small of her back. She had never been inside a police station before. Not even after living for over six years in New York City.

The door clanged open and shut, venetian blinds beating against the thick glass as it moved. The open space was divided in the middle into two small cubicles with desks and chunky off-white computers. Three rooms spanned the back wall – one with *Chief of Police* emblazoned in gold lettering across the glass door. A long table stretched the length of the right wall, an old, drip coffee maker and assorted cups cluttering one end. The sharp odor of burnt coffee and cigarette smoke tinged the stale air.

Trying to ignore the curious glances from a redhead sitting at the receptionist's desk, Sabrina forced a smile as a tall man in uniform turned from the coffee station to look at them. Dark hot liquid splashed over the mug's lip, making him curse as he quickly set it down and grabbed a roll of paper towels.

"You okay, Bill?" Jason asked, a smile in his voice. The other man glanced up at him and scowled.

"Yeah, fine." He looked at her again. It was as if a hand drifted over her skin, a prickle of dread. This man seemed to look right through a person, straight to the secrets they held close. "Aren't you going to introduce us?"

Jason cleared his throat. "Of course, though I do believe you met years ago. Sabrina, this is Chief William Wright. Bill, Sabrina Layne. David's daughter."

As Jason spoke, the man moved forward. His powerful stride sent a surge of energy vibrating off the walls. He thrust out a large hand as he reached them. "Pleasure to see you again, Ms. Layne. I'm sorry about your father."

"Thank you." She took his hand in hers, somewhat alarmed at the way her fingers disappeared in his. His quick gray eyes seemed to take it all in, every nuance, every gesture. The man would either make a valuable friend or formidable enemy.

"I'm sorry. This is lousy timing. But I do need to take your statement about the incident last night. Would you mind joining me in my office? It shouldn't take too long."

* * *

"So you have no idea who was driving the sedan?" Chief Wright asked, for the fifth time. His shrewd gaze focused on her face.

She stifled a groan and shook her head. Tension gripped the back of her neck, sending little pulses of pain radiating up over her skull. What was the man fishing for?

"No. It was dark and they were behind us the whole way up the mountain. I couldn't even be sure how many were in the car, let alone the name and address of the driver!"

The chief looked at her over top of his wire-rimmed reading glasses. "I'm sorry, but these questions are necessary. Sometimes the small details mean more than we realize."

Sabrina glanced away, kicking herself for losing her cool again. Twice in less than two hours—she wasn't going to win any personality awards today.

"Sorry," she murmured. "Is there anything else?"

"No." He removed three pages from the printer next to his desk and placed them in front of her with a pen. "If you'll just sign your statement at the bottom there."

She leaned forward, scanning the brief narrative as the man waited. Satisfied he had the facts straight, she signed the last page.

"Do you know a man named Pete Williams?"

Sabrina frowned and shook her head. "No, I don't believe so. Should I?"

"Just curious," he replied, taking the signed papers from her. "Thought you might know of him since you both lived in New York."

"It's a very big city."

He smiled, but it didn't quite reach his eyes. "Yes, that it is. Anyway, thank you for your cooperation. Now I'll speak with Jason and you two can be on your way."

Sabrina stood, glancing out the glass door at the hard plastic chairs by the nosy clerk's desk. Jason was chatting with the woman now. He laughed and smiled as if they were old friends. The sight made Sabrina's stomach clench. She pulled the door open.

"I think I'll wait outside. It was nice meeting you again." The chief took the hand she offered. A strange look flitted across his features before he turned his attention to Jason.

"Sinclair?" he called across the room as Sabrina walked out the door. "Your turn."

"Sure." Jason rose from his chair. His gaze followed Sabrina as she moved in his direction. "You okay?"

"Yeah." She glanced at the redhead filing her nails and pretending not to eavesdrop. "I just need some air. I'll get a cup of coffee across the street and meet you at the car."

"I don't know..."

"Look, Jason, I'll be fine. Who's going to bother me in broad daylight in front of the police station?"

Hesitation and concern flitted through his clear blue eyes. "You're right, but if anyone comes near you, scream."

"Fine. But if I do you'd better come running."

* * *

He watched as she walked out the door, his gaze riveted to the sultry, natural sway of her hips. When had sweet little Bree learned to walk like that? Better question—why did it affect him so deeply?

"Jason?"

He turned to look at Bill Wright. The other man's eyebrows were raised in a silent question. Jason glanced at Mary, the receptionist, giving her one last practiced smile before joining Wright in his office.

"You want to tell me what the hell is going on?" the Chief asked as soon as he shut the door.

"What is that supposed to mean?"

Wright's eyes narrowed and he stared at Jason until he couldn't help but look away. Jason sighed. "We went for a drive, Sabrina needed air and time to think. At least two men in a dark sedan chased us up Layne Mountain, taking some pot shots along the way. I outmaneuvered them and they went skiing the hard way.

"We didn't report the incident earlier because we were stranded near Layne Ridge without a car or working phone. I had Thomas call you as soon as I could. This has got to prove David's wreck was no accident, Bill. We need to find out what's going on before Sabrina gets caught in the crossfire again."

Wright swiveled his chair sideways, a frown puckering his high forehead. Jason shifted in his seat. He hated asking for help and Bill knew that all too well.

"It does seem more than a coincidence," the Chief said, lifting both arms high over his head for a long stretch. He turned back to Jason. "Thomas called and woke me up before dawn with the news of your escapades. I'm wondering why you didn't call me yourself?"

Jason held his gaze. "I like to delegate. Besides, I didn't need to hear you reading me the riot act about reckless driving."

"Not buying it, Sinclair." The Chief leaned closer. "We've known each other too long."

"Then you should know by now that my suspicions about David's accident—"

"Are just that—suspicions."

Silence lay between them as Jason waited. He was not giving Bill more than he needed to know. Not yet. Sabrina's safety might hang in the balance.

"You will tell me what's going on," Wright said. "Maybe not today, but soon. I'm a patient man. I can wait." He shrugged. "Anyway, after Thomas's rude awakening, I called everyone in and went out that way to take a look. We found the car, and the skid marks would just about prove your version of the story."

"Just about? What is that supposed to mean?"

"What that means, Jason, is that I've got two cars going off my mountain in the space of less than a month and another dead body to go with this latest! I don't like it one bit."

Jason leaned forward. "What do you know about the driver?"

Bill Wright stared at him for a long, silent moment before answering. "You should teach Thomas to keep his nose out of police work and back polishing the silver or whatever it is that man does. And next time, call me yourself, Jason. I don't like the feeling that friends are hiding something from me."

Jason held the chief's gaze despite the subtle dig. He was used to it by now, even his closest friends not trusting him, wondering at the strange life he led following a rich man all over the face of the earth. Wright looked away first.

"We haven't found the driver yet, but we did follow his trail about halfway down the mountain. I think he made it to town, if the wolves or cold didn't get him first. My deputies are canvassing the area as we speak, asking questions.

"The passenger had a wallet on him with a wad of cash totaling two hundred and fifty-six dollars, a New York driver's license identifying him as one Peter J. Williams, and a photo."

"Did you check him out?"

The Chief scowled. "Of course I checked him out. Seems Mr. Williams is formerly of the United States Army, dishonorably discharged about fifteen years ago. Since then he's made himself quite a reputation as a second rate gun for hire. He was the kind of guy someone might go to if they didn't have a whole lot of spending money and needed someone taken care of in a hurry. Last known address was New York City by way of San Quentin, where he made parole less than two years ago."

Jason took a deep breath, rubbing his eyes as he fought back the urge to curse a blue streak. None of this rang a bell. What was the connection to David Layne? To him?

Bill wasn't through. "You have any idea why someone like that would be interested in you and Ms. Layne?"

"No, not in Sabrina. They were after me. I must be getting close to figuring out what happened with David."

Bill Wright stared at him. Something in his old friend's gaze told him the world was about to tilt.

"Maybe you'd better look at this before you make up your mind on the heiress." Wright opened a drawer and pulled out a clear-plastic evidence bag.

"What is it?" Jason took the bag, turning it over in his hands. It contained a small, rectangular scrap of paper. No, it wasn't paper. The breath caught in his throat as he stared down at the photo. Sabrina's lovely face smiled back at him…younger, hair a lot longer, but definitely Sabrina.

"That is the photo we found in our hitman's wallet. I thought I recognized the face but I just couldn't place it until I shook her hand. Then I realized where I'd seen those pretty eyes before. She's involved, Jason. I'm afraid she's up to her neck in trouble."

* * *

What was taking him so long in there?

Sabrina glanced at the building, frowning, as she crushed her empty foam cup and stalked to the trashcan near a lamppost. She threw the pieces into the can. He was probably flirting with the redhead. She was busty and pretty enough. That must be what it took to hold his attention—big, round…

"Sabrina?"

She twirled around, gasping as her eyes met a familiar pair of hazel ones. The blood drained from her face, leaving her shaking and confused.

"Oh my, I can't believe it! What great luck! It really is you."

"S-Sam?" Sabrina glanced around. This was some kind of sick joke. This could not be happening.

But it was. Her ex-husband rushed forward and gathered her into his arms. His strong cologne seemed to block out all air. She couldn't breathe. He took a step back.

"Oh, I am sorry," he murmured. "I can see I've surprised you. It's just that I heard about your father. Oh, honey, what a shame! What a terrible, terrible thing to have happen."

He took her hands in his, gazing down at her with sympathy she would have found comforting coming from anyone else. Like someone who possessed a heart.

"As soon as I heard, I called my agent and told him they'd have to get my understudy to take over for a few days because my sweet wife needed me."

"Whoa!" She snatched her hands out of his grasp. "Wife? What *wife* are you referring to?"

He had the nerve to look hurt. "Sabrina, honey, I'm crushed! You know you were always the woman for me." He moved closer, his voice low and husky. It made her skin crawl. "I've missed you. I've been wondering how to approach you…how to tell you what I've been going through since you left me."

"You seemed quite happy when I left, Sam." She fought to keep her voice calm. "As I recall, Barbara seemed to be keeping you occupied."

"Barbara?" he stopped, his eyes growing wide. "Honey, I was an ass! I know you shouldn't give me a second chance but…"

"Why would you even want one, Sam? What about those things you said at Charlie's?" Sabrina watched his face go pale as he started to sputter. *Bingo. Direct hit.* "You remember that don't you? That was the night you told everyone I worked with that I was an ice sculpture in bed. Then you proceeded to ask if one of the women there might want to try and warm me up since men didn't 'do it' for me. Does any of this ring a bell?"

At least he had the grace to blush this time. Or had he learned how to do that in acting class?

"But Sabrina, honey, I was drunk! I was out of my mind with jealousy and there you were, looking so damn fine and on some other guy's arm. I was mortified the next morning when I woke up and remembered what I'd said." He gazed at her with that little boy, pleading look that used to get under her skin. She felt a rush of pride that it no longer had any effect. "Please, honey," he begged, grasping her hands again. "I heard about your father and I wanted to find you and offer my shoulder to cry on. I know what a bastard he was but you must still be in pain. We were friends once. Let me help you now."

Friends. What was he up to? Seven years ago, she had fallen for the handsome face and the great line, but she was older and much wiser. She knew what Sam really was—a conniving, philandering jerk.

But he had been good to her before romance came into the picture. He'd been a lot of fun before he realized she was *the* David Layne's daughter and heiress to a fortune. Before he set about seducing her and talking her into a disastrous marriage.

"I'm not buying it this time." She narrowed her eyes at the man she'd once thought loved her. Sam didn't comprehend the word *love*. He had no idea what it meant to genuinely care for someone like Jason did. Sabrina shook her head. She'd spent the last ten years looking for a man that could compare to Jason, but she'd wound up with someone so far from the truth, it was almost laughable. "How did you find out about Dad?"

He glanced down the street, avoiding her gaze. "I do read the papers, honey. Then I heard you were out of town and figured you'd come back for the funeral."

Sabrina frowned as she tried to decide whether or not to believe him. The wind whipped up, a section of newspaper skittering by their feet. A thought formed and she took a small step back.

"Why have you been calling me, Sam?"

He stared at her. "What are you talking about?"

She folded her arms across her stomach. "The phone calls...all hours of the night? Spouting poetry and acting all creepy. What was the point? Were you trying to scare me or was it some new acting exercise?"

His blank look made her uneasy. All along, in the back of her mind she had thought...had hoped that it was Sam. But he was never that good an actor. From the confused look in his eyes, she could tell he didn't have clue.

"Listen," he insisted, pointing at her. "I stayed away from you after that night at Charlie's. I knew I had crossed the line. I don't know what you're trying to pin on me now but I don't need any more trouble from you, princess."

She held up a hand. "No... never mind."

His wary gaze studied her face. "Are you in some kind of trouble?"

"Even if I was, you would be the last person on earth that I would trust."

Anger flashed across his angular features and Sabrina's stomach tightened. She'd seen that temper unleashed many times.

"People change, Sabrina. Maybe you'll let me prove that to you someday."

"Not this time."

"Fine. Have it your way. But if you should change your mind I'm staying at the bed and breakfast."

She shrugged, glancing away as emotions too strong and confusing to name coursed through her. Sam crossed the street, leaving Sabrina to stare after him. This week was just going from bad to bizarre. She turned back toward the police station and cringed. Jason walked toward her, his face a dark mask of unleashed fury.

Chapter Seven

"Who was that?"

She opened her mouth as if to speak, but shut it again. Instead she brushed past him on her way to the car.

"I asked you a question, Sabrina." Jason grabbed her arm and spun her around to face him. "Who were you talking to?"

She gazed up at him, frowning. He wanted to shake her. Didn't she have any idea what kind of danger she was in? Jason closed his eyes and took a deep breath. Maybe she did know. She was involved somehow. His stomach tightened. She might be using him like all the other women in his life. Women that could make love to a man and betray him before the sheets cooled.

Not that he was any better. He had learned the fine art of the one-night-stand…the use-them-and-leave-them game that came with the territory. But the thought of Sabrina – *his* Sabrina, playing such games made him feel like he'd been sucker-punched.

Anger flashed in her dark eyes. "Not that it's any of your business, but that was my ex-husband."

His grip slackened and she pulled free, turning to make her way back to the car. Jason stared, anger seething around him as he tried to clear his thoughts. Her ex? So that was the guy who broke her heart. But why was he here? He thought about the photo Bill Wright had found in the hitman's pocket. It might prove she was involved somehow but none of the alternatives were very comforting. Either Sabrina was a target or an accomplice. He wasn't sure which idea made him feel sicker inside.

Jason walked to the car. She sat staring out the windshield. He tried to figure out when things had gone wrong between them. When he saw her at the airport, he'd vowed he would keep his distance no matter what and send her back to New York as soon as possible. But that wasn't going to happen now. Until he figured out how she was involved, he'd have to keep her close.

Opening the car door, he grasped for something to say, a way to approach her that wouldn't expose his anger. He climbed in and closed the door, leaning back into the leather seat.

"I'm sorry." He stared out the windshield for a moment, unable to meet her gaze. "But as long as you're in danger, it *is* my business who you talk to and where you go."

Jason turned his head. She was so beautiful. Desire struck him full in the gut, made even more painful by the mistrust Wright's revelations had instilled. "There's a killer running loose and I have to take care of you. I would never forgive myself if something happened to you."

Her expression softened for just a moment as her lips trembled beneath the weight of a tentative smile. "I don't need a keeper. I just need a friend."

He looked away, hoping she couldn't see the surge of longing that took him by surprise. It might be the years apart or the solitary life he led, but every moment by her side intensified the urge to hold her... possess her. He clenched his jaw, fighting to hold on to his anger. That emotion was at least safe. His hand shook a little as he jabbed the keys into the ignition.

"I have always been your friend. But we can't keep hiding things from each other. Someone is going to get hurt."

She sighed. "Someone already has—my father and that man in the car. But I'm not the one keeping secrets. I have nothing to hide."

He gripped the steering wheel, knuckles turning white as held back furious accusations. "I think you do."

"What are you hinting at?" He could feel her gaze upon him, searching his profile. "I don't know any more than you do."

"But if you did?" He looked at her. "Then I hope you know you can talk to me. I hope you understand that no matter what, I will always be there for you. I want to help."

A flush crept over the high plains of her cheekbones and she glanced out the windshield. "Why? It's been ten years since we spoke to each other. Why should I believe you care now?"

The urge to take her hand in his overwhelmed him. He reached out, offering a touch that he soon regretted. Her skin was soft, her hand seemed to fit into his with sculpted perfection. Like it belonged there. Would her body fit his with such precision?

Jason pulled away. "Because it's the truth."

They sat staring out the windows at the quiet bustle of the small town at midday. People streamed in and out of the coffee shop and the pharmacy next door. Cars drove down the wide street, drivers waving at pedestrians as friends greeted one another. Jason found himself envying a small family strolling by. The couple held hands as two young children skipped ahead, smiling and laughing.

"I'm sorry," she said, emotion thickening her voice. She cleared her throat. "I overreacted. The truth is, I'm not sure why Sam is here."

"Didn't he tell you?"

Her hands twisted the strap of her seatbelt. "Yes, but it doesn't make sense. He said that he heard about my father and he came to offer his shoulder to cry on."

"But you don't believe him."

She turned her head and looked at him. "No, I don't. He's lied to me too many times for that. I can't help feeling he's up to something."

A knot of guilt filled his gut like a lead weight. Lies, so many lies. She held them against her ex, would she ever forgive *him*? But his were different. He lied to protect himself and others...he was lying now to keep her safe. In the end, would she understand the difference or would pride keep her from admitting that sometimes they were necessary?

"Do you want me to talk with Mansfield or have Bill check him out? Maybe he has another motive for showing up here."

"I don't think that's necessary. Sam is a backstabbing opportunist, but he'd never wield a real knife. He prefers to destroy egos. Besides, what would there be to gain?"

"Maybe he wants you back." Jealousy tore at him. The sensation left him uneasy. He couldn't remember feeling such intense possessiveness before.

"Yes, he might, if he suspects I inherited my father's money. That's why he married me in the first place."

He jerked around to look at her expression. Could there be something to this? Could her ex have hired the hitmen to take care of both David and Sabrina? But what would the man gain?

"I take it he's not financially independent."

Sabrina laughed. "Uh, no. He's an actor—a bad one. Otherwise, I'm not sure how he gets by, unless there's a girlfriend somewhere supporting him. He made some noise about having his understudy fill in for him while he came to my rescue, but I happen to know he hasn't worked in over a year."

"I can't figure out what a smart girl like you ever saw in the creep. He's not even that good looking."

Sabrina's eyes widened with surprise. "Why Mr. Sinclair, if I didn't know any better I'd swear you were jealous!"

He turned the key, bringing the Rolls to life. They'd strayed onto dangerous ground with the direction this conversation had taken. He had no wish to explore this particular territory yet, traversing over the landmines that were best left undisturbed.

"No, of course not. I just think your ex has a lot of nerve showing up after he dumped you and broke your heart."

"How do you know I wasn't the one who dumped him?"

"I just assumed…"

"Well, you assumed wrong. Sam is a rather untalented. While we were married, he didn't do much of anything except live off of my paychecks and go out drinking every night. I came home and found him… well, I found him in our bed with another woman. So I left and filed for divorce the next morning."

The pain in her eyes made him ache. "I wish I had known."

She shook her head, turning away from him. But he'd seen the tears. He understood it was the memories that brought them back. The pain of being betrayed by someone she trusted. Kind of like she had trusted him that night ten years ago, when he'd been so very tempted to make love to her. Even though she'd been little more than a child in an eighteen-year-old woman's body and he, a grown man of twenty-four. He hated the guilt that thought held. He didn't deserve her trust… didn't deserve *her*.

But he couldn't shake the knowledge that she was still holding back. Bill Wright had presented him with a piece of the puzzle when he'd showed him that photograph. It was one that still didn't fit, didn't mesh with any of his theories. He had to find out why the bargain-basement hitman had Sabrina's picture in his wallet and why her ex-husband had slithered into town.

"Jason, I'd like to get into some clean clothes and I've got some calls to make."

"Yeah, sure. Let's get you home."

"I hope the Mercedes can be fixed. I always loved that car." Sabrina sank back into the leather seat. "I'm glad he didn't sell it off after three years like he did all the others."

"He did." Jason looked over his shoulder and pulled out into traffic. "I bought it from him. Got a pretty good deal, too."

He glanced at the mirrors then at her again. She was watching him.

"What?" he asked, uncomfortable under her knowing gaze.

"Why did you buy it?"

Jason turned his attention to the road. He could feel the heat rising up the back of his neck. "It was in great shape and it has a smooth engine."

"It's the same one you used to drive me around in. My senior year, after you came home from college."

He glanced at her. "I didn't even think of that."

She laughed. "No, you wouldn't remember a detail like that."

"What do you mean?"

She shrugged. "Well, at eighteen, if you feel things...want things, it's hard to understand why it can't happen. When it doesn't, you're convinced the world is going to end."

He cleared his throat. "Even if I had noticed you in that way, you were the boss's daughter and a prime example of jail bait. I couldn't have gotten past that."

She looked away. "I understand that now. We were friends and I was very young. I don't blame you for not seeing me as something more. That's how life goes. Young girls get crushes on older guys. They make fools of themselves and move on."

She turned in the seat, her back against the door. "But be honest, don't you ever just wish you could stop playing games? Haven't you ever longed to talk to someone, tell them what you think and feel? What you want? Why is it okay for children to be honest and not adults? We grow up being lectured to tell the truth and then spend the rest of our lives dancing around it."

The hum of the engine filled the void between them as they drove through the outskirts of town, passing frame houses and trim, wooden fences. Life went on around them in perfect small-town bliss, though he knew nothing was really ever perfect. It was all illusion. But perhaps leaving a normal Mayberry kind of life without the intrigue and danger he put himself in wasn't such a bad thing.

He shifted uncomfortably as her words burrowed deeper and hit a very tender nerve. How could he expect her to open up when he was the one with all the secrets? But she could never understand what he'd felt ten years ago when he wasn't sure he understood it himself.

"Even if I had felt the same way, there were six years of experience between us," he said. "I'm not the same boy you helped nurse back to health after the car wreck. Life changed that."

She studied his profile. "No, you aren't the same. You closed yourself off the day you woke up in the hospital and found out Jeanine had died. I think it's eaten away at you a little more each day. From then on out, you didn't let anyone get that close to you. Isolation can't help but change a man."

He shot her a look, his jaw clenching. "I don't want to talk about it, Bree. That was a long time ago. No sense picking at old scabs."

"Jason, it's been over ten years. You've got to let it go."

"I cannot just let go of that night." He slammed a hand against the steering wheel, fighting back the anger and guilt that gripped him by the throat. Damn her for making him remember that night. Damn her for opening that wound and making it bleed anew. "I screwed up! In the worst way possible because it cost an innocent girl her life."

"It was an *accident*."

"For which I was responsible." He braked at a stop sign but didn't look at her. He couldn't. There would be pity in those eyes and that was one thing he never wanted from anyone. "Now forget it—it has nothing to do with that night at the cabin. Even if I wanted to be with you then, I wasn't what David Layne had in mind for his daughter."

"What do you mean?"

"The chauffeur's son with a bad reputation? The murderer? A guy with no direction in life? Pick one, they all worked."

Sabrina made a small, dismissive sound. "He never believed those manslaughter charges and I don't think he cared about what you or your daddy did for a living."

"Oh, he cared, sweetheart." His grip tightened on the wheel, knuckles white. "He cared more than you'll ever know."

* * *

Sabrina climbed the curved staircase, flashes of her conversation with Jason reeling through her mind. It was true. That moment at the cabin so many years ago had been a momentary lapse of judgment fueled by brandy and lust. She squelched the disappointment the revelation left behind. Knowing that all he wanted was friendship should make her happy. She felt the same way. Didn't she?

It had hurt when he walked out on her years ago. Nothing compared to that searing pain and humiliation. Her stomach ached with the memory; her body burned with the ghost of desire. The mind was a powerful aphrodisiac. One thought of that night, one chord of the song or the scent of wood smoke set her blood blazing through her veins. She had only to close her eyes and imagine Jason and how he looked during those few stolen moments when she had tried so hard to be the woman he needed.

But all her clumsy seduction had accomplished was to push him away and alienate the best friend she'd ever had. She wouldn't make that mistake twice.

She was a lot stronger this time, but getting Jason out of her system might prove impossible. He didn't want anything from her and that was what he'd get. Nothing. Her heart ached even as the thought formed in her mind. He was angry and upset, although he never said why. It seemed he didn't trust her, either. What a great pair they made.

She stepped into her room, closing the door behind her and walking across the soft scatter rugs to the mirror at her dressing table. The same face stared back at her. Strange how such dramatic events left a person unchanged on the outside while their inner core shattered.

Jason had said she was sexy. She frowned. No, she just didn't see it. She had grown into her looks rather well but her features were average, her cleavage skimpy.

She turned sideways, sucking in her belly and pulling her sweater taut against her firm breasts. No. No improvement since high school. What difference did it make if she was a failure in bed anyhow? A cold fish who couldn't enjoy sex.

Tears stung her eyes as she stood there, staring at herself in the mirror. It had hurt so much, coming home, finding Sam in bed with that bottled blonde.

It had been the final blow to a pathetic excuse of a marriage. And the last nail in the coffin containing her murdered pride.

But somehow, it hadn't hurt as much as when Jason had walked out of her life. It did make her second guess every relationship she'd ever had. In the end, she'd opted to keep emotionally distant from everyone.

It was safer that way though, wasn't it? If you didn't trust, no one could tell lies that wounded. Sabrina had been hurt enough for one lifetime…her father, Jason and then Sam.

She wiped the tears from her cheeks, took a deep breath and walked to the bedside table. Her editor would be worried and wondering how long she'd be gone. One quick call and then she could settle into a long, hot bath.

She sat on the side of her bed, tugging off her boots with one hand as she dialed the familiar number. Eric had been the first in New York to take a chance on an unknown photographer and her sometimes-skewed view of the world around them. He had been her friend and mentor, and he deserved to know what was going on. At least some of it.

The phone rang several times before he answered. "Hello, Van Horn speaking."

"Hi, Eric, it's Sabrina."

"Oh, honey, it's good to hear your voice. How are you doing?"

Sabrina sighed, the tense muscles along her shoulders unwinding in slow increments like coiled steel. "I'm okay, considering. I'm sorry I didn't call last night but everything has been hectic with the funeral and all. How are things at the paper?"

"Oh, we're fine—missing you of course, but I've got someone filling in until you get back. I do wish you had called. I was so worried about you." Sabrina wondered why she'd never noticed the whiny edge in his voice. "I've been kicking myself ever since you left. I should have gone with you for moral support."

"Oh, Eric, please don't worry about it." Her mind raced for an excuse to hang up. She was too worn out to hold polite conversation. "Listen, I don't mean to sound rude but I'm very tired. I just wanted to check in before I settled in for the night. Can I call you back in a few days?"

"Of course, Sabrina, I understand. If you need anything at all, please call." He hesitated. "How long do you think you'll be gone? You are coming back to New York, aren't you?"

"Yes, I think so. At least for a while. I'm not sure what to do. All of this is so unexpected."

"Oh, yes. I can understand that. You take all the time you need. Just know that I hope you do come back. You're irreplaceable."

An uneasy feeling washed over her. "I will let you know as soon as I can. Thank you, Eric."

"It's been my pleasure. Sweet dreams, honey. I'll speak with you in the morning."

She set the receiver down. Eric was a sweet man, shy and intelligent. Why couldn't she care about him the way she did Jason?

The thought brought her up short. She stared at her reflection, her heart thundering in her chest. She'd done it again. She'd let Jason sneak his way back into her heart. How could she be so stupid?

The phone rang, jerking her from the disconcerting truth. Lifting the receiver to her ear, she hesitated for a moment. Who would be calling on her private line?

A chill coursed down her spine. She glanced around the room, taking in every shadowy hiding place. The last time her admirer had called, her father had just died. No, he'd been killed. Breath caught in her throat. They couldn't be connected.

"Hello?"

"Sabrina, it's me—don't hang up!"

"Sam?" Her heart thudded with a mixture of relief and irritation. "I thought I made myself perfectly clear—"

"You did, but I just wanted to call and see if you'd changed your mind."

She snorted. "You've got to be kidding!"

"Come on, honey, we had some good times. Give me one more chance to make it up to you. Just dinner—you and me. No strings, no sex...unless you want there to be."

How stupid did he think she was? "No. Never. Good-bye!" Sabrina slammed the phone back into its cradle.

The bell jangled and she suppressed a scream as she snatched up the receiver. Tomorrow she would have the number changed.

"Listen, I don't care what you want. I am not interested. If you keep calling I'll have to talk to the police, do you understand?"

Silence.

"Sabrina-fair, my dearest love..."

She gasped. *Oh, no. Not here. Not now, it couldn't be.* She'd left the wacko behind in New York, hadn't she?

"The moment fast approaches," the caller continued. "I must prove my love to you. When my quest is done, you and I will be together. Forever."

She felt sick. Her head began to spin. She had to stay calm. Concentrate on the voice...concentrate. What was there about it that seemed so familiar?

A click and silence radiated down the line. Sabrina stared at the pattern of her quilt. The flowers blurred. She blinked and replaced the receiver. Her hands shook. The room moved back into focus.

"Jason," she murmured. "I have to tell Jason. He'll know what to do."

She ran from the room, taking the stairs at lightning speed. Once in the foyer, she stopped and glanced around, trying to hear above the harsh rasp of her own breath.

There, from the study, she could hear someone talking...laughing. It seemed out of place. Sabrina frowned and inched toward the closed door. No, it was open...just a crack, but enough to hear. Her throat tightened, a thousand butterflies churning in her stomach as she pushed the door another inch.

"No, no, darling," the woman's voice said, playful laughter lilting through the air. "I didn't tell her anything important. You know I'd never do that! I'm so much more professional than you give me credit for."

A male chuckle replied. Sabrina stopped breathing. Heat washed over her. She was going to be sick right there on the polished wood floor. As she swayed against the shock, she lifted a shaky hand to brace herself against the doorjamb.

Jason. She'd recognize that deep, rich sound anywhere.

"Okay, honey," he said. Sabrina squeezed her eyes shut. But it didn't stop the blinding pain that ripped through her. "I just had to make sure. You know how this game is played now, don't you?"

"Of course, darling," the woman said.

Sabrina winced at the saccharine tone. The voice seemed familiar. Shifting her position, she peered through the crack beneath the door hinge. She bit her lip to keep from cursing.

There they were, sitting as cozy as you please on her daddy's leather sofa—Jason and the Mistress of the Week, Vivian James. They sat close, his back turned halfway toward the door so that Sabrina could see part of his profile.

Jason smiled as Vivian ran her red talons up his arm, over his shoulder. The same shoulder Sabrina had nursed and bandaged. The same arm he had held her with less than twenty-four hours ago. Now she wished she had poured something really painful on his wound...something that burned.

"You poor, sweet man!" Vivian crooned. Sabrina wanted to gag. "Are you sure your shoulder is all right? I could take a look at it for you."

Jason shook his head, turning to set a glass of dark liquid on the coffee table. He was smiling and letting that bleached blonde touch him as if...

As if she'd done it many times before.

"That won't be necessary, honey," he said. The woman's hand continued to move over him, sliding down his chest to his belly, and lower. He grasped her wandering fingers in his, raising them to his lips for a brief kiss.

"I'm feeling much better now. But you still haven't answered my question. Did you tell anyone else that David's accident was suspicious?"

Vivian pouted for a moment, then sighed, pulling her hand away from Jason's grip. "No, I didn't tell anyone else, just the little heiress—as if she gave a damn!"

Jason frowned.

"She didn't even cry! Can you imagine? Her father is killed and she doesn't even shed one tear standing at his graveside. And just where has she been for the past six years, I'd like to know?"

"Miss Layne and her father weren't on speaking terms," Jason replied. Sabrina noticed the edge to his voice, the tightness in his jaw. But her heart was too busy being torn down the middle.

"Oh, I'll bet." Vivian fumbled around on the small end table for her cigarettes and lighter. "Everyone's heard the stories. She flunked out, wouldn't go back to school and stormed off to New York when her father tried to force her…" She paused to light a cigarette, puffing a few times and pulling the smoke deep into her lungs. "Tried to force her to go back but she refused. Then she married some gold-digging actor. But she sure came back quick enough for the funeral, now didn't she? Anxious to get her inheritance I bet."

"I think it's time you get home, Vivian."

She looked at him in surprise. "What's wrong? I thought you wanted to talk. I thought we were going to have dinner, at least. I'm starved! Hangovers leave me with such an appetite…for a lot of things, if you know what I mean." Vivian leaned closer, turning her head to blow smoke over her shoulder.

Jason inched away. "I'll be on duty tonight."

Vivian's face darkened with irritation. She leaned toward the coffee table and flicked her ashes into a silver bowl.

"Don't tell me the little witch has you bowing and scraping already, darling? Is she too good to drive herself around now that she has Daddy's millions?"

Jason surged to his feet, towering over the blonde. "Miss Layne is my employer. I would appreciate it if you would refrain from making any more derogatory remarks about her in my presence."

Vivian smashed her cigarette into the shining silver finish. "All right, darling, no need to get huffy."

Sabrina watched the woman's face as she stood. Understanding dawned across the smooth features. "Oh, of course," her voice lowered to a stage whisper. "The walls do have ears, now don't they? You wouldn't want the Mistress of the House getting wind of your true opinion, now would you?" Vivian sidled up close to Jason. "If you ever need to get away from the little harpy, you know where to find me. I can always help you get a better gig, darling." The red talons traced a line down his chest. "Men like you are hard to find."

Sabrina couldn't handle any more. She backed away from the door, confused about what she'd heard. Jason had acted like he didn't even know Vivian before. She turned and bolted up the steps, unable to face them and pretend nothing had happened.

Anger and jealousy tore at her. Why had he misled her about Vivian? What else was he lying about this time? Whatever his game, Sabrina was calling a time out.

Chapter Eight

She sat on her bed, her gaze darting from the telephone to the locked bedroom door. Her nerves were coiled like a roll of film wound tight in its casing. She couldn't just sit there and wait for her phantom to call or Jason to come knocking.

She wasn't safe. Her life had been violated, her privacy shredded. But the one person she longed to trust was a liar like all the rest. How could she look into his eyes without giving in to the anger that boiled in her veins?

In her mind, she still saw him sitting with Vivian, her hands moving over his body while he smiled. Were they still together? Why hadn't the woman gone home already? Maybe she'd been waiting for Jason's return…biding her time until she could sink her red claws into him.

Sabrina straightened her back, fighting off the tears burning behind her eyelids. It didn't matter. She didn't want Jason anymore. He'd been little more than an adolescent fantasy, a knight with raven hair and blue eyes she'd imagined carrying her off into the sunset.

In reality, he drove a second-hand black Mercedes and wore a huge bag of guilt strapped across his broad back instead of a sword and shield. She didn't want any part of that. If she ever gave her heart away, it would not be to a man who lied and cheated.

But was it too late? Had she let herself love him again?

Her chest tightened. Jason didn't want her. He enjoyed experienced women and no-strings sex. That was something she could never offer. He'd said it himself. She was a forever-after type woman and he was a one-night-stand kind of guy.

Tension played along the muscles of her neck, twisting them into knots. She rose to her feet and walked to the closet. It didn't matter what dangers might lie outside this house—she had to get out of it before her nerves snapped.

* * *

"May I take your wrap, ma'am?"

Sabrina stared at the teenager in the short red uniform, her smile frozen. *Ma'am?* Since when had she become a *ma'am?* She recovered and nodded, transferring her small black bag from hand to hand as the coat-check girl helped her remove her short black jacket.

"Thank you," Sabrina murmured as the girl moved away. Smoothing down the skirt of her black dress, she turned and approached the maitre-de. "I'd like a table for one, please."

"Yes, ma'am. Do you have a reservation?"

Sabrina shook her head and the man gave her a pitying smile. "I am sorry. We're very busy this evening. Might I recommend the grill in our lounge?"

She smiled, even though she felt like slinking out of the restaurant. Why had she come here alone on a Friday night? She stood her ground, thinking of the outrageous flirting she'd done to get the guard on duty to let her leave without notifying Jason or Thomas. Of all the nerve—the two of them keeping tabs on her like she was an incompetent child.

"Thank you, that would be fine."

The man led her past the rustic Alpine-lodge décor to the entrance of the small canteen set off from the main part of the restaurant.

"If I can be of any assistance, please do not hesitate to ask."

"Yes…thank you."

She slid onto an empty stool at the end of the curved bar, tugging her mid-thigh skirt down and wishing she'd worn something below the knee. With the image of Jason's *tete-a-tete* in her mind, she'd been going for a sexy look, just to spite him and bolster her sagging self-esteem. But the form-fitting, sleeveless dress left her feeling cold and vulnerable.

Glancing around the cozy room, she waited for her eyes to adjust to the dim glow of colored accent lights and flickering candles. The faint odor of cigarette smoke hung in the air.

A man in a white shirt and dark jeans pulled a beer from the tap. He glanced at her and nodded. "I'll be right with you."

"No hurry," Sabrina replied, her gaze wandering over the intimate tables for two scattered around the small space.

A few were occupied with couples sitting close together, drinking and talking, some smiling, others serious. At one table in the darkest corner, she could see a lone figure bent over a drink as if its depths held endless fascination. She felt a strong twinge of sympathy. He had loneliness written all over his tired shoulders.

"What can I get you?"

She turned back to the bartender, really looking at him for the first time. The man had a sexy smile and long dark hair tied at his nape. Like the redhead at the police station, he seemed familiar. It was as if her memory had gone soft-focus. The images were almost there, just beyond reach, the edges blurred. She couldn't remember the details; just a feeling of familiarity remained.

Sabrina realized she was staring and looked away, catching a glimpse of her own startled expression in the mirrored wall behind the bar. "Oh, I'll just have some mineral water, please, with a twist of lime."

He smiled. "Sure thing. One Castle's Purest coming up."

She looked at him. "Oh, is it local? I didn't realize we had anything bottled in Castle's Grove."

"Yep, comes right from the springs at the foot of Layne Mountain." His gaze darted between her face and the glass as he filled it and dropped in piece of fresh lime. Frowning, he set the drink on the bar in front of her. "I swear this isn't a line, but you look very familiar. Have we met before?"

Sabrina glanced down at her drink, sticking a finger in and pushing the lime wedge down into the icy water. "No, I don't believe so." Then taking a sip she looked up into his eyes. "But I was just thinking the same thing."

His smile widened. "Well, maybe we have met. Do you visit the area often?"

"I was born and raised here. I've just been living in New York City for the last few years."

He stuck out a hand. "I'm Cole Ryan, also a native. Maybe we went to school together or something?"

Sabrina stared. The name...yes, that was where she remembered him. He had been one of Jason's buddies—one of those caught in the twisted, burning metal after the accident.

She grasped his hand and shook it. "I think we did know each other, Cole. I'm Sabrina Layne."

His eyes went wide, his hand stilled. "Oh, yeah! Sabrina Layne, you have certainly grown up, haven't you?" His gaze darted over her as the smile vanished. "Oh, man. I forgot. I'm really sorry about your dad. He was a good guy."

She looked at him for a moment, wondering if he was being kind or sincerely thought David Layne was a 'good guy.' She opted for honesty at that moment. All the tap dancing and lies were getting to be too much.

"No, he wasn't." She smiled a little at his look of surprise. "But I'm finding out he wasn't as bad as I thought."

Cole shrugged. "Well, I know he treated me pretty good after..." He hesitated, his gaze slipping from hers. "But sometimes it's harder to get along with your own folks. I know I've been down that road. I was sorry to hear about what happened. Are you okay?"

She nodded. "Thanks, yes. I'm dealing with it. I'm not sure it's all quite sunk in though."

"Sabrina!" The familiar voice caught her attention and she turned in time to see Sam walking across the lounge. Her stomach rolled, the sight of him sending shock waves through her.

"Hey, honey, sorry I'm late." Sam snaked a possessive arm around her waist. His gaze moved to the bartender polishing the bar's smooth wood surface. Cole's features had dissolved into a practiced blank expression. Perfect for a man bombarded with people's troubles night after night. Sam's grip tightened. "It's good to see you. How are you?"

"I'm fine." Sabrina moved forward on her stool, shrugging off his intimate touch. "But what are you doing here?"

He stiffened. "Well, I was eating in a booth near the back and saw you. I thought maybe you'd like some company." He looked at Cole. "I know you hate to eat alone, honey."

Sam laid a hand on the small of her back. The touch made her skin crawl as anger began simmering. "I don't mind eating alone and I was just catching up with an old friend."

"You're friends with the bartender?" Sam's tone brought heat flooding into her cheeks. He sounded so pompous, so superior. If nothing else, Sam sure had nerve. He was an untalented actor looking for a free ride from his ex-wife. How dare he look down his nose at a man who knew the meaning of an honest day's work?

"Yes, Cole and I go way back." The bartender frowned a little. She held her breath, hoping he'd allow her this little subterfuge. They had known each other, if only in passing.

Sam snorted. "Oh, that's priceless! The millionaire's daughter and the boy most likely to pull taps at the local dive. Well, before you get any ideas, old boy, the lady's with me."

Sabrina stood to face him. "How dare you! You are nothing but a pompous, conceited, loser—that's all you've ever been. And to think I wasted two years of my life on you. Well, not one second more!" She snapped open her purse, dug out a ten-dollar bill with shaking fingers and tossed it on the bar.

"Sorry, Cole," she murmured.

"No problem, Sabrina. You just let me know if this joker is bothering you. We don't allow ladies to be accosted in this town." The bartender's gaze never left Sam and his deep voice lowered to a growl-like warning.

Sabrina turned back to her ex, who had gone a little pale. They had quite an audience in the dark lounge. But for once in her life, she didn't care. *Let them look.*

"I never want to see you again as long as I live, Sam. You make me sick! And just for the record—he left me everything. Every last dollar, the house, the land and every stick of old antiquated furniture. But you, Samuel Mansfield, will never see one single, solitary penny of it. And do you know why? Because you are a self-centered, egotistical bastard. If you come near me again or so much as think of calling me, I'll have you slapped with a restraining order so fast you won't be able to see through the cloud of dust! Do I make myself clear?"

Sam nodded. Good. Speechless for a change. Why hadn't she told him off years ago?

Sabrina pushed past him and strode out of the bar, hesitating only a moment as applause and cheers washed over her. She glanced around, feeling the heat in her face and the strong, steady beat of her heart as total strangers celebrated her bravado.

She left the restaurant after retrieving her jacket from the smiling attendant. It seemed her little outburst had been louder than she realized.

As she walked out into the cool, clear evening air, she glanced around. The street was quiet, no cars in sight. She walked across the brightly-lit parking lot to the gray BMW she had borrowed from her father's garage. Just as she fished her keys out, she noticed another vehicle parked several spaces over, a red sports car. Could it be? She walked toward the car, glancing about to see that she was alone. Sure enough, New York license plates. It had Sam Mansfield written all over it—flashy, expensive and not at all practical.

A quick survey showed the other cars sported Pennsylvania plates. This had to be his. No doubt he'd borrowed or rented it just to impress her. That wouldn't surprise her. But what was he up to? He had to know she wouldn't take him back.

After a moment's hesitation, Sabrina gave in to curiosity and checked the door. It wasn't locked. She let out the breath she was holding and slid down into the cramped bucket seat. What was she looking for? She didn't have a clue. Something, anything that might tell her why Sam was really here.

The sun visors were empty except for the registration and insurance cards. Someone named Maggie O'Neil owned the little red Jaguar. She'd be willing to bet it was Sam's latest love. The glove box held a Pennsylvania map folded to reveal a route from New York to Castle's Grove, and several little, foil condom packets. Sabrina wrinkled her nose in disgust. Just like Sam to travel prepared for everything. What a snake.

She had half a mind to track down Ms. O'Neil and tell her what a jerk she was involved with. Sabrina put everything back where she found it and continued her search under the seats, the pockets on the door. Beyond a few receipts for gas, fast food wrappers and a couple of beer cans, the car was clean. Then she got out, glancing around to make sure no one was watching, and tried the trunk. Locked. Probably filled with dirty laundry.

Sabrina sighed. That had been a colossal waste of time. Maggie O'Neil. She was going to have to remember that name. The woman had to be warned that Sam Mansfield was the last man on earth to trust her car with.

* * *

"Where the hell have you been?"

Sabrina jumped, then stopped at her bedroom door and glanced back. Jason stood further down the hall, his body silhouetted by the moonlight streaming in the window. She could hear the anger in his voice.

"I'm tired," she murmured, turning toward her door and pushing it open. "Please ask Martha not to bother with breakfast for me. I think I'll just sleep in."

"Where have you been?" His footsteps punctuated each word.

She caught sight of her reflection in the mirror across the bedroom. A flash of fury burst through her as she remembered what she'd seen and heard in the study earlier that night. How dare he question her like that after he'd betrayed her?

Sabrina turned to face him. "We may not be very formal around here, Mr. Sinclair, but I'll have you remember that you are the employee. I don't have to answer to you."

She saw his shoulders stiffen in response, but didn't care. She was just so very tired and disgusted. Nothing had gone right. First the frightening phone call, then seeing him so cozy with that woman followed by the confrontation with Sam. The last thing she needed was an argument from Lord Protector.

"I wanted to get out by myself so I borrowed a car and went to the Castle Club." Anger seethed through her like a volcano in the last throes of silence before it erupts. "Sam happened to be there and followed me into the bar where we staged a rather ugly scene for the other patrons. Ask your friend Cole Ryan if you want the gory details."

"What—?"

She raised a hand to silence him. "Don't worry about me from now on. I can take care of myself. As soon as I find out what happened to my father, I'll be on the first plane back to New York and I'll never darken your path again. You and Vivian can have each other for all I care."

She tried to slam the door but it bounced back again. She gasped, turning to face Jason's smoldering blue eyes. His jaw was set in a rigid line, his body stiff and unyielding.

"You *will* tell me what the hell you're talking about, *Miss* Layne." She shivered at the ice in his voice. "What does Vivian have to do with any of this and why did you go off alone with that jerk?"

Her eyes narrowed. She squared her shoulders despite the fatigue that permeated every muscle.

"I just told you. *I. Went. Alone.* He saw me come in and followed me to the bar. Besides that, whomever I choose to see and whatever I choose to do is none of *your* damn business!"

"Yes, it is," he growled. "I've made it my business since your father's accident and it will be my business until I find out who hired that man to kill me last night."

Sabrina stared. Never before had she seen him so angry. It frightened her a little. She stepped backwards as he stalked into the room. For a long moment, he just stared at her, the only sounds their harsh breathing and the pounding of her heart.

Jason shook his head and sighed. The stiffness in his broad shoulders fell a notch. He looked weary, defeated. Sabrina reached out to touch him but pulled back.

"Never mind," he mumbled. He stepped toward the hall. "I apologize. I was out of line. It will keep until the morning."

He was like Jekyll and Hyde, one moment a simmering force of testosterone, the next an almost-humble imitation of the sycophant servant. But Jason was no man's servant. How could anyone believe that for even a moment? She made a frustrated sound that caught his attention. He turned as she dropped onto the bed and kicked off her shoes.

"Jase, enough playing games. You've known me since I wore pigtails. For pity's sake, you're acting more like my brother or a jealous boyfriend than the family chauffeur."

He watched her for a moment, their gazes locked. "Sabrina, I can't take care of you if I don't know what's going on."

How she wanted to trust him, to reach out to him and tell everything that had happened. She was so very weary of standing on her own two feet and pretending to always like it.

"I want to trust you," she said. "But I'm not sure I can. I'm not sure I can let myself trust anyone again."

He shook his head and stepped inside the room, closing the door behind him. "Why? Because of what happened ten years ago? Sweetheart, I screwed up. But I told you why I left. You scared the hell out of me. I knew I couldn't make love to you that night or any other. We were supposed to be friends."

"But…"

"No but's!" Jason strode across the room, his face dark like a thundercloud.

His anger made her body tremble. But it wasn't just anger in those eyes—lust flamed there as well. He wanted her, burned for her. She hadn't imagined those things ten years ago. Maybe it hadn't been the brandy after all.

"Your father would have had me hung, drawn and quartered if I touched you. You're all he lived for—keeping you safe, making the world a better place for you. He would have had my ass locked in jail for touching his little princess. I had been warned about keeping my hands off of you."

Sabrina blinked in surprise. She didn't know what to think anymore where her father was concerned. Once she thought she had known the kind of man David Layne had been—one who cared for himself and nothing for the daughter he had sired—but according to Jason, that image had all been a lie.

"Bree, I need you to trust me now. I need you to tell me what went on tonight. Someone out there is having people killed and I'm worried you might be on their list."

She cleared her throat. "Where do you want me to start?"

"How about from where we left each other downstairs? I seem to have gotten lost in the program somewhere about then."

"Okay, first off I should have told you something." Sabrina took a deep breath, hating that she felt like a guilty child confessing to a parent. "I've been getting phone calls for a couple of months…pranks, I thought. Except they didn't stop. Then you called about Dad and I…well, I kind of put it out of my mind until I got another one tonight."

"What do you mean, pranks? Are you talking about obscene calls or what?"

"No, just weird. He spouts poetry of a sort and tells me he loves me. He calls me Sabrina-fair. The voice is muffled, but there's something familiar about it I just can't quite focus on. At first, they didn't bother me. I thought Sam was being a jerk. But then they started getting more and more creepy."

Jason took a deep breath and rubbed a hand over his shadowed jaw. "Did you report these calls to the police?" Sabrina shook her head and he sighed. "Why not?"

She shrugged. "He's never threatened me in so many words or made any obscene remarks. It's more like what he doesn't say or the words he chooses. I don't know how to explain it. But I knew the police wouldn't be able to do anything about it. I didn't want them thinking I was looking for attention."

Jason shook his head. "You have got to stop worrying about what other people think. But you are right. The cops might not have been able to do much. Did you change your phone number?"

She nodded. "Yes, but it didn't do any good."

Jason frowned. "Wait, he called tonight? Here?"

"Yes, on my private line."

His dark expression made Sabrina catch her breath. "Do you have any idea what kind of danger you could be in from a nutcase like that? Oh, hell! Why didn't you say something? Why do you always think you have to face everything bad in life alone?"

Rage sizzled through her like an electric current before a storm. *She* faced things alone? Wasn't that the pot calling the kettle black?

"I went downstairs to find you! I was going to tell you about it, ask you what I should do. I heard voices in the study. I didn't mean to eavesdrop but I heard you and Vivian talking. I saw the way she was looking you up and down like a prime cut of beef...touching you..." She looked away.

"I was trying to find out what Vivian knows about your father's death or who else she might have told about it not being an accident. After what you said about her, I thought maybe she knew more than she was letting on."

"Why should I believe you?"

"Oh, come on! We've been friends forever. Do you think an obvious piece of work like Vivian James is my type?"

She lifted her shoulders. "How do I know? I never could figure out what you wanted from a woman *except* the obvious."

Jason shook his head and turned from her, walking across the room to one of the windows overlooking the garden. He lifted the sheer curtain.

"Believe me or don't, it's up to you," he stared out into the moonlit night. "That lady is something else. She and I haven't said more than a few words to each other and yet she came on to me like…"

"Like you were old lovers?"

He turned and looked at her, one eyebrow raised. "Yeah, something like that. So you were there quite awhile."

Sabrina shrugged.

"Maybe that's what Vivian's little display was all about," he said. "Maybe she saw you and decided to come on strong to drive a wedge between us. But why didn't you say something? Why did you just sneak out without asking me what was going on? When everyone else thought I was guilty of manslaughter, you were one of the few that stood up for me. How did I completely lose your trust?"

She looked away, unwilling to admit the strength of her feelings and the dark, bitter depths of jealousy seeing him with Vivian had awakened. Heaven help her, she was in deep this time.

"I'm sorry, Jase. I didn't give you a fair chance. I just believed my eyes and ears." She looked up at him. "I know there's something you're still not telling me. Whenever I blindly give anyone my trust they've trampled it into the ground. I cannot go through that again."

He walked over to kneel on the floor at her feet, clasping her hands in his. The flicker of pain in his eyes twisted her heart. "I can understand how you feel after I walked out on you like that…after the promises I made. Please believe me, anything I've kept from you I've done so to protect you. But now you've got to be honest with me. Do you have any idea who would want to hurt you or your father?"

She looked into his eyes. The urgent pleading in his voice sent blood rushing through her veins. His nearness started a fire deep within. He was begging her for the truth and yet she had the feeling that only a certain version of it would suffice. Did she know the answers he needed to hear?

"Is it just a job? Is that all I ever was to you—the spoiled little rich girl your mama made you baby-sit?"

He stared at her, swaying closer. His gaze moved over her face, lingering on her lips. She couldn't keep still. His heat pulled at her. Beckoning. Her body responded to the beacon as if being called home from a long voyage at sea.

"No, it's not just a job. It might have been at first; not a job, but an obligation. Then while I was going through rehab, we became friends. You were so much fun to be with, to talk to. You made the days bearable. I tried…" He stared at her mouth, swallowing hard. "I tried to keep it that way when we grew up, but I couldn't. I blamed that night on the brandy but I had wanted you for a long while. You were just a kid!"

He looked down at her hands, resting in his. Turning them over, he kissed each palm. "Now, you are very grown-up and…you do things to me" His lips moved against her skin, warm and moist. "Just being near you puts very vivid pictures in my mind. But I can't take advantage of the situation. I have to take care of you and keep you safe."

Sabrina drifted closer. "I don't want a protector, Jason."

He stared at her, his eyes growing darker. "What do you want?"

One of them moved. She wasn't sure who, but his mouth hovered mere inches away. She could feel his warm breath on her lips.

"Tell me," he whispered. "Tell me what you want."

"You."

Jason shook his head. "I don't have anything to offer."

Sabrina covered his mouth with hers to stop the flow of words. Her eyes shut. He stilled as if fighting against the kiss. She felt him trying to back away. Then with a deep moan, he wrapped his arms around her, pulling her down into his lap.

She straddled his powerful thighs, the short skirt of her dress hiking up to her hips. Sabrina gasped as Jason pulled her firmly against him. His tongue teased her lips until she opened eagerly, her hands sliding into his thick dark hair. His hands moved along her back, pressing her closer.

She almost couldn't breathe but didn't care. She wanted to be in Jason's arms. She'd gladly die there. Then he abruptly pulled back, his breathing ragged as he pressed his forehead to hers.

"Bree," he whispered. "I want you so much, but…"

"…we have to stop," Sabrina finished.

He gazed at her for a long moment, regret and longing fighting each other in his blue eyes. "Yeah, we have to stop. I wish—"

She placed her fingers over his mouth. "No regrets, Jase. But tell me…do you want this as much as I do?"

Large hands moved down to her hips, embracing her and pulling her closer. Sabrina gasped and clung to his shoulders. Her gaze became trapped in the churning ocean of Jason's eyes.

She couldn't pull enough air into her lungs with him looking at her like that, pressed against her so that she could feel his arousal.

"What do you think?" he whispered, his breath tickling her neck as he bent toward her. He nuzzled her throat, warm lips pressed to her flesh, sending waves of pleasure coursing down her spine. She moaned.

"I-I can't think…" What on earth was he doing? "We don't want to do anything we'll both regret." He continued the sensual assault, his mouth roaming down her chest to the edges of her low-cut dress. "Jase? I thought you wanted to stop."

"I do," he murmured against the upper slope of her breast.

"We… can't…"

"No." He cupped her bottom, lifting her up a fraction to settle against him. Hard, rigid flesh pressed intimately against her. The sensation sent fiery darts racing along her spine. She bit her lip to keep from crying out loud. Fighting for control, she dug her fingers into his shoulders to keep the world balanced. Jason flinched and pulled away as he sucked in a deep, hissing breath.

"Oh!" She jerked her hand back. "I'm sorry! I forgot about your shoulder."

He released a whoosh air and looked at her with a strained smile. "I'm fine, sweetheart. Just hold onto me here."

He guided her hand down his biceps, away from the wound before resuming his quest. He wasn't going to stop. Did she want him to? *Yes...um, no. Not yet.* But she had to stop. She couldn't handle disappointing him. Sabrina tried to pull away.

"Uh, Jase? I-I'm not very good at this kind of thing." She swallowed. "Please, I don't...I think I might be, uh..." The word, what was the word? How could she think of it when he was doing such magical things with that mouth? "Frigid."

He didn't seem to hear her. She closed her eyes as the sensations seeped past her protective barriers, warming her body, calling to her heart. Jason stilled. Then he chuckled as he lifted his head. Her eyes fluttered open.

"Did you just say that you're frigid?"

She nodded and glanced away. She could feel her cheeks growing warm as she wished for a hole to crawl into.

"You've got to be kidding. You are the least frigid woman I have ever met. Where did you ever get such a lame-brain idea?"

Sabrina stiffened. How dare he make fun of her? Especially about this problem that had caused her so much grief and embarrassment?

She glanced around the room. Their position no longer held erotic appeal; it made her feel vulnerable. Dirty. Like having Daddy catch her in the backseat with her boyfriend's hand inside her bra. Not that that had ever happened beyond her hormonal daydreams. Nothing had ever happened in any backseat. Not even with Jason.

"Bree?" His voice was gentle as he grasped her chin and turned her head to face him. "What is it? What's wrong? Talk to me."

Sabrina cursed the tears she could feel stinging her eyes. "I-I never..." How could she tell him? How could she tell the one man that made her body burn with desire her most personal secret? "I never had a-a...you know."

Jason frowned at her as she stumbled over the word she was sure any grown woman should be able to say. But not her. The Ice Queen couldn't even name it let alone experience one. To her relief and chagrin, the light of understanding dawned on his handsome face.

"Oh!" He stared for what seemed an eternity. "You were married for two years and your husband never gave you an orgasm?"

Sabrina felt her face blazing hot and red. She folded her arms across her belly and shook her head.

"Oh for the love of...." Jason took a deep breath. "Listen, did you ever think the problem might be your ex, not you?"

She looked at him and nodded. "But, then he started parading around town with his mistresses. I mean, if he wasn't good at it, how would he get so many women into bed?"

Anger flashed over his features, startling her with its intensity. "Damn it! Why did you let that jackass treat you like that? Maybe Romeo paraded the women by because he was trying to boost his own ego. One time with the jerk was probably enough for any of them if technique was lacking."

Sympathy and disgust warred in his eyes. His grip tightened on her hips. "He could have hurt you! Didn't the bastard think about your health at all?"

The concern in his voice warmed her. No one else had ever expressed such worry. "He always used protection when we were together and when the divorce was final, I went to my doctor. I'm okay."

Jason closed his eyes and sighed. The sound rumbled over her as his arms banded around her. "Bree, why didn't you believe in yourself a little more? You are such a warm, beautiful woman. You should never have stayed with that jerk for two years."

She gasped as hands moved over her sides, burning her skin through the thin layer of fabric. "The way you react to me..." He nuzzled her throat. The rasp of his shadowed jaw sent a tingle down her spine. She shivered. "There's no way in hell you're frigid. I'd be willing to bet once you're set loose, there's going to be a heat wave of epic proportions."

Sabrina felt her body relaxing, melting into him, even while tension coiled deep within. It was nice. Very nice. A throbbing ache began low in her belly and spread downward. She burned where that very male part of him pressed into her softness.

"You could set me loose." She caressed his arms. The cotton fabric of his sweater molded to perfect biceps. She imagined them wrapped around her, protecting her and molding her body to his as he took possession. Even if she couldn't enjoy it, the thought of being loved by this man was enough to make her body pulse with need.

Jason shook his head. A reluctant smile settled on his lips. "You have no idea how tempting that offer is. But we both know it wouldn't work. I don't want to hurt you again, Sabrina. I can't offer you the kind of relationship you deserve."

She touched her lips to his, lingering for a moment. "I'm not sure what that is, Jason. But I think you're wrong." She tried to get up, her legs protesting even the slightest movement. "I think we have a problem."

"What's that?" he murmured, his gaze transfixed to her lips.

"I can't seem to get my legs to move."

A devilish gleam lit his eyes. "Maybe I can get the blood circulating again."

His hands moved down from her hips, sliding along her thighs to her knees. Then he began to massage the stiff muscles. His hands glided along the black stockings, ever upward as he gazed into her eyes. Sabrina felt her thighs tingle with warmth, the sensation moving upward until she trembled.

When his fingertips reached the edges of her stockings, Jason paused. She could hear the breath catch in his throat, saw his eyes darken. His fingers explored the bare flesh and hooks of the garters.

"Do you wear these often?" His voice was quiet, strained.

"No. I wanted to feel pretty." She gazed at him, swallowing hard as his fingers dipped beneath the edges of the black silk. She held very still despite an intense need to rock her hips against his.

Sabrina's heart thumped, driven by desire and fear. Maybe with Jason, it would be different. Her body already responded more strongly to him than it ever had to her ex. But could she trust Jason with her heart? Would she ever be able to give herself to a man knowing it wasn't forever? What did it matter? He was turning her away. Like always.

"Jase…"

He placed a finger over her lips. "I can't let it happen. We both know it. I don't think I could turn my back on you again if I tried." He shook his head. "I'm just not able to make the kind of commitment you need."

A loud knock ricocheted off the walls. Jason lifted her off his lap and they both struggled to stand. Sabrina's legs tingled, little knives of pain protesting every movement. She collapsed on the bed, straightening her skirt.

Jason faced the closed door. "Yes?"

"Sinclair?" Thomas's voice sounded surprised. Jason looked over his shoulder at her and grimaced. "Is Sabrina home?"

Jason grinned. "Hurry, get your clothes back on, we've been busted." He winked as Sabrina giggled.

"Very funny," Thomas replied. "Now open the door, please, if she's decent. I need to have a word with you both."

Chapter Nine

Jason sighed and pulled open the door. Thomas stood in the hallway, his suit creased with wrinkles, the white shirt he wore unbuttoned to his chest. His tired gaze darted from Jason to Sabrina and back again.

She felt a guilty flush sweep over her cheeks. What had gotten into her, letting Jason touch her, teasing her that way? Simple. She'd messed up and fallen in love with him all over again.

Thomas stepped into the room. "Sabrina, you can't keep running off like this! You could be in terrible danger. I don't…" He cleared his throat. "I don't know what I would do if something happened to you."

"I'm sorry. I just needed to be on my own for a while. I went into town and ran into my ex-husband at the Castle Club. We argued and I left. I just drove around for a while. I didn't realize how late it was or I would have called."

Thomas gazed at her across the room. "The chief just phoned. Two more bodies were found this evening."

She felt the blood drain from her face. "Bodies? Two *more* bodies?"

Jason looked at her, his face grim. "One of the men that chased us last night—they found his body in the car on the mountainside this morning. I didn't say anything before because I didn't want you to worry."

His words took a moment to register. He glanced away and she was left with the strange feeling that Jason was still hiding something from her. She turned to Thomas.

"What's going on?" she asked.

The butler's gaze rested on hers. The room lost focus and all she could see were his clear green eyes, comforting, lending her strength.

He cleared his throat. "The owner of the Castle's Grove Motel found a man shot to death in one of the rooms. They've identified him as an associate of the bloke that tried to run you two off the road last night. He checked in after midnight, banged up and claiming his car had broken down on the mountain. When the proprietor didn't see the man all day, he went in to check on him and found the body. He'd been killed sometime this morning."

"How?" Jason asked.

"Shot in the mouth with a small caliber weapon. It looks like a suicide, except the man's fingers are clean."

A wave of heat washed over Sabrina. "Clean?"

"There wasn't any gunpowder residue on his hand. In other words, he couldn't have fired a gun unless he was wearing gloves. Of course, the coroner will do a more thorough check, but it seems obvious someone else held the gun."

"You said *two* more bodies were found," Jason said. "Who else?"

Thomas glanced at him, then back at Sabrina. "The other man was found an hour ago in a car parked outside the Castle Club. Sabrina, I don't know how to tell you…it's your ex-husband. They've identified him by his personal effects. He was stabbed once through the heart."

Her stomach flipped as she broke out in a cold sweat. Sharp, vivid images rose in her mind—Sam, lifeless, blood spilling from his chest. Bile rose in her throat.

Jason knelt at her feet, grasping her hands in his. "Bree, are you okay?"

She shook her head and bolted off the bed. The bathroom door slammed behind her.

* * *

Jason stared at the door. He felt so powerless. Somewhere along the line, he had lost control of the entire situation—first in Sabrina's arms and now as the body count rose higher and higher. Had he had control over any of it to begin with?

"What the hell is going on, Thomas?" He speared the butler with a look that had shriveled lesser opponents. The older man didn't even blink.

"I have no idea," Thomas replied quietly, shooting a wary glance toward the bathroom door and stepping closer to Jason. "But I do think we need to revise our former hypothesis."

Jason raised his eyebrows. "I wasn't aware we even had one. So where do we stand?"

"I'm starting to doubt all these incidents are related to David's accident." Thomas rubbed his temples and sighed. "Sabrina is involved somehow. At least, if she wasn't before, she is now. I've been checking with my former intelligence connections. No one has heard of any contracts taken out on either you or David. Have you uncovered any new leads?"

Jason shook his head. "According to my FBI source, all of the felons David dealt with in the past three years are either behind bars, rotting in some third-world cesspool or dead."

"It could be someone from further in the past," Thomas added. "But it doesn't make sense them coming after Sabrina or Mansfield."

"No, and now there's a new angle. She just informed me that she's been receiving strange phone calls for several months."

Thomas frowned. "Strange? How?"

"An unknown admirer." Jason paced across the room, glancing at the bathroom door.

Thomas's face went very pale. "Does she have any idea who it might be? Has she been threatened?"

"No, on both counts," Jason replied.

"Why didn't she mention this before?" Thomas hooked his thumbs in the pockets of his tailored black trousers and walked further into the room.

"I think she was embarrassed and at first, didn't think it could have anything to do with her father's accident."

"But you think it might."

"At this point, I'm not sure. But there are a lot of things I'm not sure about. It could be a coincidence, but it doesn't seem likely."

Thomas stood silent for a moment. "Have you told her everything? About you and David—your *real* jobs?"

"No, I haven't," Jason moved closer, glancing at the closed bathroom door. He couldn't let her overhear this conversation. "You know I can't tell her. It would put her in too much danger."

"Seems to me she's already in danger," the Englishman observed. "But perhaps you're right. She does jump into situations with both feet...so much like her mother." Thomas's features relaxed as a faraway look drifted across them. "Do you know why I came here, Jason?"

The question took him aback. "No, I can't say that I do. Once I found out about David's secret life, I asked if you knew about it. He admitted that you had once been an agent but that you'd retired several years earlier."

"Several years too late," the butler murmured. He turned to face Jason. "I was assigned as a bodyguard to David's wife, Elizabeth, and their young daughter. He had been instrumental in putting a very wealthy gun-runner in prison."

"Let me guess, his involvement was somehow exposed and the other man threatened his family."

"Not directly, but that was the trend at the time, so they sent me here." Thomas paced the perimeter of the room. "David went on about his business, however, thinking he'd be the primary target. He wasn't. But we didn't know that until Elizabeth went to New York one weekend to buy Sabrina a special Christmas present. She insisted I stay here with the child."

"And she never made it home."

"No," Thomas whispered, pain filling the short syllable. "Her car was run off the road. They never caught the other driver." The older man turned to look at him, the desolation in his eyes almost too painful to witness. "I failed, Jason. I couldn't protect her. That's when I realized it wasn't worth it anymore. I resigned the day after her funeral."

Jason watched as Thomas stood there a moment, his gaze darting around the walls. It came to rest on a small, color photograph above the nightstand. A young woman with dark hair and eyes smiled back at them.

"Why did you stay after she died?"

"I stayed for the same reasons you came back, young man. This is my home and I love Sabrina."

It felt as if Thomas had punched him full in the gut. Jason shook his head, fighting to deny the truth. "That's not why…"

"You can lie to her all you want, but isn't it about time you were honest with yourself?"

Jason stared at him, a lump forming in his throat. "I can't…" He swallowed hard. "I don't know how to make her happy. She doesn't belong in my world."

"Then leave it and make a home in hers!" Thomas stepped closer, anger tightening his features. "It's a job, Jason, not a life. Give it up before you're in too deep. I made that mistake, and so did David. We kept in there, thinking we were making a difference somehow, until it was too late for us. Then everything…*everyone* we loved was gone."

Jason jerked away from his friend's stark truth and thrust a shaking hand through his hair. "Hell, Thomas! I can't just quit. It's not a job you just leave behind at the end of the day. What would I do? I can't offer her what she needs. I don't think I can love one woman like that…forever."

"How do you know if you haven't even tried?" Thomas shook his head. "You've lived by your own rules as long as I've known you, Jason. So change them! Make new ones and give yourself a chance."

The men turned as the bathroom door opened. Sabrina stood there, her face pale, her dark eyes red and brimming with tears.

Jason watched as Thomas hurried toward her and drew her into his arms.

He envied the butler at that moment. He felt like an intruder watching something too personal, too intimate. Jason didn't want to be an outsider. Not with Sabrina. He realized that he wanted…no, he *needed* to be a part of her life. He didn't want to wind up like his old friend—alone and mourning a life never led. A love never satisfied.

The phone on the nightstand rang, jarring him from the sudden realization the butler had forced him to confront. Jason picked up the receiver on the third ring.

"Yes?"

Silence.

"Hello?" Jason frowned.

"I'm sorry," a male voice replied. "I must have the wrong number. I was trying to reach Miss Sabrina Layne?"

"Yes, you have the right number. She's occupied at the moment, however. May I ask who's calling?"

For a moment he thought the man had hung up. "Yes, of course, my name is Eric Van Horn—Sabrina's editor? I was just calling to see how she is. I was under the impression this was her private number."

"Yes, yes, it is, Mr. Van Horn. Like I said however, she can't come to the phone right now so I'll let her know you called. Does she know how to reach you?"

Another moment of silence. Did they have a bad connection?

"Yes, of course she knows how to get in touch with me." The sudden tense note in Van Horn's voice caught Jason's attention. What was with this guy? "If you would be so kind as to give her the message—tell her I need to speak with her as soon as possible."

"Yeah, okay, will do. Good night." The other man had already hung up. Jason stared at the receiver. Something didn't seem right. But his insides were so twisted at the moment, he couldn't think. Couldn't contemplate anything but the possibility that he might be very much in love with Sabrina.

"I'm sorry." She pulled away from Thomas, wiping at her eyes with the handkerchief he'd given her. "I seem to be blubbering way too much these past two days."

Thomas smiled. "I say it's warranted."

She shook her head. "Maybe so, but it's got to stop." She took a deep breath and sat on the chair by her dressing table. "Who was that on the phone?"

"Oh, your editor, a Mr. Eric Van Horn," Jason said, forcing a light tone that he didn't feel. "The man sounds like he could use a personality transplant."

"Oh, be nice, Jase. Eric's a stuffed shirt, but he's okay."

"Yeah, well, he could use some lessons in phone etiquette. He would like you to call him as soon as possible."

She frowned. "Thanks."

Jason sketched a mock bow. "Always your humble servant, *Mademoiselle*. I hate to break the mood, but I think we have some policemen who are going to want to speak with us."

Sabrina's face paled another shade. "Do they know who killed Sam?"

"They haven't made an arrest," Thomas said. "But they've asked that you both come in for questioning."

"Tonight?" she asked.

"No, Wright told me the morning would be soon enough." His gaze flickered to Jason and back again. "They've sent the murder weapon and the car to the state crime lab in Philly. All he asked was that you not leave town."

She looked at him, her eyes growing wide. "They think I did it. I argued with him in front of witnesses. I don't have an alibi since I was most likely alone in my car when he was killed. I have motive, means and opportunity…hell, I'd arrest me. Why are they waiting until tomorrow?"

Jason sighed, pushing a hand through his tousled hair. She'd been the one running her fingers through it…what was it? Twenty minutes ago?

"You are their primary suspect at the moment," Thomas said. "But they don't have any proof, so they won't arrest you—yet. They have to have something concrete, not just conjecture."

"Okay, so say if they found my fingerprints on the murder weapon...or, uh, in his car?" Sabrina asked. "That would be incriminating?"

Jason narrowed his gaze. "Please tell us you didn't get into his car."

Sabrina grimaced. "I had to know what he was up to! I thought...oh, I don't know what I thought I'd find. But he didn't just show up out of the blue. No one knew where I was going but Eric and I know for a fact that he would never tell Sam. They hate each other."

She sighed, crossing her arms over her stomach and walking to the bed. Jason fought the urge to take her in his arms and love away the pain she was going through. He'd only hurt her more in the end.

"Damn!" She dashed at the tears streaming down her cheeks. "He was such a jerk! But to be killed like that...!" Her voice broke. "It's just so horrible. I could never, ever do something like that." She looked up, her gaze flitting between the two men. "Please believe me! I hated him, wanted him out of my life, but I couldn't kill anyone."

"What did you touch?" Jason asked.

She sat for a moment, her brow furrowed as if in deep thought. "The steering wheel, the glove box and the dash. Oh, and I looked under the seats and in the sun visors."

He stared at her and realized his mouth was gaping. Shutting it with a snap, Jason turned to Thomas. But the Englishman stood, staring at her with wide eyes. "What? You didn't check the boot?"

Sabrina felt her cheeks flush. "Well, I tried to open it but it was locked and he'd taken the keys with him."

"Bloody hell!" Thomas turned and started pacing the room, his face as dark as a thundercloud.

Jason shook his head and took a deep breath. *Don't panic. Circumstantial evidence could not get a conviction.* "So her prints will be on the trunk, the door and…well, just about everything but the murder weapon." Then he glanced at her. "You didn't touch a knife tonight, did you?"

"No," she said with confidence, then stilled.

"Sabrina!" Jason took a step forward as panic began a tap dance in his chest. "I repeat, did you touch a knife?"

"I-I don't think so."

He and Thomas groaned in united frustration.

"Well, not that I can remember! How am I supposed to remember every single thing that I touched? What kind of knife was it?"

Thomas sighed. "Wright said it was a hunting knife of some sort, a common enough weapon in this area. But I really doubt we have much to worry about anyway."

"Oh, sure, no worries here," Jason snapped, wishing he could bury a fist in the punching bag that hung in the weight room.

"An individual would have to have superior upper body strength in order to wield a knife with enough force to penetrate a grown man's chest cavity," Thomas said.

"So…" Jason grasped at the hope Thomas's morbid words held. "…Sabrina wouldn't be able to shove a knife into her ex's heart?"

"Exactly," Thomas agreed.

"The slant of the wound could also be enough to cause reasonable doubt," Jason continued, picking up momentum. "Her ex was about three inches taller…"

"Enough!" Sabrina shouted.

He jumped, staring at her as she swayed on the bed, her complexion as white as new snow. He could hear her swallow.

"In case you gentlemen haven't noticed, this conversation is going way past morbid and bordering on the gruesome," she said. "Please. Get out."

Chapter Ten

Shadows spilled across the floor, slithering closer and closer, moving as if they'd come to life. A voice whispered somewhere in the darkness.

"Sabrina...Sabrina..."

Her gaze darted around the room. Where was it coming from? She couldn't move. Fear snaked around her, closing her throat and trapping her voice deep inside.

Her heart began to pound so hard she was sure it would burst from her chest at any moment. Jason. Jason would help her. She swallowed past the lump in her throat, his name forming on her lips. But the sound wouldn't come. She could feel the shadow now, just beyond the edges of moonlight pouring through the open curtains. There in the blackness beyond the silver gray light, something moved, shifted, changing shape.

Sabrina bolted upright on the bed, her body shaking as she glanced around. Her heart pounded in her ears, hands fisted the covers, drawing them upward. A dream? Had it all been a dream?

A shadow beside the open bathroom door moved. She stared at it, trying to focus on the wispy shape. Tree branches swayed across the windows, silver moonlight chasing the inky black and mottled gray phantoms across the floor and walls.

Sabrina held her breath. It was a dream. The floor creaked. The shadow loomed closer. *Oh, God, it's real!*

The blood froze in her veins, a chill coursing over her spine. She couldn't move. Wind howled, shaking the windows. A scream split the night. Shadows flew about the room in a swirl of dancing limbs and moonlight.

She screamed again and the bathroom door slammed against the wall. The figure disappeared through the open portal. There was rush of icy wind. The howling grew louder, more shrill.

Pounding. Was it her heart? She stared at the space where the shadow had been, unsure how to breathe, wondering why the pounding wouldn't stop. Over the roar, she heard her name, then a thud, followed by another and another. There was a sharp crack of breaking wood and the heavy oak door burst inward, splinters flying from the frame.

"Bree!" Light flooded the room. She huddled against the headboard, frozen like a deer in the headlights. Jason's hand on her arm made her jump and cry out.

He jerked away. "Are you all right? Bree?"

She shook her head. "No, someone…in the bathroom."

He swung around, his body stiff and alert.

"Don't!" Her voice came out a whisper, hoarse and breathless. He waved a hand at her without a word. She watched as he walked toward the doorway. Fear clogged her throat.

Thomas tore through the battered doorway as Jason stepped over the other threshold into the dark. The butler skidded to a stop, glancing at him and then Sabrina. His face twisted into an expression of relief as he rushed to her side. "Are you hurt?"

Sabrina shook her head, her gaze riveted to the bathroom door. A light switched on inside and her breath hitched. Time stood still. She could hear nothing but the rush of wind and blood in her ears. After a moment, the howling stopped.

Jason reappeared unharmed. She let out the breath she'd been holding, tears of fear and relief mingling in her eyes.

"There's no one here," Jason said. "But the window was open and there's mud on the sill. It's big enough for a man to get in and out."

Thomas sat with a protective arm about her shoulders. She let her body sag against him.

"Bree, what happened?" Jason asked.

She tried to breathe, a sob escaping her lips. For a moment, she closed her eyes. "I-I was having a dream. A nightmare. When I woke up, I saw a shadow move by the door. I-I think I screamed and he ran into the bathroom."

Thomas switched on her bedside lamp and reached for the phone. He pressed a small red button. "Yes, this is St. John. We've had a break-in—set off the alarms and lock down all gates. We'll need to contact the police." He and Jason exchanged a look. Jason shook his head.

"No," the butler continued. "This is not a drill. An intruder was in Miss Layne's suite. I want the house and grounds searched and everyone called in for around-the-clock surveillance until this person is caught. No one is to leave this house until either I or Mr. Sinclair have questioned them, is that understood?"

He slammed the receiver down, his arm tightening about her shoulders. "I can't believe with all the high-tech garbage we've installed someone still managed to get in. This is absurd!"

Jason sighed. "Thomas, as soon as everything is secured and we're sure the intruder is gone, I want you to go over the surveillance videos with whoever is on duty."

He started pacing but stopped, glancing down at his feet.

"What is it?" Thomas asked as Jason bent over, retrieving something from the rug at the foot of her bed.

He held four large pieces of torn paper in his hands. Lamplight reflected off their glossy surface as he shifted the bits around. Jason looked up at Sabrina, anger chasing stark fear across his features.

"It's a photo...or it was." He handed the pieces to Thomas. Sabrina glanced over the butler's arm as he held the torn fragments in place. She gasped when she realized the image they formed—her own smiling face.

Jason spun around, pacing to the far wall. He lifted the curtains and examined the windows. "We need to figure out where the security breech occurred and how the hell it happened. I want to know where all our hired professionals were during the past three hours and if I don't get any satisfactory answers, heads are going to roll!"

The butler nodded as he stuffed the ruined photo into the pocket of his bathrobe. "Of course." He turned to Sabrina. "How are you?"

She shrugged. "Okay, I think. You go ahead and do whatever you have to do."

Thomas gave her a brief hug and rose from the bed. "Jason, would you stay with Sabrina, please? She may think she's fine, but once shock sets in, it might be a different story."

Jason looked down at her and nodded. "Of course, but I'm sure she'd rather have you stay."

"Don't be an idiot. As soon as she's settled, you can take over. We'll likely have several hours of tapes to plow through." Thomas turned to Sabrina. "Do get some rest. I promise no one will ever get that close to you again."

"Thank you." She smiled up at him, sensing he wanted to say more. But the butler left, closing the door behind him.

She glanced up at Jason. He stood, staring at her, his eyes dark even in the lamplight.

"You don't have to stay."

"Do you want me to?" His low voice slid over her skin. Their gazes held.

"Yes."

"Then I will."

She fought against the familiar pull, looking away for a moment. The air between them sparked and crackled. Danger lurked in the remaining shadows, a ghost of the terror she'd felt moments ago. It heightened her senses, vibrating in an uncomfortable rhythm across her skin. She longed to feel his arms wrapped around her, knowing Jason could still the shaking. He could keep the shadows at bay.

Sabrina dared another glance, this time taking in the broad expanse of his bare chest and traveling lower, following the firm plain of his belly to the waistband of his low-slung pajama pants. He was so beautiful.

She heard him clear his throat. "Maybe I'd better get dressed first."

He turned to go and she jumped off the bed, lunging forward as she reached out to grasp his arm. Her gaze lifted, caught in the dark, ocean depths of his.

"Please. Don't leave me."

A warning look passed over Jason's features. Danger. Did she realize what she was inviting? She saw his throat move as he swallowed.

"Are you sure?"

Sabrina nodded. "Please hold me."

She watched him for a moment, wondering at the thoughts behind his shuttered expression. Wondering how it would feel to lie in his arms. Beside him. Beneath him.

"Bree, what are you trying to do to me?" he whispered.

She smiled at him. He looked like a wolf cornered by the rabbit. Unsure and confused.

"Please?"

She watched as his eyelids lowered, his gaze moving down her body. For the first time since she awoke, Sabrina became very aware of the skimpy black teddy that did little to conceal her curves. Her skin warmed beneath his appraisal. Tension radiated from him, filling the room with pulsing energy.

Deep disappointment twisted in her stomach when he turned away. Then she realized he was only turning off the main lights. A flick of the switch by the door left them in the dim glow of the lamp by her bed.

When he took her hand in his, Sabrina sighed. He kept watching her as he led her to the bed where she sat down. The mattress dipped with his weight, tossing her nearer as he knelt beside her on one knee.

"Turn off the light, Jase. I don't want to be afraid of the dark anymore."

He leaned across her and flicked off the lamp. His warmth washed over her, filling her senses as her heart tripped in her chest. Jason moved closer, sitting as he drew her to his side.

"I'm just going to hold you." He didn't sound convinced.

"Okay," she whispered.

His fingers danced over her bare arm. "What is this thing called that you're wearing?"

Sabrina smiled. "A teddy. I'm sure you've seen one before."

She felt him shrug. "I could never keep all the terms straight. It's...ah...nice." She could feel the whisper of his ragged breathing against her hair. The beat of his heart thumped beneath the cheek she pressed to his solid chest.

"Why did you marry that creep?"

The question threw her off kilter for a moment. "I thought it was the right thing to do. I was alone and he was a nice guy. Well, he seemed nice on the surface. He's one of those negative-image people."

"What do you mean?"

Sabrina shook her head. "Sorry. That's what I call people who seem one way to the outside world and yet inside, they're very different. My photography instructor at college used that expression and I just picked it up. It's an artsy way of saying you can't judge a book by the cover."

She sat silent for a moment, trying to sort out her feelings during those events almost seven years earlier. But the heat of Jason's skin beneath hers made it hard to think. Her body quivered as the deepest part of her twisted in anticipation.

"But didn't you...I mean..." He stumbled over the words, took a deep breath and bore on. "Why would you marry the guy when he couldn't satisfy you?"

"We didn't go to bed together before we got married. He liked making-out but he always stopped short with me. I thought it was because he respected me. I liked that. I never wanted casual sex. I wanted my first time to be with the man I'd spend the rest of my life with."

With him. She had longed for the first time to be with Jason and no one else. But he'd walked away and never come back. Sabrina felt her cheeks grow warm as the silence stretched between them. How naïve could she be to think he'd understand?

"I'm sorry," he murmured. "I never knew you felt that way."

Sabrina shrugged. "It's not something I discuss with anyone. My mom wasn't around for long, but she did teach me to respect my body…that sex is something special."

She straightened and looked up into his shadowed face. He stared at her for a moment. She wished she could see the expression in his eyes.

"Did you love Sam?"

"No," she whispered, caressing his cheek with her fingertips. "I needed to feel loved, but I couldn't give him my heart—you never gave it back to me."

He shook his head. "Don't love me. I'm no good for you."

"I don't believe that," she insisted. "You've always let me just-so-close before pulling away. What are you afraid of?"

"I'm not afraid." He moved away from her.

"Yes, you are," she said. He wasn't going to run this time—not without an explanation.

He shook his head and stood up, pacing to the other side of the room. She watched his back, waiting.

He turned, the moonbeams framing his chiseled body in cold light. "I'm not hiding anything. You know what happened—you were there. You saw how I screwed up. People suffered and died because of me. My life is no more stable now than it was back then."

She felt the pain in his words as she saw a hint of the specters that still haunted the strong, solid man. A child lived inside, aching with guilt that had never been laid to rest. Why hadn't he forgiven himself?

His face and emotions were obscured by the shadows, but she wasn't frightened. She just wished she could see his eyes. She longed to ease his pain, to make it her own and lift the burden from his broad shoulders.

In a moment, she was moving toward him, arms outstretched. "You made a choice. You were drunk and let someone else drive. That's what you're supposed to do. You cannot have known Jeanine would lose control of the car. Stop punishing yourself. It was no one's fault."

"It's not that easy," he murmured. "I can't chance something happening to you, Bree. I wouldn't be able to live with that."

She shook her head, wishing so much that she could heal this proud, gentle man. So strong and yet so very alone—how had he survived such aching isolation?

Her fingers traced the lines of his arms. A rigid biceps jumped beneath her touch. "Let me love you."

"Bree…" Her name whispered past his lips as his hand reached out. Sabrina tensed, waiting for his touch.

The shrill cry of the telephone cut through the night. She spun around to stare at it on the nightstand. Her heart thudded.

"It's him."

Jason brushed past her and snatched the phone from its cradle. "Hello?" He glanced at Sabrina over his shoulder. "Yes, okay. Thanks." He set the receiver down. "That was Thomas. They may have found the point of entry already. But our man is long gone."

She folded her arms as guilt hit her hard in the stomach. Tears sprung to her eyes. "I thought…I thought I was safe. I'm sorry. I should have told you about the calls sooner." Her voice broke. "It's all my fault! Sam…my father…! Someone killed them because of me, didn't they?"

Jason pulled her into his arms, cradling her head against his shoulder. "We don't know that. But we have to find this guy, no matter what. Do you have any idea who it might be?"

"No."

She snuggled closer against his chest. His heartbeat sped up, pounding against her ear. Sabrina moved one hand up over his ribs and higher. Her fingers wove through the thick black hair. She breathed in his essence, intoxicated by the scent of soap and warm male. He felt so good. So strong. Sabrina wondered again what it would be like to lie in his arms. His breathing was labored, ragged. His warmth drew her onward, giving her boldness she'd never possessed.

Magnet and steel. She turned her head, eyes closed. Her lips brushed against the hair on his chest as she sought the warm skin beneath. She found her quarry, lingering at the taste of him. Standing on her toes, she trailed kisses to his throat, beneath his ear, his jaw. She heard an incoherent moan as she slipped both hands up into the hair at the nape of his neck. It was soft and thick.

"Bree..." he murmured. His hands fisted once, hesitating on her back before sliding down. He cupped her bottom and pulled her tightly against him. She strained to get closer, her pelvis pressed to his. She could feel him hot and hard through the slick silk and warm cotton between them. Her body quivered in response.

"Jase..." she whispered, then flicked her tongue against the sensitive spot beneath his strong jaw. "Make love to me."

He stilled, pulling away to look down into her eyes, his expression hidden in the shadows. She felt the heat rise in her face. What if he walked away again? How could she face him in the morning? She waited, wondering if he was about to rip her last shred of self-esteem into confetti.

"For you," he whispered. He bent at the waist and wrapped his arms beneath her bottom. Jason stood, lifting her off the floor. She gasped. "Tonight, this will be for you."

She didn't understand, but didn't care. He walked toward the bed. The mattress bumped against her legs as he stopped. His hold loosened and she slid down his body, every hard inch of him creating delicious friction with her softer curves. It was a good thing his arms were around her or she might have collapsed on the floor.

"Lean against me. I won't let you fall."

His deep, husky voice made her insides quiver. Fear crept up and wove its way through the intense need the feel of him evoked. What if she was a lost cause? What if even Jason's love making couldn't bring her to that mythical peak of ecstasy?

His hands moved over her back, burning through the thin silk. "It will be good. So very good."

"Pretty sure of yourself, aren't you, Sinclair?" Her voice sounded shaky, even to her own ears. But his words made a fire burn low in her belly. She reached out and caressed his unshaven jaw. The moonlight colored his face in the cold tones of a black and white photograph. But there was nothing cold in the way he was looking at her.

"Jase…"

She swallowed, trying to keep the note of panic from her voice.

"Ssshhh," he whispered as he bent his head to kiss her bare shoulder. "Let me show you, sweetheart. Trust me."

She looked into his beautiful eyes, dark and devoid of color in the silver light and shadows. She saw the longing that sparkled there with the moonlight, a reflection of her own churning desires. Once she would have run the other way, but she had learned one thing from her father's death—life was too short to play it safe.

Sabrina took a tremulous breath. "All right. I trust you."

Jason's hands moved over her, caressing as he probed the edges of the thin, silk teddy. With gentle pressure, he urged her down onto the bed. She gazed up at him as he loomed above her in the shadows. The distance between them felt like a vast chasm. She reached out and grabbed his arm, pulling him down on top of her. They bounced and the bed creaked in protest at the shift in weight.

He chuckled, his breath vibrating against her ear. "Don't be in such a hurry, sweetheart. We have all night and I intend to take my time with you…all of you."

The words sent a shiver down her spine. Her body began to throb in the most sensitive places. Jason nuzzled her neck, nipping and suckling until she squirmed beneath him, wet and ready for their intimate dance. His hand moved over her breast, a whisper of touch through the silky fabric. But it wasn't enough. She cried out for more.

"Oh, Jase...please..." She could barely breathe. The air seemed thin and hot, like something foreign and strange.

"What?" he whispered against her skin. His tongue flicked against the hollow of her throat. "Tell me what you want."

"Touch me."

She heard his shallow breath, felt him tense for a moment. Then he melted over her, pressing her deeper into the mattress as his hands moved in sure, downward strokes from her shoulders to hips. He traced the swell of her breasts, his touch firm but almost reverent in its gentleness. She closed her eyes, fighting to keep from crying his name out loud as she shuddered.

Then he was moving, crawling down her body, his mouth feeding on her through the silk. The hot, wet trail of his kisses turned cool as the damp material lay on her skin. An erotic pulse beat deep inside her, thrumming faster and faster until she gripped his head to stop the torture.

"Jase...I-I don't think...I can't do this. It won't..."

"Yes," he whispered. "You can...you're halfway there already. Just hang on, sweetheart. It's going to be one hell of a ride."

Sabrina couldn't think. She could only feel as he focused his energies on playing her body until she was burning with need. Every muscle, every cell seemed to be taut and ready for his touch, for the moment when he would fill her.

His hands slid over her, firm and possessive. She could sense the passion just below the surface in the way he held himself back. He was probably afraid of scaring her or losing complete control. Like she was losing it now.

He slid the straps of her teddy down over her shoulders, then rose to his knees, straddling hers. "Let me undress you."

Sabrina gasped as he peeled the garment away from her breasts. She started to cover herself and he grabbed her hands. "No…let me see you."

She obeyed. Moonlight washed over them both. She felt exposed in the cold gray light. She shivered at the look in his eyes, the heat of which seemed to spark in the air like a sizzling crescendo of lightning. Her heart thundered beneath her naked breasts.

"You are so very beautiful." Jason's hushed tone made her want to dive beneath the covers and hide. Lust and passion she could handle, but his tenderness might be her undoing.

She laughed nervously. "I'm too small."

"No." He tugged the garment down over hips as she lifted her bottom to help. The clingy material whispered down her legs. Jason lingered a moment, devouring her with his eyes. "You're perfect."

He lowered himself between her thighs until they were pressed together from chest to knee. She raked her fingers down his back, digging in when he captured one breast in his mouth. A moan escaped her lips and her body arched toward him, pressing against his swollen erection.

His hands roamed lower, moving over her belly and down to the curls at the juncture of her thighs. His fingers delved deeper and she gasped, her body jerking in response. He lifted his head.

"Relax, sweetheart," he murmured. "I won't hurt you."

Then there was nothing but the sounds of their breathing and the feel of his hot breath against her skin, his fingers swirling over her sensitive flesh in teasing circles. But never giving enough. She wanted more, so much more.

With a steady thrust, his fingers moved inside her and he suckled her breast like a man dying of hunger…a hunger only she could satisfy.

Sabrina moaned, moving with restless energy. He increased the rhythm. He seemed to know her body better than any instrument; which way to move, how hard to suck her nipple as he patiently worked magic with his hands and fingers, urging her closer and closer toward that peak from which she had never flown.

Then her own instincts took over. She rocked against his hand. Her fingers tunneled deep into his hair as she held him to her, lost in the warmth of his body over hers, the mastery of his hands and mouth on her flesh. She reached higher…higher still. It was there. She could feel the tension vibrating as it reached the pinnacle. *So…close …*

The tempo increased, the angle shifted slightly. Jason lifted his head and whispered her name, but she couldn't respond, couldn't slow down her breathing enough to form the words.

"It's coming," he whispered, urging her on as he let her set the pace. "You're almost there…just a little more."

Then a small tingle…a ripple of pure pleasure that bordered on pain. She grabbed his hand and held it. A shudder of breath and she cried out his name in wonder. Her body rocked with sensation, every cell alive and vibrating as years of abstinence left her shuddering with orgasm after orgasm like a tide pounding the shore.

The intense pulses ebbed and Sabrina sighed, her limbs going limp against the mattress. Jason leaned over and kissed her mouth. She tried to open her eyes but even that motion seemed to require too much energy. Their heavy breathing filled the air but Jason didn't move; he held very still as if waiting for her. After a moment, she was finally able to speak.

"I've never felt anything like that in my life." She looked up at him, her mouth curving into a smile. "How did you…? I mean…I didn't know I could feel like that."

He chuckled and kissed her again, darting his tongue in and out between her swollen lips. "You just needed some coaxing. Someone to care enough to take his time with you. Some women need that more than others."

She felt as if she'd been slapped in the face. It had seemed so special—so wondrous, and yet she had always known Jason would not have led a celibate life as she had. She swallowed back the sudden tears that edged up her throat. This experience had been almost sacred to her, but how did he feel?

"Have you… have you been with a lot of women?"

Jason sighed as he withdrew from her. "No, not that many. But the past doesn't matter now. It's done." It felt as if someone had thrown her into an ice cold shower. She turned her head but he gently guided her face back toward him. "I can't change what I've done. But we can start over. If you want to…?"

Sabrina gazed up at him and tried to read the emotions that went with the words. Was he talking about a fling or forever? Did she dare ask? Though her heart ached to tell him she loved him, she chose to play it safe instead.

"Yes, I'd like that, Jase." She reached up and caressed his rough jaw with her fingertips. "But what about you? Don't you need something, too?" She slid her other hand down his side to his hip before reaching around to stroke his erection. He was so hard, so hot…she longed to pleasure him and ease the tension that seemed to permeate every muscle.

Jason grabbed her wayward fingers. "No, sweetheart. This night was for you—to prove something."

"Jase…" She bit her lip at the needy sound in her voice.

"I don't have any protection with me. I'm not taking any chances with you."

She glanced down. "Maybe I could…help you. If you show me what you like."

He closed his eyes briefly and swallowed hard. "You're a little vulnerable. I won't hurt you for anything—no matter how earth-shattering the final result might be."

Sabrina looked back in to his eyes, trying to gauge the mixture of emotions she saw glimmering in the dark ocean depths. He looked so vulnerable at that moment, an observation which surprised her to no end. Jason was scared to death—of her.

She leaned forward and kissed him, teasing his lips with her tongue. Jason wrapped his arms around her and rolled them both over to lie side by side, her head pillowed against his good shoulder. "Try to get some sleep, sweetheart," he said.

Sabrina fought against the weariness that tugged her down into the deep black abyss. She wanted to be awake, to talk to this amazing man that had brought her such pleasure. But exhaustion hit her so hard, with such intensity that she couldn't resist. The last thing she felt was warmth of the blanket he pulled around their bodies and the gentle pressure of his kiss at her temple.

Chapter Eleven

"Damn, damn, damn!" Jason slammed his fists into the punching bag. Left, right—one, two. The dull thud ricocheted off the gym walls. Blood pounded in his ears as the blows jolted his torn shoulder.

"Are you trying to kill the thing or just cause internal bleeding?"

Jason stopped and turned toward the deep voice. Thomas stood in the doorway, staring at him with a glass of orange juice in one hand.

"What's that supposed to mean?"

Thomas shook his head. "Just that you look like a man on the edge and ready to do some damage. If you're not careful, that wound will start bleeding again." He walked further into the room and offered the glass to Jason. "Here, try this. They say it's good for you. It may brighten your mood a bit."

Jason gave the butler what he hoped was a very sour look before lifting the drink to his lips. The juice was cold and slightly bitter. It made his tongue tingle. He gulped it down, then looked at Thomas with as he wiped his mouth with the back of his hand. "Thanks. I needed that. I didn't get much sleep last night."

"I don't think any of us did—or will until this mess is cleared up." Thomas cleared his throat. "Jason, I realize you and Sabrina are both adults and I did insist you stay with her last night, but I'd rather not hear any details."

Here came the famous tactful yet blunt speech. Jason thrust the glass back at the Englishman. "Before you get your shorts in a knot, let's set the record straight, shall we?" Jason was not in the mood for tact. "I did not have sex with Sabrina. Not that it's any of your business, old boy. If I had, I would not be bragging about it like some locker-room stud."

So he left out a few details. Like their little sexual experimentation and the way she had managed to reach right inside him to twist his heart around. Whatever had gone on between him and Sabrina would stay just between them. Jason forced the moonlit memories from his mind as Thomas spoke.

"Why are you trying to kill the punching bag?"

Jason pushed sweaty hair out of his eyes and sighed. "That photograph last night. I don't mind telling you it's got me spooked."

He walked to the weight bench that sat near a mirrored wall. The gym had everything anyone could need to stay in shape—hand weights, barbells, a rowing machine, treadmill, and two stationary bikes. Jason had spent many hours working out there, trying to burn off the extra energy he built up waiting for the next assignment. He sat and hefted a fifty-pound weight out of its cradle with his good arm.

Jason curled his arm, his biceps bulging beneath the strain of the metal weight. He extended his arm, took a breath and repeated.

He fought off the image of Sabrina the night before, wrapped in moonlight and black silk. Scared and vulnerable. Sexy as hell. He could still hear her breathing as he brought her to her first orgasm.

Form...he had to concentrate on his form not on Sabrina's curves and the mind-blowing experience of loving her. His arm jerked. Pain knifed across his shoulders, radiating down his arm. *Love? No, damn it!* He couldn't—

"You better take it easy until that wound heals," Thomas admonished. Just like a father, one who had known before he did how very much he cared about Sabrina. How had he let her twine so completely around his heart?

He extended the weight and pulled air back into his lungs. Then again up, breathe out, down, breathe in. Two reps later, he was done in. It was not a good day's work for a guy who ordinarily pressed two hundred pounds every morning. But his shoulder burned and his arm ached. Not to mention his concentration was about nil. All he could think of was the smooth silk of

Sabrina's skin and her erotic cries of ecstasy. The way she'd made him laugh afterward…the longing in her eyes as she'd offered to pleasure him in return.

He looked up at Thomas and nodded. The Englishman helped him lift the weight back onto the stand.

"Bloody hell, Jason! What does this all have to do with David?"

"I don't know." He took the towel Thomas offered to wipe his brow. "Sabrina thinks this whole mess is her fault, that she's the common link. She's right about that. The one thing David, the hitman and Sam Mansfield have in common is her. But why?"

"Why not?" Thomas asked. "If the man who's been calling her is deranged, there's no telling what he might do. She could be in grave danger."

Jason shook his head. "But it doesn't feel right. We both know stalkers follow a pattern. They tend to be egomaniacs and lone wolves. I don't think he would hire someone to take care of an obstacle. He would do it himself. And why would he have them try and kill us both? It doesn't make sense. She said he never threatened her."

"Until last night."

Jason scowled. "Yeah, until last night."

Thomas turned and began pacing in front of the mirrors. "Maybe the caller is up to something else and is using the guise of a stalker to throw us off track. Someone had to be inside the house to figure out how to bypass the security gates and obtain entrance. It must be someone we all know. Maybe one of the guards."

"What other rooms were infiltrated?"

"None. That's what worries me most of all. As far as I can tell, Sabrina's room was the sole target. You saw yourself that the image caught on tape couldn't be identified. We can't even be sure if it was a man or woman."

Fear snaked over Jason's skin, squeezing his chest so that it hurt to breathe. Who would want to hurt Sabrina? How was he going to keep her safe when he wasn't sure who to trust?

Thomas continued. "If it wasn't for that, I would say you were the target. It was dark that night you two were shot at. Perhaps the men didn't realize she was in the car. But now…"

"But now that theory doesn't explain the intruder last night or the not-so-subtle threat he left by Sabrina's bed—that torn up photograph."

Jason wrapped the towel around his neck. He stared at his reflection in the mirrored wall. Vivid, terrifying memories flashed across his mind—Sabrina's expression, her terrified screams in the middle of the night and the suffocating fear that had gripped his heart as he raced across the hall to her room.

The fear lingered, threatening to knock his legs from under him every time he thought of what he could have found behind her bedroom door.

"He could have killed her, Tom. She was alone and no one would have been able to get to her in time. If I hadn't moved across the hall…"

The butler placed a hand on his shoulder. "Don't dwell on it, Jason. She wasn't harmed. You mustn't think beyond that right now."

"I have to be thinking, Thomas. All the time. I have to keep one step ahead of this lunatic. I can't let anything get past me. I have to keep her safe. I won't let someone else I care about die."

Thomas sighed. "Let it go, Jason. Stop punishing yourself for Jeanine's death. It's time to move on with your life instead of acting like a guilty man on death row."

"Everyone thought I was guilty. Maybe I am."

"If that was true, you'd have spent a few years in jail at least. But you aren't guilty, Jason." Thomas met Jason's gaze in the mirrored wall. "There's a young lady in this house who has cared about you almost all of her life. Put the ghosts to rest and take hold of her with both hands. Don't live in the shadows forever—they won't keep you warm, Jason. Someday you'll wake up all alone and wonder where the hell your life has gone."

He turned to leave. "You have a phone call to return, by the way. And I have some more tactful queries to make. Bill Wright is waiting for the two of you. See that you don't spend all day staring at yourself in the mirror."

Jason smiled. Butler. Who was he kidding? What a complicated man Thomas St. John had turned out to be: staid domestic, tragic romantic hero, former international spy.

Put the ghosts to rest. Maybe he needed to take those words to heart. But how could he just quit? How was he going to convince Sabrina to forgive him when she found out the truth?

He thought of her again…a goddess in moonlight. His body tightened at the memory, his heart skipping to a faster beat. He sat and stared at his own reflection as perspiration cooled across his skin. He loved her. She had somehow burrowed deeply beneath his skin and branded her image on his heart. *Damn.* This was not part of the plan.

* * *

Sabrina sighed and stretched before opening her eyes. She blinked against the morning sun streaming through her windows and smiled.

Jason.

She turned her head. The pillow beside her still bore the imprint from where he'd slept. She took a deep breath, inhaling the intoxicating scent of his cologne that lingered on her sheets.

He'd done incredible things to her. Amazing, wonderful things that she'd never dreamed were possible. Then he'd spent the night with her cradled to his chest, wrapped securely in his arms while she slept. She wondered if he had gotten any rest.

Sabrina slipped from the bed and headed for the bathroom, humming to herself as she almost danced across the floor. There was nothing wrong with her; in fact everything was quite right. The last six years of disgrace and fear just melted away. She stopped at the sink to stare at her reflection in the mirror. No, she didn't look any different. Not unless she counted the glow in her cheeks and the way her eyes sparkled. But that wasn't just from great foreplay. No, that could be nothing but the radiance of a woman who had fallen in love.

Sabrina hadn't thought she could care about Jason more than she had at eighteen. She now knew that thinking had been flawed. He'd shown her such tenderness, such passion that her heart had filled to bursting. She felt like laughing and crying all at once. Jason, the boy of her dreams, who had once broken her heart, had become a man of honor. Once she'd trusted him, he'd taught her things she'd never known about herself. She never knew how much she could love another human being until now. The thought sent a wave of panic over her. She loved him, trusted him and that meant she'd given him power. He might leave her again. He might decide that he wanted nothing more than a casual tryst. In giving him control over her body, she'd left her heart wide open. Would it be shattered like before? She knew it was a little too late to worry about such things.

After a quick shower she dressed in a pair of blue jeans, a red pullover, warm ankle socks and her favorite white tennis shoes. She grabbed her coat and camera bag out of the closet and headed downstairs. Fresh air and a brisk walk were in order. Time to clear the cobwebs and sort out the sensual memories in the light of day.

Her thoughts swam with images of Jason washed in moonlight, hidden in shadows, leaning over her, caressing her. His strong, hard body pressed to hers. Sabrina closed her eyes, breathing deeply to cleanse the heat from her veins. She glanced down the quiet, empty hall toward the kitchen. Tantalizing aromas drew her from her original course. Sabrina burst through the swinging door, smiling at Martha, who was busy cooking as country tunes blared from a radio nearby.

"Well, good morning to you, dear," Martha said, her round face filled with affection. She reached over and turned down the volume. "I see you're up bright and early for a change. I couldn't sleep with all the fuss going on. Those men never know when to call it a night. If you ask me, that security system is a lot more trouble than it's worth – going off at all hours for no reason."

Some of Sabrina's energy faded as she thought of the events the night before. She wasn't sure how much Martha knew or much she needed to know.

Sabrina hated the thought of scaring the woman, so she said nothing and plopped herself on a high stool at the island where the cook worked.

"I guess I never was much of a morning person, was I?" Sabrina recalled. She glanced around, inhaling the perfume of Martha's kitchen: eggs cooking in creamy butter, bacon frying to crisp perfection, blueberry muffins cooling on the counter, the tantalizing aromas of fresh melon and coffee brewing.

She sighed. "I've missed this so much, Martha. No one cooks like you do."

The woman chuckled, lifting the skillet to spoon fluffy yellow eggs onto a platter. "Well, I don't have anyone to cook for anymore, so this is a treat for me." She glanced up and smiled. "I've missed you so, young lady. Can't say this place has been the same since you left it. Too quiet. These men don't know the first thing about roses and not a one of them listens to country music."

Sabrina slipped a wedge of cantaloupe off the cutting board and sucked on the sweet orange flesh. Heaven. She swallowed and finished the wedge in three bites.

"But don't you cook for Thomas and Jason? Then there's...what's his name? Abe, the gardener? And all those security guards they've got coming and going? I would imagine cooking for that many men would keep you busy."

Martha shook her head, her gaze averted as she lifted the bacon from the frying pan. "None of them want to stick around for a full meal. They take juice and coffee in the morning with a bagel from the bakery, a sandwich for lunch—if anyone is about—and then everyone's off for dinner. That restaurant in Castle's Grove gets more business than I do these days. Before...before your father died, I was thinking of retiring. Maybe moving to Arizona to be with my sister."

The thought of Martha leaving and moving across the country made Sabrina's throat tighten. "Are you sure that's what you want?"

"No. I mean, someday I want to see what all the fuss is about in Phoenix, but this house has been my home for over forty years. I would miss it, but I can't stay where I'm not needed. I hate being useless. It makes me feel old."

"I can understand that." Sabrina studied the problem in her mind as she ate the food Martha set before her. There had to be a solution. Something that would give the older woman a sense of purpose and allow her to stay in her hometown until she felt ready to move on. "Don't worry, Martha. Dad left me everything and as long as I'm living here, you'll at least have me to cook for."

Martha set a cup of coffee by Sabrina's plate. "That's wonderful of you, dear, but I know you have a life of your own in New York now. You're not going to be able to stay here forever."

"Well, I've been considering moving back home again," Sabrina said, somewhat surprising herself. Had that thought been at the back of her mind all along? It sure had appeal. Especially after last night. "I miss it here. I like New York, don't get me wrong, but I think I need a slower pace now."

"I don't suppose Jason has anything to do with that decision?" Martha's eyes twinkled.

Sabrina felt her face heat. She looked down and stabbed at the fluffy yellow eggs. "No, of course not. Why would you think that?"

"Oh, maybe because I know how you used to moon over him when you were a youngster. Plus I've seen the way he looks at you and how you've been looking back since you've been home." She took a long sip of coffee before continuing. "Is there anything you want to talk about, dear?"

Sabrina shrugged, unable to meet Martha's knowing gaze. "I think I messed up. After...after my divorce, I was sure I'd never get involved with a man again. Now..."

"Now?"

"I don't know. I don't think I ever stopped caring for Jason. But there's too much going on...too many problems. This isn't exactly a normal situation we've found ourselves in and I'm not even sure that he feels anything for me."

"I don't know what to tell you," Martha said with a smile. "But when you love someone, you have to take chances. Someone has to be the first to put their heart on the line or chances are you'll both wind up alone. Some women would consider you to a lucky girl. Not too many of us find our first loves again after so many years."

It hit Sabrina like a flash of light, a burst of revelation from above. Her problem hadn't just been Sam's lack of attention or skill, but that her heart had always belonged to Jason. Of course he could touch her and send her reeling—her body always responded to him. Her heart recognized him. It had never erased the image of his countenance. She had always loved him.

She needed to tell him. Now. She had to let him know how much she cared for him, that last night had been more than just a sexual awakening. It had rekindled her heart as well. Maybe he needed to hear the words as much as she did.

"Thank you, Martha," Sabrina whispered, then jumped to her feet. "Do you know where Jason is?"

The older woman smiled, but shook her head. "No, but I'm sure he hasn't left. He works out in the weight room every morning and then takes a sauna. He might still be there." Sabrina leaned over and kissed Martha's round cheek, then turned to bolt out the door.

"Go get him, girl!" Martha called after her, laughing.

* * *

"I know what we agreed on…" Jason stopped and listened. "I don't think it's that simple anymore… no… no…" He ran a hand through his damp hair as dark rage twisted his features. "I've got to bring Wright in on this—I should have done that in the beginning. When this mess is over, I quit. No… no, I will not reconsider. There's not enough money in the world that would make continuing this relationship worthwhile."

More silence as he listened, his jaw clenched. Sabrina backed away from the open door to the weight room. She'd come down the steps with spirits soaring and her heart on her sleeve, only to be caught up short by the sound of Jason's angry voice.

At first, she thought her plan to surprise him with a sexy sauna for two would have to wait until whomever he was arguing with left. When she peeked around the corner and saw he was on the phone, however, cold dread had washed over her. Just like his call at the cabin—angry, secretive. She was sure if she walked in, he would hang up and try to pretend nothing was going on. Sabrina felt as if someone had punched her in the gut. He was still hiding something from her. But what?

Sabrina crept back upstairs to the kitchen and retrieved her camera and jacket, thankful that Martha had left the room for a moment. Heading out the front door, she forced her lungs to draw slow, steady breaths as she fought to hold up the crumbling weight of her bloodied emotions.

"Not enough money in the world…"

Had he been speaking about her? Was she just his assignment, as she'd been when they were children and his mother had forced him to be nice to her? The notion that his love-making had been part of a job made her want to curl up and die.

The crisp spring air stung her cheeks. She looked up, marveling at deep, cerulean blue of the sky. Fluffy white clouds drifted by, skittering over the mountains like children playing leapfrog. Sabrina's coiled feelings unwound inch by inch. First the fear was dispelled in the bright sunshine, followed by doubt and then a great amount of anger. Her heart skipped a tremulous beat.

It was stupid to jump to conclusions without checking her facts. She took a deep breath, thrilling in the way the cool air tingled in her lungs. Then she struck out to photograph the grounds that she had once taken for granted, but would never see the same way again.

Sabrina followed the sprawling outline of trees that surrounded the house. Here and there, she noticed the signs of budding spring blossoms and the stirrings of wild animals that inhabited the five hundred-acre estate. Through the viewfinder she searched the dense growth of trees and the rambling rose garden for images that might capture the spirit of her mountain home.

"Hey, there, beautiful."

She glanced up, her pulse racing. The sight of Jason standing across the garden path, smiling at her, took her breath away. He had a gleam in his eye that brought back vivid memories of the night before. Sabrina felt a wave of heat wash over her face.

"Hi," she whispered, mesmerized by his smile and the way he moved toward her. A wolf stalking the rabbit. Smooth grace, sure stride. Powerful. Beautiful.

He stopped a foot away, gazing down at her with those eyes that made her insides melt. Every nerve in her body seemed to come to life, yearning for his touch, replaying his sensuous caresses from the night before. Sabrina swallowed and looked away so he couldn't see the desire his nearness sparked.

"Are you okay, sweetheart?" The gentle tone of his voice threatened to sneak past the barrier she was fighting to erect.

But she had to remember he was hiding something from her. She couldn't trust Jason, no matter how much she wanted to.

"Yes, I'm fine." She still couldn't meet his gaze. "I guess I'm just feeling…a little shy. You know, after last night."

It was the truth, in part. The memory of what they'd done together in the moonlight—what he'd done *to* her, left her feeling exposed and vulnerable in the light of day.

"Fair enough." There was something in his voice that told her he didn't quite buy it. Sabrina glanced up but he was turning away, moving deeper into the garden toward the back of the house and the wide French doors that led into the kitchen. "But there's nothing to be ashamed of," he added. He opened the doors and waited. His blue eyes darkened as his gaze slipped over her, warming a path along the lines and curves of her trembling body. "You were incredible."

Sabrina's face heated, but she didn't look away. He was so sexy, dressed all in black. The jeans hugged his lean hips and the pullover molded his

169

sculpted chest. His hair laid in sleek, damp waves, glinting blue in the sunlight streaming through the treetops.

Her insides twisted. She loved him so very much. How could she face the pain if last night had been a farce?

"So were you," she whispered.

On impulse she brought up her camera, a shield against his heated gaze. She watched through the lens as he frowned, looking more uncomfortable than in all the years she'd known him.

"What are you doing?" he asked.

The camera clicked once, twice, film advancing through the body with a subtle whisper. "I'm taking your picture."

"Why?"

Sabrina couldn't help but laugh, though there was little humor in the sound. "Because you're standing there looking like a Greek god and I need to use up this roll of film." He didn't look convinced.

"And I just realized I don't have any pictures of you. Nothing recent anyway. I'll need something to remember you by when…" Much to her chagrin, her voice caught on a sudden surge of tears. She swallowed. "When I go back to New York."

He stared at her a moment. Then his long legs were eating up the distance between them until he loomed over her, close enough to smell the light odor of soap and subtle aftershave he used. Jason reached out, cupping her cheek with one hand. He bent his head and leaned toward her, his gaze fixed on hers.

"Bree…you don't have to go back. This is your home and I…I'd like you to stay."

Another lump formed in her throat. "You would?"

"Yes." His warm breath whispered across her lips.

"Why?"

Jason searched her face, his gaze lingering on her mouth before meeting her eyes. "Do you have to ask? After last night?" When she didn't answer, he shook his head in confusion. "After everything we shared, why do you even have to ask?"

"What did we share, Jase? Was it just a mindless moment of lust? Is…is there something more?"

She heard him clear his throat, saw the glimmer of raw fear in his eyes. "You know there is, sweetheart. You've got me so wrapped up inside that I don't know if I'm coming or going."

Her breath caught, lodging in her throat. "Is that good?"

He smiled, his thumb caressing the curve of her mouth. "It's scary as hell. But I think I like it."

Chapter Twelve

The last little coil inside her heart unfurled beneath the vibrant April sun and the love shining in Jason's eyes. He hadn't said the words but she could see the emotion in the warmth of his gaze. Her heart tripped and soared away with the clouds. Jason loved her.

He pressed his mouth to hers, a gentle, reverent touch that knocked the last of the doubt from her mind. With a sigh, she leaned into him, her arms sliding around his strong neck. She felt his deep moan rumble against her chest as his hands blazed a path down her back to her bottom and up again.

After a moment, she felt him pull away. He pressed his forehead to hers as they both breathed in ragged, shallow gasps.

"We need to go into town this morning." Jason swallowed. "Chief Wright wants to take our statements."

She grimaced. How callous had she gotten? She had almost forgotten all about Sam. Poor, stupid Sam.

Was it her fault? She looked up at Jason as panic spread through her. The distress must have shown in her face. He gathered her body close to his, cradling her head against his shoulder.

"I can't do this," she murmured. "What if they want me to identify him or…or something?"

"They've already done that. He had plenty of I.D. on him. The owner of the car was flown in very early this morning. I think they had her do that. I'll go in first and talk to Wright. I want to ask some questions you might not be comfortable hearing…about Mansfield's death. I think you should wait in the coffee shop until I come to get you, okay?"

Sabrina nodded. "I'm in no hurry to talk to the sheriff again."

"We'll be fine, sweetheart." She felt him kiss the top of her head. "Just remember—keep it simple and tell the truth."

"And the truth shall set me free?"

Jason chuckled; the sound vibrated against her ear in a soothing and familiar rhythm. "Something like that." His arms tightened around her. "When this mess is over, we have a lot of talking to do. There are some things I need to tell you."

"Just talking?"

He looked down into her face and gave her a slow, sexy grin that made her heart race. "That's something we can figure out together…after we talk."

* * *

"So our lady has an admirer." Bill Wright's voice dripped with sarcasm. He was not a happy policeman, that much was obvious. Like Sabrina, the man hated to be lied to.

"Yes, you could call it that. Loosely." Jason strove to keep his escalating temper from showing. It wouldn't do any good to lash out at his former classmate. Bill had a right to be angry. "But I think the more fitting term is 'stalker.' He's been calling her for about a year, anonymous and non-threatening, so the cops couldn't do anything."

"Did she ask them to?"

Jason sat up straighter. "What?"

Bill shifted on his chair, turning from the computer monitor to look Jason in the eye. "Did Miss Layne ask the police to do anything about her supposed stalker?"

Jason stared at him a moment. Anger welled up so hot and fierce that he had to fight back the urge to plant his fist in Wright's placid face. Bill thought Sabrina was lying.

"No, she never notified the police about the phone calls."

Bill nodded. "Uh-huh. Seems to be a lot of that going around lately—withholding evidence and all that. No wonder you and the little heiress are so chummy."

Jason's gaze narrowed. "Just what is that supposed to mean?"

"Not a thing, Jason. This is my job, asking questions. A lot of people are getting antsy over all this violence taking place in their hometown, especially so close to carnival time. The damn thing is scheduled to open in two days and we've had more unexplained accidents and violent deaths here in the past month than in the last five years all total!"

Bill sighed, rubbing the back of his neck with one hand. Jason watched as memories of their youths came flooding back. Playing one-on-one, cutting class to go swimming at the lake. They had been almost inseparable, the three of them: Jason, Bill and Cole Ryan. And they hadn't done anything together since graduation...no, since that night almost a year before they had graduated, when a few too many beers and a twisting mountain road had changed their lives forever. He hated to think how much the accident had taken from them all; how many of his relationships had disintegrated due to neglect.

"Listen, Bill, I realize this is going to be a P.R. nightmare for you and the town council, but Sabrina is in danger. The bastard got into her room last night!"

The Chief looked at him and frowned. "What do you want me to do? She's a suspect, Jason, like it or not. It doesn't matter how improbable this all is. Her fingerprints were all over Mansfield's car—"

"I know that!" Jason interrupted. "She told me she searched the car after their argument. That doesn't prove that she killed him—it just proves she's as nosey as ever. You've got to know she doesn't have enough physical strength to plunge a knife that deep."

Bill looked at him. There was something in his old friend's eyes that sent cold dread through his veins.

"No, she doesn't. But you do."

Jason stared. "You've got to be kidding." But the look on the Chief's face told him it was no joke.

Wright cleared his throat. "You have motive, means and opportunity."

"And what is my motive?"

"You have a thing for Sabrina. Mansfield was a rival or maybe you were angry at the way he treated her."

"Now wait just a—"

"*None* of the staff at the Layne estate remember seeing you after nine o'clock last night, when it was first discovered that Miss Layne had left the grounds." He glanced down at Jason's hands, fisted on the arms of his chair. "You have the strength. I know you've been bench-pressing at least two-hundred pounds for the past five years."

"The motive stinks and you know it," Jason said through clenched teeth. He sat forward on the hard metal chair, took a deep breath, counted to ten. "Bill, you know me better than most. I might have snitched a candy bar or two in my day and I even tried pot that once in the back of your daddy's garage. Then there's the time I helped you swipe a six-pack and a bottle of Jack Daniel's from his stash so we could tie one on at the lake. We all know how well that turned out." Wright flushed. "But I could never kill anyone in cold blood!"

"All right, simmer down," the Chief urged in a harsh whisper. Bill leaned forward, his gray eyes intense. "We've got a game going here that neither one of us expected. First you come in here, dropping a bomb in my lap about David and his extracurricular activities. And now the heiress has a stalker? So who the hell is our suspect, Jason? A gun runner or a psychopathic freak?"

"Bill…"

"No!" Wright shoved a finger in Jason's face. "You didn't confide in me from the beginning and it seems we were both barking up the wrong trees.

I've been trying to figure out the money angle, but apparently I was wrong. There are too many other motives to choose from! If I had known everything—"

"I couldn't tell you," Jason interrupted.

Bill shook his head. "Oh, you *could* have. You *chose* not to. But we don't have all day to argue over this."

Wright sat back against his cushioned chair, his chest heaving as he reined in his anger. "I don't have enough manpower to guard her, and you know that."

"I don't expect you to. All I want is a little help investigating."

"Hold it right there! You are a civilian, Jason. This is no longer your affair—it's mine. I want you to start at the top, relay any and all information you have and then stay the hell out of my investigation. Do I make myself clear?"

Jason stared at his friend, eyes narrowed. "I understand that, Bill. And I understand why you're angry. But we need to work together now."

"Can you give me one good reason why I should agree?"

"Yes, I'll give you three: your lack of manpower, the carnival and Sabrina's life. If we work together, I think we can draw the killer out and capture him before he strikes again. Maybe even before opening night."

The Chief frowned, his gaze shrewd and assessing. "I assume you have a plan in mind, Mr. Hot-Shot CIA?"

Jason sighed. "Yes, I do. I think we need to bait a trap. If we can control the situation and be ready when he shows, then there's less of a chance that someone else will get hurt."

"Just who do you plan on using as bait?"

"Sabrina." Fear gripped him by the throat even as he said her name. It wasn't the brightest idea he'd ever come up with, but he couldn't just sit around waiting for the cold-blooded murderer to jump out of the shadows. If he could be prepared and waiting, they all had a better chance of surviving.

"And I'm guessing you're the man that will be guarding our little heiress." Bill stared at him for a moment. Then his somber face suddenly melted into a slow, sly grin. "I'll be damned. You got her in the sack."

Jason sat up straight, anger shooting to the surface like a geyser. "Watch it, Bill, or I'll forget we're friends."

"Whoa! Take it down a notch." The Chief shook his head. "Man, you've got it bad for her. I hope she's worth the trouble. I haven't found a woman yet who is."

"Yeah, she's worth it." Jason relaxed against the seat. "She's…amazing."

"Have you told her everything you told me? About her father?"

"No, not yet. But I will as soon as she's safe."

"Damn, you're going to be the one needing a body guard at that point." Bill chuckled and shook his head. "Okay, Jason, from the top—I need to know what happened from the moment David Layne's car took a header off my cliff."

Jason snorted. "*Your* cliff? You've been at this job too long. You're starting to take things way too personally."

"Maybe so, but this mountain is my domain, even if half of it still belongs to Sabrina's family. So, let's start putting the puzzle together."

* * *

Sabrina stared out the window of the coffee shop, well aware of the eyes that watched her. The morning camaraderie had quieted to a self-conscious murmur when she'd entered the café an hour ago. It hadn't gotten any more comfortable.

She sipped her cold espresso, wondering what Jason and the police chief were discussing for so long. Her, no doubt.

Sabrina glanced around the café, looking for a familiar face. Everyone sat, busy with their own conversations. A few who were glancing her way shifted their attention. All except one. Sabrina straightened her shoulders and smiled, lifting one hand to beckon to the man across the crowded room. He smiled, then rose to his feet and joined her.

"Hey, Miss Layne, nice to see you again," Cole Ryan said.

She grimaced. "Please, call me Sabrina. I could use a friend right about now."

She glanced around the room at the barely concealed curiosity of the coffee shop patrons. Cole followed her gaze and grinned, then leaned over to whisper near her ear.

"Hey, you want to give them something good to gossip about?"

She couldn't help but smile back. "Like what?"

"Well, I could sweep you off your feet and carry you out of here." He glanced around as if searching out the best exit. "Or I could grab you and lay one on you that will make their eyes bug out." He looked at her then, the twinkle in his eyes making her laugh.

"There," he said, a satisfied look on his lean face. "That's much better. Jason always did say you could light up the East Coast with that smile."

Sabrina felt her face grow warm and she laughed self-consciously. "Flattery will get you everywhere, Mr. Ryan. Here, have a seat."

"Not unless you call me Cole."

Sabrina chuckled. "You've got a deal."

He sat in the chair opposite her and took a sip of his drink before setting the cup down. His dark gaze studied her face. "So, are you doing okay? This must have been one rough week."

Sabrina tried to smile but gave up, directing her attention to the espresso sitting in front of her. "It hasn't been one of my better ones. I guess you've heard all the gruesome details of what happened after I left the bar last night."

He nodded. "I think you should know something. I was the one who found your ex-husband's body."

She stared at him. "What?"

"Yeah." He cleared his throat. "I was heading for my car and noticed somebody slumped over the steering wheel of this little red Jag. I stopped to see if I could help."

"They think I had something to do with it."

"I know." Cole placed a hand over hers on the table and squeezed. "That's why I'm here this morning. I spent most of the night with the police, answering questions."

"What did they ask?"

"The usual, I suppose. Did I see anyone or anything unusual? Were there any cars in the lot besides the victim's?"

"Did they ask about the argument?"

Cole nodded. "I just told them he came in, got a little nasty and you told him off. Which he deserved, by the way. Just for the record, I don't believe for a moment that you did that to your ex. Jason doesn't vouch for just anyone." He leaned over the table. "I saw the body, Sabrina. You were angry, but not that angry. Whoever took him out had to have been high on pure rage."

Sabrina shuddered. "I wanted Sam out of my life for good. But every time I think of him…butchered like an animal, I just…" Her voice broke. She looked down, biting her lip blinking to keep the tears at bay. Wouldn't the town gossips love to see her break down and cry in a crowded restaurant?

"Hey, it's okay," Cole said. "Wanting someone gone and wanting them dead are two different things. It's not your fault."

She nodded and tried to smile, taking a deep breath as she straightened her shoulders. "Sorry, I guess this is just all caving in on me at once. I was kind of numb after Dad died, and then…then I started finding out all this stuff about him."

"Hang in there. They don't have any proof. You were just in the wrong place at the wrong time. Not to speak ill of the dead, but if Mansfield was always such a charmer, there's got to be at least half a dozen suspects the cops could choose from."

Sabrina sighed. "But I'm the one seen arguing with him just before he died."

Cole shook his head. "Don't worry, Sabrina. They'll figure out this mess. Jason's not going to let you take the rap." He cleared his throat. "After the accident…after they accused Jase of killing Jeanine…you and your dad were among the few people in this little burgh that stood by him. I don't think you realize how much that meant to all of us—and Jason, in particular."

"I knew he had to be innocent…that there had to be another reason for what happened," Sabrina said. "Jason may have been a little wild at times but he was always a decent guy."

They sat in silence for a moment, the gentle drone of voices filling the air. "Cole, did you see Sam talking to anyone else? Was there anyone around that might have seen something?"

"Like I told Bill, after you left, he ordered a whiskey and slinked back to one of the tables by the wall. I think he used a cell phone. I watched him, waiting for him to go after you so I'd have an excuse to lay him out flat."

She took a deep breath, forcing the worry back. It wouldn't do any good to panic now, even if there weren't any other suspects. She had to keep her cool and not let the police chief shake her up.

"It'll be okay," Cole said. "Just stick with the facts and you should be fine. Wright's okay…a little stiff, but okay."

Sabrina smiled. "You know, you sound a lot like Jason."

"Well, hey, we've been friends forever," he admitted. "I wouldn't be surprised. If he wasn't such a good guy, I might try and convince you to run off to Mexico with me." He winked and Sabrina couldn't help but laugh.

"So, what's the punch-line?"

She looked up to see Jason standing a foot away, his face impassive. But the odd glint in his eyes made Sabrina wonder which one of them he was angry with.

"We were just talking about you," she said.

Jason looked from her to Cole.

"Oh, don't try and protect me, Bree," Cole replied, an impish gleam in his dark eyes. Jason frowned at the other man's use of her nickname. No one but Jason had ever called her that. Sabrina had a feeling Cole knew that fact all too well.

"I was just trying to convince her to run off to Mexico with me." Cole sighed. "But it's no use. You've got her bamboozled into thinking you're some kind of knight in shining armor or something." He shook his head as he rose from the seat. "Guess I'll have to find another pretty lady to sip margaritas with on the beach."

Jason grunted, grimacing as Cole clapped him on his sore shoulder. The bartender leaned in closer. "Listen, buddy, I've got your back. Just yell and I'll be there."

Jason nodded, his gaze shifting back to Sabrina as Cole turned and sauntered out of the café. He lowered himself into the vacant chair, pushing his friend's discarded cup toward the center of the small table.

"So, you want to tell me what that was all about?" His gaze lingered on the table as he drew small circles on the smooth surface with his fingertip.

Sabrina shook her head and drained the cold, bitter dregs of her cup. "I think he was just trying to cheer me up. I remembered him from our trips to the lake. He told me he's the one that found Sam."

Jason's hand drifted across the tabletop to cover hers. She looked up into his face and tried to smile. Tears blurred her vision.

"Never let 'em see you cry," he murmured. "Come on. Let's go."

"I'm scared."

He smiled. "I know. But we'll be fine. I'll take you to Wright's office now. You'd better get this over with."

"Will you stay with me?" She hated to ask; hated sounding and feeling weak.

"You can't get rid of me. Until this mess is cleared up, just think of me as your shadow."

Sabrina smiled. That sounded nice. Shadows stayed very close.

* * *

"I did not kill Sam," she repeated. "I know that it looks incriminating but—"

"Oh, I don't think you used the knife yourself, Miss Layne," Wright told her. "I doubt you have the physical strength for that."

She frowned. "But I thought—"

"However, you do have motive and means to, say, hire someone to take care of things for you."

"What?" She rose from her chair, her body quaking with mixture of fear and anger. This could not be happening. The chief glanced at Jason, who stood behind her. Sabrina frowned.

"What's going on?" She didn't like the way the two men were looking at each other. Sabrina glanced back at Jason. "Let me get this straight. You think I hired *Jason* to kill my ex-husband?"

"No, I doubt you hired him to take care of your ex." He looked at Jason then, his expression calm. "Hiring involves being paid. All you'd have to do is bat those big brown eyes at Sinclair and say please."

Sabrina gasped and turned to face her silent lover. "Jason? How can you just stand there and say nothing while he accuses you...while he accuses *us* of murder?"

"Calm down, Bree," Jason murmured.

She looked at him and shook her head. "You've got to be kidding! How can you let this man say these horrible things?"

Jason glanced over her shoulder at the police chief. Sabrina again had the feeling that he was hiding something from her.

"Are you going to let me in on the joke, or do I just go ahead and get fitted for the orange jumpsuit?" she demanded.

"*Bree.*" The quiet urgency of his voice caught her attention. She looked at him for a long moment, then glanced back at the police chief. The man had a face of granite. She wondered if he ever smiled or laughed.

Turning toward him, Sabrina squared her shoulders. "I've told you everything that's happened—everything I know. I have no idea why those men would want to kill my father or me. I'm not sure why Sam came here, unless he heard about my dad and thought he might be able to sweet-talk himself into a reunion and my father's fortune. I didn't think he was dumb enough to believe I'd fall for him again, but Sam wasn't a rocket scientist and he had an over-inflated ego."

"Not exactly a grieving widow, are you, Miss Layne?" the Chief interrupted.

She felt the anger rise up, but swallowed it back. Taking a deep breath, Sabrina counted to ten before trusting her voice.

"No," she agreed. "I'm not. For one thing, I'm not his widow—we were divorced. But you know that. For another thing, he was a low-life, womanizing, ego-destroying leech. I'm sorry if I don't shed more than a tear or two at his passing. Sam made my life a living hell. I'm sorry *anyone* had to die like that, but I'm not responsible and neither is Jason."

The Chief just stared at her, and she could see the wheels turning behind his eyes. He rose from his desk and walked to the glass office door. Sabrina had wondered why they left it open when Jason had ushered her inside minutes ago. The receptionist must be having a field day eavesdropping on their conversation.

"Mary?" Wright called to the receptionist. "Why don't you go across the street and get us some good coffee and a couple dozen donuts? It's going to be a long afternoon."

Sabrina heard a chair roll over the linoleum floor in the other room. Soft footsteps made their way across the room. Other muted sounds followed, but she kept her gaze focused on the Chief's desk. The outer door clanged open and shut. Mary must have known when she was being dismissed and made no bones about it. Sabrina couldn't help but wonder how much the other woman would tell the café gossips.

Silence fell over the room as she fought to stay on top of the panic threatening to overcome her. This was all too surreal, like a nightmare that had come suddenly true. Chief Wright took a deep breath and exhaled.

"All right, here's what we're dealing with, Miss Layne. You and Jason are our prime suspects in the murder of Sam Mansfield."

Sabrina felt the blood drain from her face. The room started to tilt.

"That's the official story," he added.

"There's an unofficial one, then?"

Wright glanced at Jason and then back at her. "This is just between the three of us at the moment, understand? Take a seat, please. We need to make this fast. I've been looking into your father's wreck." He glanced at Jason and scowled before continuing. "I just didn't buy the idea that it was an accident, but who would want to kill him? As far as I knew, you were the only one who stood to gain anything. Since my manpower is limited and I didn't want anyone local to start rumors, I brought in a private investigator from Philly to check out your father's financial records."

He paused for a beat as she absorbed the information.

"Do you realize there's a discrepancy between the invoices and the actual stock at the warehouse for Mountain Layne Antiques?"

Sabrina just stared at him. "That means...?"

"Someone's been cooking the books," Wright supplied.

She shook her head. "But who? You can't think that I had anything to do with that? I haven't even been here in six years!"

He held up a hand and smiled. It didn't quite reach his eyes. "No, I don't think you did it, Miss Layne. But I did wonder if you had any idea who might have? Who in your father's employ had access to the computers, invoices? Someone no one would suspect? Someone that might be able to go in and out of the warehouse without attracting too much attention?"

"I think I can answer that better than Sabrina might," Jason interjected. "Just about anyone employed with Layne Enterprises could do what you're suggesting if they knew their way around a computer. As to who would be able to move around without gaining undue attention…that might narrow the field bit. There are three or four other employees that have periodic business being at the warehouse."

"Names?"

"Myself, as David's chauffeur and number one flunky. Vivian James, company secretary, Cole Ryan and Greg MacNeil…we use them as drivers to haul imports to and from the airport and docks in Philly."

"Wait," Sabrina said. "Okay, I'm the one who dropped out of business school. What are we talking about? What would anyone gain from falsifying invoices besides screwing up the inventory?"

Jason sat on the chair beside hers. "It's an old trick but one that still works. Say I make up a bogus invoice for a car and pay for it through the company's accounts, but there is no car and I just reroute the money into a dummy corporation or private bank account."

A light bulb went on in her head. "Oh, I get it! Unless someone was to check the invoice against the actual assets, you've gotten away with embezzling."

"Yeah, not a new way to pull a scam but it works," Jason replied, then looked at Wright. "The thing is it can't last forever—you're going to get caught. So how much are we talking about here?"

The Chief shrugged, casting a glance out his office door before continuing. "That's what I'd like to know. This info hasn't been the easiest to obtain, since I've had my man checking on things unofficially because the coroner ruled Layne's death an accident. We have all invoices for the past two years locked up tight and my man is trying to piece the trail together. I didn't want to raise suspicion where there shouldn't be, not with this nightmare of a public relations fiasco looming on the horizon. The Layne name alone would make even a hint of a rumor front page news across the state."

He glanced out the window again. "Listen, Mary will be back soon. Here's the gist of it—I think we have an embezzler on our hands and Jason tells me we have a stalker in the picture. We both agree that part of this equation is dangerous, but which part? We're going to set a trap and we need your cooperation."

Her stomach pitched, a sick sort of feeling settling in her gut. "You want me to be the bait."

"Yes," he said, his stormy gaze holding hers. "You can say no, but Jason and I both agree that someone is very interested in you, Miss Layne. We both feel that the only way to catch the killer is to flush him out before he strikes again. He's not operating with a full deck, I can tell you that much. Your ex-husband was murdered in one of the most brutal ways I've ever seen."

She felt Jason's hand on her shoulder, squeezing as he tried to offer his strength. Sabrina laid her hand on his and nodded. "Okay, just tell me what to do. I don't want anyone else hurt."

The outside door clanged and Chief Wright jumped up. "Play along," he whispered, then drew himself to his full height until he towered above her. "You've got a hell of a lot of nerve, Sinclair." Sabrina jumped at the thundering anger in the Chief's voice. She glanced over her shoulder as Mary entered the station house, balancing a cup-carrier with four tall, Styrofoam cups on top of two large white bakery boxes. The door banged shut. "You don't have a decent alibi, but you expect me to just believe you didn't do it because we've known each other for years?" Wright bellowed.

Jason frowned and leaned forward on his seat. "You're the one with nerve. Takes a hell of a lot of imagination to come up with that kind of scenario. Where did you get your training from anyway? The Police Academy or the Theater of Dramatic Arts?"

"That's enough! I could toss your ass in jail right now and throw away the key just for tampering with evidence and obstruction of justice."

Sabrina stared, mouth gaping. The transformation from civilized conversation to testosterone-fest had been so swift, so convincing that it took her by surprise. She tried to gauge the secretary's reaction.

"You just try it!" Jason shouted as he grabbed her by the arm and pulled her from the chair. "I'll have you brought up on harassment charges so fast, your head will spin!"

"Jase?" Sabrina tried to pull away. He looked at her, the twinkle in his eyes belying his harsh tone of voice.

"Let's get out of here," he said. "We don't have to stand around and take this kind of abuse." He turned back to the Chief. "If you wish to question Miss Layne any further, I suggest you contact her lawyer."

Jason pulled her out the office and toward the front door. As they passed the gaping secretary he smiled.

"Thanks, Mary," he said, lifting two cups from the tray on her desk and handing one to Sabrina. "We'll take ours to go."

Chapter Thirteen

Sabrina followed him outside, letting the door slam shut behind them. She hurried to keep pace with his long stride. "What are we doing?"

Jason slid an arm around her waist as they moved toward the car, holding her close. "We're causing a scene and starting rumors. I've got to get you somewhere safe, sweetheart."

"The mansion?"

Jason shook his head. "No, the cabin."

"But security…"

"Can be bought and paid for, as can a breach in that security. I still don't know how that guy got into your room last night and I'm not taking any chances."

"What is that supposed to mean?"

"It means I'm not one hundred percent sure who to trust now, so I'm taking you away from everyone." They reached the dark Rolls Royce and Jason opened the passenger door. "Get in."

"You're kidding, right?" She was getting more confused by the second. "If we're in real danger—"

He leaned forward and kissed her. His lips claimed hers in a full, wet possession that stopped the flow of conversation as well as her thoughts. When he lifted his head again, Sabrina felt a little weak. She held the doorframe with both hands.

"What was that for?" she whispered.

"Do you trust me, Bree?"

She stared for a moment, fighting the cowardly urge to look away. "I'm trying to."

Jason nodded. "That's fair enough. So let's just get out of here, okay? We can talk more in the car."

She looked at him. "All right, Jase." Then she ducked inside, sliding across the leather seat with Jason following after. A moment later, the big engine roared to life and they pulled out into lunchtime traffic.

"Why the cabin?" she asked as he slowed for the blinking light in the middle of town.

"It's home turf. There's only one way in by car and one way out. It'll be easier to keep an eye on things."

She grinned. "Why do I have the feeling you're just trying to get me alone again?"

"As a matter of fact, the thought did cross my mind."

"The mansion would be easier to defend."

"Yeah, but our man might not try a second time while we're locked behind acres of security alarms, fences and ten-foot stone walls."

She looked at him, eyes wide. "Don't you think it's a bit foolish to try and flush him out when we're alone in a secluded cabin?'

"Don't worry, sweetheart. Just do what I say when the time comes and we'll both be fine."

"I'm assuming you have some sort of plan here?'

"Of course," he said and turned that dazzling smile her way. "Don't I always?"

Sabrina shrugged and looked away, focusing on the winding road. Bare trees and evergreens whipped by, keeping rhythm with flashes of jumbled thoughts. They were in this mess together—first because of Jason's sense of duty and now by a common goal of proving their mutual innocence. But what would happen once they discovered who the killer was? Would Jason want to continue their relationship and take it to a deeper level? Or would she once again be left alone?

"It's been so long, Jase, I don't know."

His hand touched her knee, lingering a moment. When he spoke his low voice sent a shiver up her spine. "Trust me, sweetheart. I promise I won't let you down. Not this time."

* * *

Why did he feel like a used car salesman? *Trust me.* Yeah, great line. Jason cringed, lifting his hand from her knee. He placed it back on the steering wheel.

Just a few more hours and this mess should be over. If he didn't screw up again. If he could keep the smart, sexy woman he loved safe. Then maybe, just maybe they could find a way to make this thing between them work. Provided she forgave him for not telling her the whole truth.

Trust me. Oh, hell, she was going to skewer him alive when she found out. But she had to understand. She had to see the necessity of his secrets and that all of it was for her.

He savored the nearness. Every moment with her was precious. He longed to take her to the cabin, carry her inside and forget all about the chaos around them as he buried himself deep inside her. When they were safe once more, he vowed to do exactly that.

"How long do we stay at the cabin?" Sabrina asked.

Jason shrugged, swallowing as images burned through his mind. Control. He had to remain in control.

"As long as it takes."

He sensed her gaze on him. "So, who's watching us?"

"What do you mean?" he asked, trying to sound casual. Why did he bother? She was too smart for this.

"Jase…"

"Okay, sorry. Thomas, Bill and a couple of our most trusted security guards are going to take shifts."

She sighed. "Good, I'd hate to think of you trying to face down this lunatic on your own." She turned in her seat to face him. "I don't want you getting yourself hurt or killed—do you understand?"

Jason smiled and nodded.

"I can help, you know. I took a few self-defense courses in New York. I'm not a little shrinking violet or debutante, I've fended off my share of men."

His hands tensed on the wheel. The thought of Sabrina with other men made his gut clench with jealousy. Damn. He never thought he could feel this possessive of any woman, let alone the sweet kid he'd watched grow up. But that had changed the moment his lips had first met hers. He'd run away from those feelings over ten years ago, never dreaming they'd haunt him forever.

"Jase?"

He shook his head, willing away the memories. "I'm sorry. What?"

She chuckled. "If I didn't know you better, I'd be offended by your spacing out on me." He glanced at her, the light in her dark eyes letting him know that her humor had returned.

"Busted," he quipped, trying to keep his thoughts from wavering again.

"I don't want you protecting me and getting yourself killed. I can help. I can watch for the bad guy. I'll even parade up and down the driveway if you need me to."

He smiled at the hopeful note in her voice. But she didn't understand. He wasn't sure he did himself. It might be a caveman attitude, but Jason had to keep her from getting hurt, no matter how much his actions might bruise her ego.

"Believe me, sweetheart, if I need your help I will ask. But let's both hope it doesn't get to that point. If your admirer is watching you and everything goes according to plan, the only one that'll be tangling with him is the chief or one of his deputies."

She watched the road for a moment. "So, does he have any suspects?"

He sighed. "No, not really. That's why we're posing as bait."

Together. Alone. In a romantic setting where he had almost given in to the desires of his body and heart. Not a bright move for a guy who was still lying and yet wanted the woman he loved to trust him when all was said and done. But he'd do the right thing. This time. He wouldn't take it too far.

"So," she murmured, moving a little closer. "Any ideas on what we can do while we wait?"

Damn. His groin tightened at the not-so-subtle suggestion in her tone. Her hand slid across the seat and up his thigh. The steering wheel nearly came off in his hands. Jason cleared his throat to disguise the groan that he couldn't control.

"Bree, I think we need to slow things down," he said, even as part of him—a very insist part—screamed at his noble self to shut up. "I need to keep watch and you need to get some rest. This whole ordeal has got us both wired tight."

"Oh."

The small syllable held so much hurt that guilt hit him right between the eyes like a bullet. He felt as if he'd just kicked a puppy.

"I-I didn't mean to presume. I just thought you...you know...wanted..." She waved a hand in the air between them before it fell back into her lap.

The silence was deafening.

"I do," he murmured, fighting to concentrate as he pulled the car off the long driveway to the cabin. "But I think it would be better if we waited until we're safe and we've had a chance to clear the air about some things."

"Sure, yeah. That sounds like a good idea." She had unfastened her seatbelt and jumped out almost before he had the Rolls in park. He watched as she scampered up to the house without looking back, shoulders hunched beneath her coat.

"Smooth, Sinclair," he murmured. "Real smooth."

* * *

He stepped through the shadows toward the doorway, listening. Flames crackled in the hearth below, the light dancing against the ceiling and walls.

Peering down the ladder, he tried to see into the dark corners of the room. What had he heard? Something wasn't right but he couldn't quite place the sound that had nudged his senses awake.

It came again—a soft gasp followed by a quiet, almost inaudible sob. He started forward, ready to leap down the steps and rescue her. But a memory surfaced, stopping him in his tracks. Jason's stomach clenched. He remembered that sound. Sabrina was crying. Desperate, aching sobs that she held in check, burying the noise with sheer force of will.

He sank to the floor and waited as a thousand thoughts flitted through his mind. Should he try to comfort her or leave well enough alone? He knew somehow the truth right now wouldn't ease the pain—it would make it worse. At least for a time.

The sobbing quieted. Jason shifted, easing himself back to his feet.

"It's okay," she called, her soft voice drifting up to him. "You can come down now."

He felt the heat creep up into his face, but it was useless pretending so he made his way down the ladder.

"I'm sorry," he said, watching her head as she gazed toward the fire. Light shimmered across the silky strands of her hair. "I didn't mean to intrude."

He stopped, frustration mounting with every word. Why did everything have to be so hard? He longed to take her in his arms and make love to her, to bury himself in her warm, welcoming body. In her embrace he'd found peace…solace. He knew she could help heal the scars his spirit bore. She could help him live in the light again. In time. If she spoke to him again after discovering the truth.

She swiped a hand across her face before turning to look at him. "I'm glad you woke up. I could use some company."

"You want to talk?" He walked toward the futon and sat down on the opposite end.

She nodded. "It's silly. I feel like I've been crying for a solid week. He's gone. I've accepted that. But I was sitting here and it hit me again like a steamroller. My father's dead. No more chances to make things right with him. Until you told me he loved, I didn't realize I wanted a second chance."

Her pain ripped at him worse than any knife could. He wanted to take her in his arms and absorb it all, keep her from feeling this way. But he knew he couldn't.

She looked at him, tears sparkling in the firelight. "For so many years I wondered what I did wrong, why he didn't love me."

Jason moved then, unable to stand it another moment. He drew her into his arms and lifted her up into his lap. Rocking her like a child, he whispered reassuring words against her ear as he stroked her back.

Sabrina cried even more. Great, gulping sobs shook her body. He held on. They would get through this together. They had to. She was light to his darkness; a beacon of hope, a ray of laughter drawing him out of the shadows that had held him captive for so long. Maybe Thomas was right. Maybe he should leave his world and join Sabrina in hers.

Her torment shook him to the core. The truth clogged in his throat. He needed to tell her everything before he wound up hurting her again. But the words wouldn't come and no matter how hard he tried, he could not think of how to even begin.

"Bree, it's all right," he murmured, pressing kisses against her neck. "I swear to you, it'll be okay. I know you can't see that now, but it will. I'll take care of you, if you'll let me. I love you, no matter what happens you've got to remember that."

She sniffled, her body going stiff before she drew back to look into his eyes. "You do?"

His gaze roamed over her face—flushed and wet with tears, her eyelashes spiky, nose red. He'd never seen a more beautiful sight in his life. His heart squeezed in his chest.

"Yes. I do." His stomach churned at the thought of telling her the rest, the betrayal in her eyes, the harsh reproach.

"I love you, too." Her fingers caressed his jaw, roaming upward to the faint scar at his hairline. "I have for a very long time."

She wiggled in his lap in a way that made him want to groan. He closed his eyes and stroked her back faster. He longed to lift her into a different position, straddling his lap like that night in her bedroom. They would be so good together. In her arms, he could give in to every dark desire and she'd be there welcoming him. But he should wait. He couldn't take her to bed when he hadn't told her everything.

"I don't want you to protect me, even from yourself," she whispered. She gazed at him, eyes dark and hot with longing. "Help me forget the pain. I like the way I feel in your arms. Please, I won't ask you for tomorrow. Just give me tonight. I need all of you."

Jason swallowed even as his body responded. "This isn't a good idea. Not now...not yet."

She covered his mouth with her own, her tongue caressing his lips in urgent, pleading strokes. Jason groaned. He couldn't resist. Didn't want to. In the morning, he would regret giving in to lust, but tonight he didn't care. This is what he wanted...no, what he needed. He needed Sabrina.

No matter what happened when she found out, Jason would keep her by his side. She loved him. Somehow she would forgive him.

She leaned back, breathing hard. "I trust you."

He almost jumped from the futon. She knew there was a secret, but she believed in him. Hadn't she always? In that moment, Jason wondered if he deserved the woman in his arms.

All thoughts vanished as she stood, bathed in firelight, and shed her sweater and jeans. As she stood there in her bra and panties, Jason thought she looked like the creation of some artist. Too beautiful, too perfect to be real.

She held out a hand and he joined her, hoping he wouldn't make a fool of himself and collapse at her feet. Then she reached for the hem of his pullover, tugging it up and off as he lifted his arms above his head. Her hands moved over his chest, her gaze following. Then she closed her eyes and pressed her lips against the flesh near his wound. Fiery darts of pleasure radiated across his skin.

Long tapered fingers roamed downward, over his flat belly to the waist of his jeans. The soft touch made him shudder...he could feel his groin tightening with every caress. A flick of her thumb and she unsnapped his jeans, sliding the zipper down. Colored lights burst beneath his eyelids as her fingers brushed over his taut erection. Oh, yeah. This was not a good idea... but it felt like sheer heaven.

"Careful," he warned, his voice a mere rasp. Sabrina glanced up at him and smiled.

"Don't worry," she whispered. "I wouldn't want to damage the merchandise."

Jason chuckled, then gasped and swayed a little as her fingers slipped inside, brushing over him with soft strokes. Then her warm hand slid out again and she pulled his jeans down to the floor.

"Bree," he murmured, fighting for sanity. "Remember...remember you said that you wanted to wait for sex until you were married?"

He saw her nod as she tugged at his jeans. "Lift your foot out, Jase," she commanded. He obeyed, leaning on her shoulder with one hand.

Jason swallowed, his erection throbbing as she stood and trailed kisses up his stomach to his throat. Her fingers slid along the waistband of his black silk boxers. His nerves coiled like hard steel as he anticipated her touch.

"Maybe...uh, we should wait...you don't want to rush...something as great...uh...important as this."

Sabrina stopped and gazed up at him with a frown. "Are you trying to talk me out of having sex with you?" He nodded and Sabrina laughed. "Tough. It's not going to work. I'm a grown woman. I make my own choices, Jase. This is not ideal, but this is what I want and I'm willing to accept the consequences. Are you?"

He stared at her, his conscience and heart fighting a major three-way battle with the heat in his groin. Was he willing? Her hand slid inside his boxers to stroke him to the point of agony. *Oh, yes. Yes, yes, yes.*

"My pants…" he reached down, hooking his jeans with one finger and fishing out his wallet.

"What are you doing?" Sabrina's frown turned into a satisfied smile when he held up a foil packet. "So, you came prepared?"

Jason grinned. "Just hoping, sweetheart…for future opportunities."

She reached behind her back and unhooked her bra, letting it fall to floor atop the other discarded clothing. "I hope you have more than one because I'd say the future is now."

He pulled her against his body, blood pounding in his veins. She melded to him like hot, tempered steel. They sank down onto the futon. His body pushed her deep into the cushion as he explored her mouth with his tongue and initiated a rhythm his body ached to replicate.

Desire and love mingled, flaming into an emotion he'd never imagined. It threatened to consume him, to take him over the peak and beyond. Crash and burn. But he couldn't stop now if the house itself was on fire. He had to have her like he needed air to breathe. There was no turning back.

"Perfect," she murmured, grinding her hips into his until he hissed in pain. He was going to lose it. Any second now he was going to explode like a teenager. "Jase, let me put it on you."

He obeyed, his mind and body disconnecting as she tugged the boxers off and ripped open the condom. She stroked him through the barrier as she rolled it over him, smoothing it down from tip to hilt. He clenched his jaw and grabbed the upholstery with both hands to keep from jumping off the edge before they even started.

"Bree…" He choked on her name, not caring at the note of begging in his voice.

"Yes, I'm ready Jason." She laid back and pulled him on top of her. "Make love to me…fill me. I've dreamed of this."

He cupped her breast, worshipping the shape of her before leaning forward to take her nipple gently between his teeth. She moaned and he replaced the teasing touch with a gentle, sucking motion. She was so sweet. The taste of her breast on his tongue, the scent of her skin and desire drove him higher and higher until his body ached.

"You make me melt," she whispered. "I love you so much."

His heart soared high above the darkness. She moved again, wrapping her legs around his waist. "Oh, please, Jason...now, I want you now."

"Anything the lady wants," he murmured, then grasped her hips with both hands and sank deep inside her.

She gasped as he threw his head back and groaned. She was so tight, but so ready that she yielded easily to his penetration. It felt like someone had knocked the breath right out of him. He fit her body perfectly. They were designed for each other from the beginning of time.

He let her set the motion—slow and steady, testing the union with experimental strokes. It almost killed him and took more self-control than he thought he possessed. Then something began building like a flash flood on a stormy night, like that night in her room when he'd used his hands and mouth to make her come. She writhed beneath him, hands grasping for him as the tension spread across her beautiful face.

They became as one in body and spirit. He swore he could feel her emotions as heart beat to heart, soul spoke to soul. Then it burst around him—her body convulsed, milking him in smooth, needy strokes. The perpetual darkness surrounding him dissipated...fading into the shadows like a mist.

Her hips began moving faster, harder. She wasn't done...his temptress wanted more. He smiled and let the rhythm drag him under, hoping he could hold out a little longer for her. He thrust deeper with each stroke and watched through glazed eyes as she rode him closer and closer to the edge. Her fingers grasped his wrists. His hands tightened on her hips.

"Oh, yes, Jason."

Harder...faster. Then she gasped, her body stilling for a second in time. He felt the contractions again, drawing him deeper yet. She cried out his name and the throaty plea pushed him over the edge. Wave after wave jolted up and down his spine. He held on to her hips, pulling her so tightly against him that she couldn't move as he came again and again. But he couldn't help it. He was afraid of letting go. Lights flashed behind his eyelids, searing heat seemed to explode from every cell.

"Bree..." he groaned, her name sounding like a plea for mercy. And it was. His heart felt so full of love that it couldn't hold it all. Jason opened his eyes and blinked once, twice before he smiled at her. She was looking up at him, as dazed as he felt, her dark eyes huge and luminous in her beautiful oval face. His chest heaved from exertion.

"I love you," he whispered, and dropped on top of her to press kisses on her throat. "I love you."

Sabrina hugged him closer. "I love you, too, I always will."

* * *

In the soft gray shadows of morning, Jason drew Sabrina close. She nestled against his side, sighing in her sleep. He smiled. Amazing. It was amazing the changes one night and an entire day of lovemaking could bring. He had Sabrina at his side and in his bed. They could weather the storms, no matter what. But he'd be glad when they had blue skies to go by.

She stirred, stretching and yawning as her eyes fluttered open. "Good morning, beautiful," he murmured. Sabrina smiled, a faint blush creeping over her cheeks.

"Good morning," she replied, then lifted her head off the pillow to examine his face. "Are you always so incredibly handsome? Don't you ever have a bad hair day?"

Jason chuckled. "No, never. Not when you're around."

"Well, that's just not fair," she said, reaching up one hand to feel her hair. Her eyes went wide. "Oh, I'll bet I look like a bag lady!"

He grabbed her as she tried to bolt off the bed. In between sessions of lovemaking that first night, they'd made their way to the bed in the loft. Frequent naps, a quick early morning trip to the town pharmacy, occasional forays for food and long, hot showers for two had kept the passion simmering at mind-blowing levels.

"You are beautiful," Jason insisted, tracing an imaginary line between freckles on her arm. "You just look like you've been thoroughly ravished. I think it's all the Pirate's fault."

Sabrina laughed when he winked at her, sharing their own private joke about a discussion regarding sexual fantasies. Many of which he'd gladly offered to help her fulfill.

"You, sir, are a cad!" she teased in her most unconvincing southern drawl. "Now unhand me so that I might use the facilities."

She jumped up, grabbing for a blanket to wrap around her naked body, but not before Jason got a good long look. He sighed, leaning back into the pillows as she fumbled with her covering and tried to back down the ladder.

Sabrina glanced up. "Enjoying yourself?"

He grinned and nodded. She shook her head in mock disgust and managed to make it downstairs.

"Bree?"

"Yes?"

"Don't forget, we're on to Plan B tonight." He waited, imagining her lovely face and the characteristic frown he knew must be creasing her brow.

"Is that tonight?"

"Yes, sweetheart. He didn't show up here, so we have to draw him out. Now stop frowning and hurry up down there. I want some more time to ravish you before we have to leave."

He heard her snort as she moved toward the bathroom. "Are you sure you're up to it, big boy?"

"Come and see for yourself."

She laughed and he heard the bathroom door shut. After a minute, he could hear the shower running. Jason sighed, resigning himself to getting out of bed, and went downstairs without covering up. He found his discarded clothes, slipping his boxers back on before grabbing the cell phone.

"Thomas? We're awake. So is everything still on or did you all manage to sew up this case overnight?"

"Very droll, Jason," Thomas said. "There were a few more calls to her line, but nothing traceable. So, we're sticking with the plan unless something happens in the meantime. You and Sabrina arrive at nine o'clock by the front gate for your grand argument. When she goes back to the car in the back lot, we'll be ready to follow her every move. If that bastard is out there, we'll grab him."

"Everyone needs to be in the right place on time. We don't want a crowd around getting in the way. They're expecting a record attendance but most should be inside the gates by eight o'clock."

"Wonderful." Jason sighed. "All right, we'll go through with it, but I'm still not sure I like the whole set-up. You tell Wright if anything happens to Sabrina, I'll make his life a living hell until one of us dies. Do you understand?"

"Yes, but as dramatic as that may be I'm sure it won't come to that. None of us want to see her hurt. With such a large crowd nearby, it's doubtful he'll try anything right away and yet he'll feel safe enough to make some kind of move."

There was a slight pause.

"I hope you two take good care of one another when this is all over with. Just know I'll back you up when it comes time to tell her the truth."

Jason smiled. "And just why would you do that for me, Tom?"

"Because I see how much she loves you. It won't be easy when she finds out you've been lying to her."

"No, it won't. But she'll understand why I had to do it. She'll forgive me."

As he hung up the phone, Jason wondered why he didn't feel as confident about that as he should.

Chapter Fourteen

Sabrina glanced over her shoulder, a sudden chill making her body quake. Someone watched from the shadows. She could feel a gaze on her like a physical caress.

Sabrina quickened her steps. Gravel crunched beneath the soles of her flat-heeled shoes, echoing across the deserted lot, bouncing off the cars parked in long, narrow rows. Her heart pounded in her chest. Blood roared in her ears.

She fought back the panic, forcing her lungs to take in slow, steady breaths. Slow, deep breath. She could do this if she didn't freak. She would be okay.

The carnival noises drifted toward her on the crisp evening breeze. She kept her gaze riveted on the dancing lights in the distance. The Ferris wheel rose above the fair, revolving against the dark sky.

She could hear laughter and music, snatches of happy sounds that drew her forward, toward people, toward safety. She and Jason had faked an argument and she'd come back to the car alone as planned. But something didn't feel right. If she hadn't listened to Jason, she would be there now, instead of waiting alone in a half-lit cow pasture for some psychopath to jump out of the shadows.

They would have a little talk about this later.

A barker's voice rose on the wind, drifting and twisting over the parked cars. She couldn't make out any words, only the deep, resonant sound of the male voice. Jason. *Oh, please let Jason be nearby*. He'd said they would be watching her. But something must have gone wrong. Unless they were even better at their jobs than she realized.

Why had she parked at the very outskirts of the lot some three-football fields long? *Stupid, stupid.* Just like the girls in the slasher flicks she used to love. Images flashed through her mind—blood, knives, and senseless, hideous violence. How had she ever thought that kind of thing was entertaining? She shuddered.

She stumbled over a rock, catching herself upright and stopping for a second to steady her reeling senses. She gasped. There it was again. The sound of soft-soled shoes treading on the rocky ground. Behind her and coming closer.

Sabrina jerked around, scanning the shadows. The parking lot was an old pasture on the outskirts of town. It had been lit every twenty yards. Small pools of light reached out, then dimmed, leaving a good third of the space in varying degrees of darkness.

The town ought to splurge on better lighting for this major event. She'd bring it up at the next council meeting. Whenever that was. If she was still alive to see it happen. She shook her head even as she turned to flee. *What an ironic time to get civic-minded.*

She held back, moving at a brisk pace but not allowing herself to run. If she ran, he would, too. He'd overtake her. Let the hunter think he was still hidden, unknown. The prey had to use cunning to make it to the other side alive.

Turning her head, she listened for the soft steps behind her. But as the carnival loomed closer, the cacophony of sounds seemed to swallow her predator's pace. She couldn't hold her breath steady. Shallow gulps of cold air filled her lungs, a faint cloud of mist puffing out of her mouth with each exhalation, trailing behind as she moved faster and faster.

She tilted her head again, slowing down just a bit. A loud crunch told her the assailant was gaining. She panicked and ran, instinct taking over.

"Sabrina, wait!"

The familiar voice stopped her. She skidded on the gravel, stopping just beneath a lamppost. Squinting into the darkness, Sabrina gasped for air. Her heart slammed against her ribs while every instinct screamed to run. She stood her ground. If she had to fight, she would. She was so tired of running—from her feelings, her life and now from shadows.

"Don't be frightened."

The sound came closer, an indistinct shape moving forward. She knew the voice, but couldn't think. It wasn't in the right place. He shouldn't be here.

"Darling, are you all right?'

"Who is it?" She hoped the small quaver in her voice wasn't obvious. The shape moved closer to her circle of light, edges sharpening into the form of a man.

"How can you ask that?" the voice replied, the tone petulant. The man stepped into the bright white glare and Sabrina sighed with relief.

"Eric?" She frowned, taking a small step backward. "What are you doing here? How did you find me?'

Eric stopped short, a look of frustration washing over his fine features. "When I didn't hear from you again, I decided to come down and make sure you were safe. You should have called me back, Sabrina. You know how I worry about you."

Something in his tone, the glimmer in his green eyes didn't seem right. A cold chill washed over her. She took another step back.

"That doesn't explain how you found me here at the carnival."

Eric didn't move, but she could feel the tension radiating from him across the small space. He glanced away before answering. "I called your house, and someone there told me where you'd be tonight. It's just pure luck that I found you."

No. Everything in her told Sabrina that he was lying. There were too many coincidences happening and no one at the mansion knew of their plan except Thomas. Sam had just *happened* to find her and now Eric?

He cleared his throat and Sabrina stopped breathing. Her heart seemed to skip a beat. That was it. That's what always seemed familiar about the calls. It wasn't the voice, but the short, muffled pauses in between his ramblings.

When he was nervous, Eric cleared his throat. On the phone, he'd always cover the mouthpiece to muffle the sound. It was Eric. It had to be him.

Sabrina took a small step backward, ready to run for her life. If only she was closer to the carnival. No one would hear her scream at this distance, not with the level of noise surrounding the attractions. Jason should be there. Where was he?

"Sabrina? Why are you afraid of me, darling?" Eric inched forward. "You must know I wouldn't hurt you for anything in the world. You are so precious...so pure and good. My finding you here—it is our destiny."

"I-I don't understand." Her mind raced for an idea even as it screamed at her to run. "What destiny?"

His features softened into a smile, the feral light of desire glittering in his eyes. He moved nearer, his gaze unwavering.

"You and I...we were made for each other. It was ordained from the beginning of time."

"What do you want from me?"

A hurt expression passed over his face. "Sabrina, what could I possibly want *but* you? You are the world to me. I'm sorry I frightened you, but I was trying to get you to lean on me. I thought...I thought if you needed me, then you'd stop looking at me like a piece of furniture."

"I never thought of you as furniture." Panic outweighed any real regret she might have experienced. She could see the hurt in his face, hear it in his voice. But there was something else, as well. Anger. Slight, almost undetectable amid the other emotions.

"No. I might have been a friend or even a mentor in the beginning, but then you never saw me. I might as well have been a table or chair for as much as you paid me any attention!"

"That's why you called?" she asked. "That's what this was all about?"

He stopped, heat washing over his face. "I know—it was juvenile of me, but I didn't know how else to make you see me, how to make you rely on me." He stared at her for a moment before reaching out one hand. "But it didn't work, did it? You still had to do things your own way. Why don't you need me? Why don't you want me as much as I want you?"

She jerked away as his hand touched her arm. The anger surfaced then, blazing, fierce rage that made her gasp. She'd never seen him so intense, so violent. He lunged for her, grasping her wrist with his long, thin fingers.

"You will love me, Sabrina-fair." He pulled her close against his body. "I'll show you how good it can be."

Bile rose in her throat but she swallowed it back. His breath was hot and moist against her skin. She had to play along or she'd be dead. Sabrina steeled her nerves and looked up at him, smiling with as much warmth as she could muster.

"Eric, you have no idea how long I've waited for this. I wish you had shown me this commanding side of yourself."

He frowned, drawing back to study her face. "Don't play games me with me. I'm not stupid."

She shook her head. "Of course you're not—I've always known that. You are very clever. How did you get into my room past all that security?"

Her praise stroked his ego. "I wish I could take the credit, but it wasn't that big a deal. I think there was something wrong with your system because I got right inside without as much as a dog barking."

"You frightened me."

"I am sorry, darling…but I saw you with that man." His face darkened. "I had to let you know how much that displeased me."

She moved closer, repressing a shiver of disgust as she leaned into him. "Forgive me, Eric. If I had known how you felt, I never would have looked at him twice. You have no idea how sexy you are right now."

The heated look in his eyes told her the act was convincing. She lowered her lashes and calculated how far she had to run.

"Take me away from here," she pleaded even as she glanced sideways. "I need to be alone with you—somewhere private. Someplace where I can…touch you."

She could feel his breath on her face, feel his heart pounding beneath her hand. "Oh, yes…yes, of course," he murmured, his voice husky with lust. "I-I have a hotel room. We can go there if you'd like?"

Sabrina almost felt sorry for him, the desperate, needy note in his voice. How could she have known him for so many years and never seen this in him? It didn't matter. All that mattered now was getting away.

"Yes, that would be wonderful. Where's your car?"

He stood up straight, pulling away from her. She could see his hands were shaking. Sabrina wasn't sure if she should be flattered or disgusted.

"It's over there." He waved at a row behind him. Damn. She was hoping he'd be closer to the carnival, not further away.

She smiled up at him. "Good. Let's go."

"Yes, of course. I'll take care of you, my darling. I'll take good care of you."

He squeezed her hand and turned, guiding her out of the light and back the way they'd come. She lagged behind half a step, reviewing all the moves she could remember from her self-defense class. Too bad she hadn't practiced any of them. How could she know what would work and what would just make him angry?

"Sabrina!"

She turned, her heart racing. Jason jogged toward her, dodging between the parked cars. He was the most beautiful sight in the world at that moment. As he passed beneath a light, something glinted in his hand. Eric turned with her, a sharp curse hissing past his lips.

"You lied to me!" he bellowed, his face distorted with anger. "You lying little bitch!"

She tried to wrench free of his grip. "Let go. It's over, Eric, just let me go."

"No!" Eric cried.

Jason skidded to a stop a few feet away, leveling a revolver at the other man. "Let her go, Van Horn. I'll drop you here and now if you don't back off."

Eric went white. He stared at Jason for a split second and dropped Sabrina's hand. "Okay! I didn't hurt her...n-now put the gun away. I'm not going anywhere."

"You're damn right you aren't. You won't be going anywhere but jail." He held the gun steady with one hand while retrieving a cell phone from his jacket pocket. Flicking it open with his thumb, he motioned for Sabrina to hurry toward him.

Eric's jaw went slack. "For making phone calls? For caring about someone? Since when is that a crime?"

"It's called stalking," Jason said. "That and a little case or two of murder. As far as I know, killing someone has always been a big no-no."

"Murder?" Eric's eyes went wide with horror. "I didn't kill anyone! Are you crazy?"

Jason waved a hand at him and spoke into the phone. "Yeah, I've got Sabrina and her admirer. She's fine." He looked at her for confirmation and she nodded. Jason turned his gaze back to the other man. "Okay, I'll wait here for you. We're near..." He glanced at the nearest lamppost. "...row thirty-eight B. Hurry up will you? I've got better things to do than watch this jerk sweat all night. No, I won't do anything foolish."

Sabrina smiled as he flicked the phone closed and slipped it back into his pocket. "Thomas?"

Jason nodded. "Of course. I'm sorry things got screwed up, sweetheart. There was an accident around the front gate—Wright's patrol car and some drunken teenagers in a pickup. They had to take two of them to the hospital and were still clearing the wreckage when I gave up and ran over. I got here as fast as I could."

Sirens wailed in the distance, the sound growing stronger as the police cars drove closer. Red and blue lights flashed, filling in the dark voids left by the sporadic lighting. Sabrina sighed and glanced at Jason's profile as he stared at Eric, who was crying and proclaiming his innocence. It was over. Life could go back to normal.

Would Jason be a part of that life?

* * *

Jason leaned against the wall in the small interrogation room. The claustrophobic feel made it more like a broom closet with a table in the center. A pendulum light hung down from overhead, its bare bulb casting stark, yellowish-white light on the man seated there, the man who had been stalking and terrifying the woman Jason loved. The man that might or might not have hired two dead hitmen to kill David and him.

"I'm only going to ask you this one more time, Van Horn," Wright said. The man had a deadly edge to his voice Jason had never heard before. He shifted, folding his arms across his middle and waited. "Why did you hire Williams and Reilly to kill David Layne?'

"I didn't—"

"Don't give me that crap!" Wright shouted. "What? Did you think you could pull off a crime like that in Hicksville? Did you think it'd be easy to get around a small-town cop?"

"No! I—"

Wright slammed both hands down on the pressed wood table. Jason flinched. Van Horn cowered against the back of his metal chair. He swallowed, his gaze flickering about the dark perimeter of the room. "I only wanted Sabrina's attention. I didn't kill anyone. I didn't hire anyone to kill her father."

Wright snorted, straightening his tall body inch by inch until he towered over the blonde man shaking beneath the glaring light. "Now why should I believe a sniveling little coward like you? You are exactly the type that would hire another man to do his dirty work."

Jason narrowed his eyes and waited. There was something wrong with this whole mess. Something missing. But he couldn't quite put his finger on it.

Van Horn shook his head, glancing at Jason with a strange mixture of anger and fear in his eyes. His mouth twisted into a grimace. "There's no reason you should believe me. But Sabrina can tell you—I'd never hurt her, or anyone for that matter. I love her." His gaze flicked back to where Jason stood in the shadows. "She would have been all mine if he hadn't interfered. He's nothing but a servant with the devil's eyes and a serpent's tongue. He defiled her like a common whore!"

Jason lunged forward but an iron grip wrapped around his forearm, pushing him a step back.

"Don't do it, Jase," Wright whispered near his ear. "He isn't worth it."

"Listen you psycho son of a—"

"Jason, let it go!" Wright said. "Get out. Let me deal with this. I shouldn't have let you in here in the first place."

Jason hesitated, clinching and unclenching his fists as he imagined popping Van Horn right in his thin face. He could almost imagine the sound of his nose snapping. Wright seemed to read his thoughts.

"What would Sabrina say if you followed through, buddy? Think about it."

He did. She would be incredibly ticked if he got himself arrested for bludgeoning her former employer. That alone made him take another step back. They were going to have enough to deal with once she learned the truth. He took breath and let his tight muscles uncoil a notch.

"Fine. I'm out of here. But if you have to set him loose, I want to be notified first. Got it?"

Wright gave him a half-smile and patted his shoulder. "Got it. But believe me, he's not going anywhere for a long time."

Jason directed his gaze at Van Horn. "If you ever come around her again—if you so much as think about her—I'll kill you with my bare hands. Do you understand?"

He heard Wright sigh as his grip loosened.

"He's threatening me!" Van Horn shrieked. "I want to press charges. I want a lawyer!"

"I didn't hear any threats," Wright replied quietly.

"But—"

"Who's going to believe the word of a murderer over that of a federal agent?" the Chief interjected. "And your lawyer is on his way."

"I don't care what you all think," Van Horn insisted, lifting his pointed chin. "I didn't kill anyone or hire professional killers. All I'm guilty of is loving a woman."

Jason sneered in disgust and opened the door, walking out into the brightly-lit police station.

"Rough night?"

He turned at the sound of the deep English voice. "You could say that, Thomas. He's not even close to confessing to murder."

"Well, at least they can hold him for terroristic threatening and attempted assault. The man bloody well confessed his stalking in front of you and several state troopers."

"I know. But that's not nearly enough to put him away for good. I want this bastard behind bars until he's old and gray."

Thomas held a foam cup out to him. "Here, take a swig of this. It's been sitting for a while, so it should be nice and strong."

"What I need is a stiff drink."

"That may be, but you'll be driving later and I don't think that's a good idea."

Jason's glanced around the station house. It was bustling with activity, as the state troopers that had been called in as back up sat around drinking coffee and exchanging war stories.

A tingle spread over Jason's skin. "Where's Sabrina?"

"What do you mean?" Thomas asked with a frown.

"I mean, where is she? Did she go for coffee or something?"

213

"Jason, she said she was going home. I assumed you had discussed it with her. She was tired and since one of the troopers had already taken her statement, I didn't see any need for her to linger until you were finished."

Jason pushed a hand through his hair and sighed. Thomas was right. She didn't have to stay under his watchful eye any longer. The danger was past.

But why were his senses tingling as if someone walked over his grave?

"Jason, what is it?"

He looked up into the Englishman's concerned gaze. Something was wrong. Something didn't fit…

"Stalkers…they rarely work with others. They work alone."

Thomas shrugged. "Yes. That's the common psychological profile. But we both know not all criminals follow patterns."

"Van Horn insists he didn't hire Williams and Reilly. He swears over and over that he didn't kill anyone. He's obsessed with her…but…"

Jason stared at the wall without seeing it. The wheels turned, images and voices taking shape, combining with hours of forensics and psychology classes he'd taken years ago. If Van Horn wasn't the killer…

"Oh, my God," he murmured.

"What?"

"There's someone else. The money…the phony invoices. Thomas, we've been barking up the wrong tree."

The butler's eyes grew wide. "And Sabrina…"

"…is alone!" Jason gasped. He whipped out his cell phone as Thomas rushed by him toward the interrogation room. He dialed the mansion's main line, the one that should have been answered directly at the guard's station. It rang ten times and he cursed, hanging up just as Thomas came back.

"No one's answering at the estate. Something's wrong."

"Van Horn isn't budging in his statement. Either he's the world's best actor or Sabrina could be in real danger."

Fear gripped his heart, squeezing so tightly, he couldn't think for half a second. Then Jason ran out the door, calling back over his shoulder. "Get some of these guys to the mansion!"

Heedless of Thomas's cries to stop, he flew down the steps to his car, flicking open the phone again as he slid behind the wheel. As he started the ignition, Jason pressed a familiar number.

"Hello?"

"No time to explain. We have the wrong man and Sabrina is alone at the mansion. The guards aren't answering."

"Oh, God. Do you think—?"

"There's no time to discuss what I think. You're closer. Get in there and find her. I've got a bad feeling…"

"Jason—"

"No! She could get hurt!" The thought almost choked the air out of him. He swallowed hard. "Please, no more chances. If anything happens to her…"

"I'm already out the door." The line went dead and Jason tossed the phone onto the seat beside him.

She'd be fine. One of them might even beat her to the house. They would find her before…

Again the thick darkness seemed to swirl through him. He fought down the panic. They had to find her before the killer did. There was still so much to tell her, to explain.

Jason sped through the flashing yellow light at the center of town and up the dark mountain road.

* * *

Sabrina pulled into the driveway alone, her mind still reeling from the knowledge that her friend had actually been stalking her for months, playing some sick head game. It was then that she realized Jason had never given her the security codes. She didn't even have a cell phone to call anyone. She hated the idea of driving all the way back to Castle's Grove.

She stopped the car, staring up at the gates. *Wonderful,* she thought. *What now?*

Bright white headlights filled her rearview mirror as another car swung in the drive behind her. She smiled. Could it be Jason? The light filled her vision, making it impossible to discern the silhouetted figure behind the wheel. Sabrina rolled down her window and stuck her head out.

"Hello?" she called. The other driver got out, leaving the door open as he approached. She squinted into the shadows beyond the halo of the high beams.

"Sabrina, dear girl, what on earth are you doing out here this time of night?" She let out a breath, not realizing just how tightly strung her nerves were till now.

"Marcus, you scared me," she admonished, smiling as the lawyer walked toward her. "I just got back from the police station."

His eyebrows arched. "Police? Are you all right?"

"Yes, I'm fine," she said. "A lot has happened since you left, but I'm so tired and I really need to change my clothes. Can you get us inside? Jason never gave me the security codes."

"Ah, yes, of course. I don't know the code myself, but the guards will let us in. Hang on a minute." He turned his back to her and opened the door that revealed the keypad. Then he pressed a button and spoke into the box. "Yes, this is Marcus Talbridge. Miss Layne and I are at the front gate and I'm afraid Sinclair didn't give her the security code. Would you be so kind as to let us pass?"

She frowned, wondering why she hadn't thought of trying the intercom system herself. Maybe because she'd was almost too tired to think at all. A buzzing sound filled the still night air and the gates clinked open. Marcus turned back to her with a smile.

"There we are, young lady. Now if you'll go ahead, I'll just drive in behind you. The other set should open, as well."

"Thank you, Marcus. I probably would have thought of that myself eventually. It's been a very long day."

"I can well imagine." He returned to his car without another word and she put hers back into drive.

A minute later, they rounded the last bend. The mansion loomed in front of her, as dark and somber as a tomb. Marcus's headlights were almost blinding in her mirrors.

Climbing out of the BMW, she wondered if there had been a power failure. They weren't uncommon in this region, but normally occurred in the winter or during storms. That still didn't explain why the generators hadn't kicked in.

She switched off her engine, leaving the keys in the ignition as she climbed out. Marcus pulled up directly behind her. She was still watching the house when he got out, engine still rumbling. His footfalls crunched on the small gravel.

"Did you hear anything about a power failure?" She turned to look at him and froze, blinking several times to clear the absurd image her sleep-deprived brain had conjured out of the headlights. But it wasn't a mirage. Marcus had a gun aimed right at her.

"W-what are you doing? Marcus?"

He gave her a rather grim, regretful smile. "I am sorry, dear girl. But you do have the worst timing. Please, get inside."

He waved the barrel at the house and she felt a moment of panic before taking a deep breath. This was Marcus—someone she'd known since she was a child. He couldn't be serious.

But he seemed very serious as he followed her up the concrete steps to the front door that stood ajar. Her heart began to race. What was going on?

She stepped inside and fumbled along the wall for a light switch. *Click, click.* Nothing but blackness.

"They won't work," he informed her. She jumped as he grabbed hold of her arm. "I don't want to hurt you, child. If you just do what I ask, you can leave. Can you tell me where your father kept the invoices? That idiot Sam

217

couldn't find them. I don't want to hurt you, but if you don't get them for me…"

"…he will."

Sabrina turned toward the quiet, feminine voice behind them. Vivian James stood there, holding a kerosene lantern as she gazed at Sabrina with undisguised hatred in her eyes. The yellow glow from the lamp cast their shadows in long, grotesque silhouettes over the entry walls.

"I don't understand," Sabrina said, looking from the secretary to the lawyer. "What's going on, Marcus? What is she talking about?"

"What I'm talking about," Vivian sneered. "Is the fact that you have caused us nothing but trouble, Miss Layne. Tell us where your father kept the invoices and maybe, just maybe we'll leave the country without killing you."

Sabrina gasped. "It was you all along?" She looked at Marcus, shaking her head as the information sunk in. "You and her? You killed my father, didn't you? And Sam?"

The lawyer's lips curled into an evil grin. "Well, I can't say that either of them didn't get what they deserved. Your father had it coming to him for years. And that ex-husband of yours was such a greedy imbecile. Didn't your poor mother's death teach you to choose your men with care? As for that bumbling idiot Reilly—well, I told him not to put you in danger, but the bastard didn't listen. He became a liability."

"Oh," Sabrina murmured. "I…I almost forgot about him. You killed him, too?" Marcus's brow lifted in mock surprise. She fought off the wave of nausea. "Why? How could you do something like that?"

"It wasn't all that difficult…" Marcus began.

"Come off it, bitch!" Vivian hissed, stepping forward to grab Sabrina's other arm. Her claw-like nails dug into her flesh. Sabrina winced as anger roared to life. She was very tired of being called a bitch.

"We did it for the money of course! Lots and lots of money!" The woman glanced at Marcus, disgust barely concealed on her face. "I told him I'd run away with him if he helped me siphon a little money out the accounts. Just a million or two—heaven knows your dear old dad had enough of it to go around. But, of course, he had to screw it up. Your father got wise and made some noise about hiring a new attorney. We both knew what would happen then, didn't we, darling?"

Sabrina almost groaned. It was so simple. They'd been chasing shadows the entire time when the answer had been right under their noses. Instead of looking for a crazy stalker, they should have been following the money trail.

"A change in command would mean an audit of the books," she murmured, stopping when she saw Marcus staring.

"You are so much like your mother," he said. "So beautiful and intelligent. Your father never deserved either of you. Neither does Sinclair. He's the real killer, you know. My dear niece, Jeanine would be alive today if it weren't for him."

Vivian snorted. "You do have lousy taste in men, don't you, princess? There's Sinclair, the failure and your ex-husband, the imbecile. I think he'd have sold his mother's soul for a few hundred dollars."

"How did you know Sam?"

"I thank lover boy here for that." Vivian glanced at Marcus, her mouth twisting in disgust. "He hired that idiot to get close to you and help us get into the house past the security system. I told him I could handle it, but you know men—if a certain part of the anatomy isn't involved they don't listen.

"All I had to do was pretend to pass out after the reception. A day or two of the royal treatment and full access to your humble abode—just like that. It was easy to charm one of guards into showing me the big, complicated computer system. I slipped in during a bathroom break and infected it with a small virus—nothing too invasive. But it took one group of sensors down for a day or two with no one the wiser."

She looked Sabrina over, grudging admiration flitting through her eyes. "You wouldn't let that loser ex of yours close enough to do us any good. Another waste of money."

Marcus turned. "But I got most of it back, my love, after he tried to blackmail me."

The look in his eyes made Sabrina shiver. She had to think fast. She and Jason had a lot of catching up to do. They had a future to figure out. She wasn't going to let it end like this.

"Listen," she began, looking from one to the other, but finding no pity in the other woman's face. "All you have to do is tie me up or something. You did me a favor, you know, getting rid of Sam and my father. Dad never cared about me no matter what I did. Now the money and the company are all mine. I don't care how much you took. Like you said, there's plenty and then some. If you both leave and get out of the country, no one will even be looking for you for at least twenty-four hours. They have my editor in custody and by the time they figure out he's innocent—"

"Shut up!" Vivian yelled, squeezing Sabrina's arm. "Marcus might buy the song and dance but I am not that stupid."

"Darling, perhaps—" Marcus began.

"Oh, don't be a fool!" the secretary shouted. "The little bitch will run for the cops or her boyfriend as soon as we're out the door. Now find something to tie her up with while we keep searching. If they can't find the invoices, they can't prove anything."

Vivian pulled a scarf from around her neck and threw it at the lawyer. "Here, use this. I can buy a dozen more once we get to the islands."

He glanced at Sabrina, something akin to sympathy in his eyes. "I am sorry, young lady." He turned her around and wrapped the material around her wrists. "I had hoped if you came home, I could convince you to keep me on for a few months—at least long enough for me to hide the losses better."

After her wrists were bound, Marcus led her down the dark hall, following the glow of Vivian's lantern.

"Why didn't you leave?" Sabrina asked, trying to stretch the scarf. "I mean, the money's yours. You could have been long gone by now."

Vivian snorted. "Oh, sure. And have police and FBI dogging our trail forever? No way! If they don't have any evidence, then they can't get a conviction. They'll give up sooner."

"Maybe you should have just cut your losses instead of killing my father!" Sabrina shouted, angry that this evil woman had taken so much from her, all for the sake of the almighty dollar.

Marcus pushed her into her father's study after his accomplice. "No one would have been the wiser if the attorney here had hired someone who knew their business instead of some bargain-basement hitmen!" Vivian's gaze narrowed. "But I thought we did you a favor, princess? Ah, the composure is slipping now, isn't it?" The blonde smiled. "Tell you what. Help us find the invoices and we might let you live to see daylight."

Vivian walked across the room, sweeping the lamp up and down, casting its light across the bookshelves and furniture. Marcus joined the search, rifling through desk drawers as they systematically tore the room apart.

Sabrina backed toward the door, still working at the scarf. "If you wanted it to look like an accident, then why did you make noise at the reception about it being suspicious?"

Vivian shrugged even as she began picking up books and shaking them, then throwing them on the floor. "By then Jason knew the car had been tampered with. I was just trying to divert attention. Like you said, why would I say anything if I were guilty?"

Sabrina watched as books and papers were dumped. They weren't going to find what they wanted. She knew Chief Wright's investigator had taken everything as evidence. Soon they'd get tired of looking.

"Did you try the warehouse?" Sabrina asked, twisting her wrists as panic tried to take over. It budged a little, encouraging her to keep trying.

"Of course we tried the warehouse!" Vivian snapped without looking at her. "The file cabinet and the safe were empty, almost as if…" She stopped, her gaze darting around the walls. "That's it! A safe! Marcus, darling, where did David keep his personal safe?"

The lawyer frowned, looking around the room like a sleepwalker. "I'm not sure." He glanced at Sabrina. "Where is your father's safe?"

Sabrina swallowed hard. This was it, her one chance. She couldn't wait around for Jason to arrive on his white horse.

"It's hidden behind one of the paintings," she lied. "I don't know which one, though."

They both turned away to examine each painting, feeling around the edges for access to the wall behind. Sabrina inched backward, the faint light from the lamp guiding her steps to the door and freedom. She stepped out of her shoes, hoping to move faster and more silently on bare feet.

The hall loomed behind her, dark and yet somehow comforting. Back and to the right…she should be able to get out the door and down the driveway before they even noticed. Then she could hide in the thick woods surrounding the house. And pray.

Sabrina gained the hall just as Vivian lost her patience. "It isn't here! Where the hell is the damn safe?"

Sabrina turned and ran, her arms trapped behind her. Stumbling through the dark she cursed as she heard Vivian's shout. "She's getting away! After her, you idiot! I told you we should have killed her."

Heavy footsteps came up from behind as she reached the open front door. A hand grabbed her arm and Sabrina screamed. Then she was pulled outside. She looked up and froze as the clouds drifted away from the moon. The light shone down on a familiar face. Sabrina swayed on her feet.

It…it's not possible, she thought, stunned. *It can't be him…it can't…!*

"Get down!" the man shouted, pushing her to the hard concrete stoop as he spun around toward the doorway.

It's not possible!

She had no way to brace her fall. As if in slow motion, the world tumbled beneath her and something slammed into the side of her head just as a loud pop rang out nearby. She felt the pain through the numb fog that surrounded her mind. The shadows went in and out of focus as she lifted her head just in time to see Marcus Talbridge's face, ashen and pale, his eyes wide with terror.

"David?" he gasped.

Daddy? Sabrina thought, and then she fainted.

Chapter Fifteen

Sabrina opened her eyes, blinking against the glare of the lamp by her bed. Had it been a dream? She glanced around, a sharp pain lancing through her skull as she tried to turn her head.

"Hold still, honey. The doctor said you have a mild concussion but you should be fine in no time."

She looked toward the voice, steeling herself for what she would see. Her heart lurched, tears burned behind her eyes.

"Daddy?"

He leaned closer, nodding his head. She noticed tears shimmering in his blue eyes. "Yes, honey, it's me. Everything is going to be all right now, I promise."

"Wait, I...I don't understand." She scooted back on her pillows. A jagged pain slashed through her head. She dropped back against the headboard, squeezing her eyes shut. "What's going on? Why aren't you dead?"

David chuckled as he rubbed the back of his neck with one hand. "I'm sorry, it's just that you're about the fifth person tonight to ask me that. I'm beginning to wonder if everyone wishes I was." He looked at her, the glimmer of pain in his eyes belying the teasing note in his voice.

"I never meant to hurt you." She knew he wasn't just talking about the past week when she had thought him dead. "I've never been very smart about how I lived my life, never understood how to deal with things or people. Especially people."

He sighed, reaching for her hand. When she didn't pull away, he seemed to gain courage. *Funny*, she thought. *Millionaire, international businessman—made nervous by his own daughter.*

"I'm tired of the games, honey. There are some things you need to know about me, about my life." He looked down at their joined hands and smiled. "When I was a little younger than you are now, I went to Vienna on a business trip. I witnessed a man being forced into a car, and I tried to help. I failed and wound up in the hospital.

"Months later, I was contacted by someone in the CIA. I found out then that the man who I had tried to rescue was a former Soviet officer that had defected some years before. The kidnappers were KGB agents."

She shook her head, wondering why her father was making up this made-for-television plot. "I don't understand...what does...?"

He squeezed her hands. "Wait, let me finish. I should have told you this story years ago." David cleared his throat. "The short of it is, I was recruited to work for the CIA because of my position, especially in the international community. They do that sometimes when they find civilians that are exemplary in their fields of expertise." He laughed, the sound lacking any real humor. "I was good with women and I could get into the homes of the filthy rich all over the world. Those were my main qualifications. I accepted because it was exciting. I felt like my life finally had a real purpose, some meaning."

She stared at him, her head beginning to spin. "You're telling me that...that you're a spy?"

He gave her a crooked smile. "Yeah, a spy. Didn't know your old man had it in him, did you?"

"Did mom know about this?" This couldn't be real. It was time to wake up, to get on with her morning routine and out of this nightmare.

"Yes, she knew. I told her before we got married. She lived with it because I loved it all, but there were many times when she begged me to quit." His face twisted into a mask of sheer pain.

"I made a mistake and got caught...and they hired someone to kill her. To punish me." He looked up at her then, his eyes brimming with tears. "I am so sorry, Sabrina. It was my fault that you lost her. I hope someday you can forgive me that."

It slammed into her then with the intensity of a speeding locomotive. It was true. It was all so absurd and surreal…but the pain in his eyes, in his voice was all too real.

She jerked her hands away and bolted off the bed, heedless of the pain and dizziness that had her rocking back on her heels.

"That's why…that's why you never let me close? Because you were playing James Bond? Because you were afraid someone would kill me like they did Mom?"

"Yes. I was afraid I'd screw up again. I was afraid you'd be hurt…I-I couldn't stand to lose you, too."

She held her throbbing head with both hands, squeezing her eyes shut to block out the sight of him for a moment. "Why did you let them tell me you were dead?"

"Jason called you right after accident. I'd had a business associate in the car with me, but no one realized it at the time. I was thrown clear but he…he wasn't so lucky. I was unconscious for a while and once I made it back up the mountain, everyone had been told I was dead. I made Jason help me. I thought if I could lay low, let them think they'd succeeded, it might be easier to uncover the killer's identity. We didn't count on them coming after you and Jason. I thought you'd be safe."

She stared at him, fighting to breathe normally as panic seized her chest in a vice grip. He had known. Jason had known her father was alive.

"Oh, God. That's what he's been keeping from me." She felt the edge of hysteria brush by her, but she held on for a moment, waiting. Harsh, bitter anger quickly took its place. "He told me you loved me. He stood there and watched my grief tear me inside out, and he did nothing. He didn't tell me the truth."

"He couldn't, honey. He promised me he wouldn't—he had his own job to do."

She stared at him. "He…he's a spy, too? Oh, isn't that cozy? And what about Thomas? And Martha? Does she bake little coded messages into her muffins?"

David shook his head and glanced around the room uneasily. "Thomas was an agent, but he resigned several years ago. He just decided to stay on here, but you'll have to ask him about that yourself. Martha…none of the others are involved and they don't know. This isn't a house of spies, Sabrina. And in another week, it will be all over. I'm resigning."

"Marcus said you were going to fire him."

He shook his head. "He's been with me for years but I was worried about his health. He'd been acting peculiar. His own father had a mental breakdown when Marcus was quite young. I was afraid the stress of working might be driving him to the brink so I *suggested* he take early retirement. I still can't believe he was stealing from me…that he hated me so much."

Sabrina wrapped her arms around her churning stomach. "Did you kill him?"

David shook his head. "No, just nicked his shoulder. I think the shock of seeing me alive did more damage than anything. He's at the hospital and Vivian is in jail."

"Is Martha okay? The guards?"

"Yes, they were all tied up. Beyond some bad headaches, they'll be fine."

He glanced around the room, his gaze resting above her nightstand on the photo of her mother. "These last few years I watched you from a distance, seeing you grown up and standing on your own two feet. I realize now what an idiot I've been. I could have had so many years with you and your mother if I had just been satisfied with myself. But I insisted on trying to be some kind of hero. Please, do you think you can give your old man another chance? Even if I don't deserve one?"

She blinked back the tears, but they slipped down her cheeks anyway. There were too many to contain. Had there been too much hurt to forgive? Sabrina looked at her father, saw the pain in his face, the desolation in his eyes.

"I'm not sure, Dad. I want to forgive you, but...I need some time. I don't know if I trust you."

He nodded and cleared his throat. "Fair enough."

A knock on the door brought him to his feet. "Come in."

Jason stuck his head in the door, his wary gaze darting between them. "Wright needs to take your full statement now, David." He looked at Sabrina. "Bree? Are you okay?"

She shrugged and looked away, a traitorous part of her wanting to run into his arms even after the way he had deceived her. "I-I don't think I want to talk to you right now. I don't think I want to talk to you ever again. Please just leave."

* * *

Jason shrank back. She was dismissing him. He had lied to her and she was telling him to leave her alone. But he wasn't going to let her get away that easy. Not this time. She loved him and he needed her more than air. They had to get past this.

"Bree..."

She held up a hand, her eyes flashing fire across the room. "Don't call me that. Not now."

David tried to intervene. "Honey, Jason was only—"

"Lying to me!" She glared at both of them and Jason winced. It was a wonder the look she aimed at him didn't set the room ablaze. "I told you everything—I bared my soul to you." Sabrina looked away as her cheeks turned red. "You lied to me. I trusted you, Jason. I trusted you with my heart and you let me suffer worse than I ever have in my life. You could have helped me...you could have told me the truth and trusted me to be careful."

Jason shook his head. "You're not being fair. You knew there was something I wasn't telling you. You told me you trusted me."

"I thought it was something about yourself! I didn't know what it was but I never even imagined…! I felt like I was dying inside—you *knew* that! You saw it all but instead of being honest, you told me half-truths that made things even worse." She took a deep breath. "Just leave me alone. I need you to just leave me the hell alone!"

After everything that happened between them, she still couldn't forgive him? Trust him? Jason felt his blood begin to simmer with rage.

"Fine. Have it your way, Sabrina. I've had enough of this dysfunctional family to last me a lifetime."

He stormed out the door, ignoring David's pleas. Rage colored the world red as he made his way down the hall, the stairs and out the front door. When the heiress decided to come down off her high horse, then maybe they'd have a chance. Until then, she could just stay in her lonely little castle. He'd had enough.

Within an hour, he'd thrown most of his belongings into a couple of suitcases, loaded them in the Rolls and roared down the driveway. He was better off without Sabrina and her problems and her father's money.

So why the hell did it feel like he'd just been gutted?

* * *

Sabrina stared at the walls of her tiny New York apartment. She'd come back to wrap up her affairs and gather her things. The place looked so bleak in the light of day.

Her father had been true to his word. They'd made progress in the last three months, doing things together that she'd never dreamed he would enjoy. It seemed that David Layne's close brush with death had given him a new perspective.

She had decided to move back to Castle's Grove for good, convinced now that her father was serious in wanting to be a family. He had already gained a large portion of her trust.

Sabrina paused for a moment as she packed the last of her sparse treasures. Her fingers wrapped around a small glass statue Jason had given her for her sixteenth birthday, the figurine of a horse. Thomas' words to her before she'd left echoed in her mind. He had been part of the deception all along.

"Why can you forgive my deceit but not Jason's?" he had asked the day before she had returned to New York.

Sabrina frowned. "Because I love him. He knew what I was going through. I let him close...he knew it was wrong."

"But you love me, too."

"That's different!"

His eyebrow rose. "How so? And don't tell me it's because you think of me as a father figure and him as a lover. You let Jason close because you love him—we both know you have for a very long time. Trust is trust and love isn't easy to find in this world, young lady. We all make mistakes. Maybe you need to consider whether or not Jason's mistake is worth throwing away an entire relationship, an entire future together."

Sabrina had stared at him, not knowing what to say, and somewhat angry that Thomas had seen things so much more clearly than she had.

She lifted the glass mare to her face, pressing the cool surface to her cheek. He'd given it to her during her horse phase. Jason always seemed to know what she liked, what she needed. Those hours in bed together had shown what a giving, thoughtful man he'd become. He seemed to know just where to touch her and when to take things to a more intense level.

But it was more than just being the perfect lover. He had made her laugh, had listened to her as if he cared. He had been the one through it all who had seemed to understand.

But he had lied to her. He had looked her right in the eye and told her...told her what? That her father's car had gone off a cliff; that he had always loved her and was proud of her. Not lies as much as leaving out a very important truth—that her father was still alive. But he had done it to protect David.

Glancing around the sad apartment, Sabrina realized it wasn't the place itself that seemed so lonely. The ghostly outlines of framed pictures adorned the bare walls, a chilling reminder of how fleeting things really were. The room was cold, empty…like a photograph of a playground devoid of smiling, happy children. She would never take a photo like that, yet she was living in it.

Yes, something was missing—the man she'd thrown out of her life three months earlier. The one who had always been her best friend. He had protected her ever since that horrible day her mother had died. All she was left with was her pride. It was a very poor substitute for the strong, warm arms of the man she loved.

Oh, damn. Tears filled her eyes. She was going to cry again. What had she done? Would Jason forgive her?

*　*　*

"Honey, I don't know where he's gone," David insisted. "After he packed his things and left, I received a letter of resignation in the mail. You can't blame him."

He glanced up at her from his paperwork. There'd been a lot of investigating involved to find out how much Marcus and Vivian had stolen, but things were getting pieced together. David had impressed his daughter by suggesting the significant amount they had recovered be donated to build a community center in town.

"But can't you ask his father? His parents must know where he's gone." She stopped talking, her throat clogged with unshed tears. "I love him, Dad. I know he loves me. He can't just disappear forever without a word. We have to resolve this."

David shook his head, glancing back as he signed his name again. "I talked with the Sinclairs while you were in New York, but they haven't heard from Jason in a couple of weeks."

He looked up and smiled. "Honey, why don't you pack some things, take your camera and go up to the cabin for a week or so? The change in scenery will do you good and I'd love to have some good shots of the place now that the trees have all blossomed. I'm thinking of putting it on the market."

"What?" she squeaked. "You're selling the cabin?"

David shrugged. "I'm just thinking about it. I haven't made up my mind. I stayed there for a day or two after the accident and realized I don't use it enough to warrant keeping it. Why?"

Sabrina fought back the wave of pain and regret. "It's just that I love that place. I'd hate to see it leave the family."

"Now don't worry. If it bothers you that much, I'll reconsider selling. Don't you worry about Jason, either. Once he's done nursing his pride, he'll be back, you mark my words."

"Thank you, Dad," she said, then leaned over to kiss him on the cheek. "I hope you're right."

It felt good to be able to give in to such familiar gestures and to share her life with her father. David blushed a little. "Go on, get out there and bring back some good shots."

"Yes, sir!"

* * *

The mountain air smelled clean and fresh, like the calm before a storm. Sabrina gazed up at the cabin nestled among the trees. It seemed dark and desolate with thick, black clouds blanketing the sky. The weather cast the perfect reflection of her own mood.

She sighed, opening the trunk to retrieve her bags and camera equipment. Slamming the lid shut, Sabrina turned and walked up to the house, taking the key out of her pocket. She couldn't help but smile at the memories that surrounded her as she opened the door. Tears followed close behind. She blinked them back. Crying would do no good. She'd screwed up, but as soon as she figured out where Jason was, Sabrina was going to find him and beg his forgiveness.

She struggled with the door and the load slung over her shoulders and back, and didn't notice anything different at first. Once inside, she dropped her bags and closed the door. Sounds and smells assaulted her senses all at once. Music played in the background, low and with a familiar country beat. The wonderful aromas of Italian spices, tomato sauce, and garlic filled the air.

"Martha? Did Dad put you up to this?" She walked toward the kitchen. The bathroom door jerked open and she shrieked, jumping back as a pair of startled blue eyes met her gaze. "Jason?" Her heart hammered against her ribs.

He blushed, glancing around as if wondering where to hide. "Uh, yeah." He made a face of self-disgust. "Your Dad said it would be a couple more hours. I was hoping to have everything ready before you…"

She launched herself at him, filled with relief as his arms came around her and held on tight. "I'm sorry! Oh, Jason, please forgive me for being such an idiot! I love you—I've always loved you! I know you did what you thought was best and I had no right to get so angry with you."

Sabrina froze as the realization sunk in that while he was holding her, he hadn't tried to say anything. Maybe he hadn't forgiven her. Maybe he couldn't.

"Jase?" she whispered, scared to back away and look into his eyes. She was so afraid of what she'd see there. The stormy sky rumbled in the distance. "Please…please give me another chance. I'll do anything you want, just please don't leave me again."

She felt him sigh. His arms tightened about her. He turned his head, his lips brushed against her neck.

"You spoiled everything."

Sabrina felt the blood drain from her face as she pulled away. "What?"

He laughed and shook his head. "I had this huge 'forgive me' speech all worked out. I even made dinner and everything from scratch. Then you come barging in here, throwing yourself at me. How's a guy supposed to grovel if the lady won't let him?"

She sighed, overwhelmed with relief. "Oh, Jase, don't ever scare me like that again."

He chuckled and drew her into his arms. "I promise, for as long as I live, I will never scare you. At least not regarding how I feel." He gazed down at her, his blue eyes darkening with desire, brimming with love. "I love and adore you, Sabrina. I don't want to live another day without you." Jason swallowed. "I've quit the CIA. I've put all of that life behind me and now I want to build a new one here with you…if you'll have me. Will you please marry me?"

For once, she couldn't speak; the words were stuck in her throat along with a million emotions, all of them powerful and good. Sabrina nodded and pressed herself to him, burying her face against his throat. Thunder rolled over the cabin, shaking the walls as lightning blazed a trail through the dark clouds.

Jason sighed. "I'll make you happy, sweetheart. I promise I'll do everything and anything I can to make you the happiest woman on the earth."

She shook her head and looked up at him. "You already have, Jase. But we'll make each other happy. This is a two-way street. We both deserve that."

He looked down at her and smiled. Then his mouth was on hers, soft and gentle at first, but soon devouring. Jason moved against her and she felt his desire. Hands explored as the kiss deepened. Sabrina's heart raced and she couldn't seem to get enough air.

"Jase," she said, gasping as she pulled away. He trailed kisses down her neck, his fingers fumbling at buttons of her blouse. She slid her hands beneath the hem of his T-shirt. "Please…make love to me."

He chuckled against her skin. "I've created a monster." She smiled as he lifted her feet off the floor, her body pressed intimately against his from chest to hip. "A lusty, insatiable monster."

Sabrina nodded, nipping at his jaw. He carried her to the ladder that led to the loft and put her down. "I think we need a real house with real stairs."

"But I like it here," she whispered, reaching to help him take off his shirt. "There are a lot of good memories in this old house."

He grinned at her, that slow, sexy smile that made her melt from the inside out. "How about we make some new ones?"

"Good idea." She stood on tiptoes and kissed the hollow of his throat. "But maybe you'd better turn off the stove first."

~~The End~~

About the Author

To learn more about Meg Allison, please visit http://megallison.bravehost.com/, you can also email Meg at meg_allison_author@yahoo.com.

Alex Rossi leads a double life, and it may cost Grace Nolan her son.

72 Hours
© 2006 Shannon Stacey

The Devlin Group: A privately-owned rogue agency unhindered by red tape and jurisdiction.

Grace Nolan walked away from the Devlin Group carrying Alex Rossi's child in her womb and his bullet in her shoulder. But a ghost from the past has kidnapped her son, Danny. The ransom—Alex Rossi. To get her son back, Grace will have to step back into the life she'd left behind and reveal her secret to Alex.

With vengeance for his mother's murder nearly at hand and a deadly substance on the loose, the last thing Alex Rossi needs is to find himself at the business end of Grace's gun. Now the clock is ticking as they race to save a child and stop a madman bent on destruction.

But Alex has a secret of his own, and it may be the ultimate betrayal.

Available now in ebook from Samhain Publishing.

Enjoy the following excerpt…

Alex watched her jump when he opened the door, her mouth opening in a quick exclamation of surprise.

She looked the same, yet so different. Her mass of chestnut curls was pulled back in a loose clip, and she needed no makeup to enhance those big sapphire eyes.

Her body had changed. Her breasts under the lightweight sweater were a little fuller, as were her hips. No doubt the changes lingered from giving birth to her son, but they didn't stop the sudden, hot urge to feel her body under his.

If anything, his want was intensified. The lean girl was gone, and in her place was a woman with a body to make a man want to come home at night.

He stepped back, giving her room to enter and close the door. It was only then he realized she was watching him as well. In his pajamas, probably still coated with the sweat of his nightmare, he guessed he probably made an interesting picture.

Alex watched Grace stare at his body, but he didn't let it get to him. She wasn't here to play. And she looked like hell.

"To what do I owe this pleasure, Grace?" he asked. He made sure the words were slow and lazy, but the back of his neck tingled in warning.

That was fear in her eyes. The list of things that scared Grace Nolan was pretty damn short, and he sure as hell wasn't on it. So what was?

"What are you doing in Key West?" she asked. Stalling—gearing herself up for something.

Instead of moving toward her, trying to intimidate her as he'd done in the past, he stepped back. He might need some room. For what, he didn't know, but he had a feeling he was about to find out.

"Just a job," he said. "It's me, remember? The guy who doesn't know how not to work?"

"Devlin told you I was coming?"

Alex nodded, hating the lie even more when looking her in the eye. "But not why."

She took a deep breath, and he noted the slight hitch. "I need to know…I need—"

Damn. Alex rested his hand on his hip, closer to the Glock tucked at the small of his back. This woman never *needed* anything, especially from him. But today…something was very wrong.

He blinked. Her arm moved. He blinked again, and found himself staring straight down the barrel of her Sig .38.

"I need you to get dressed and come with me, Alex."

He spent a few seconds eyeing the barrel of the gun while he slow-breathed his pulse rate down.

What the hell was Grace into? And who was she into it with? She was supposed to be doing boring-as-hell computer support for the feds, not kidnapping people at gunpoint.

He shifted his gaze to her eyes, and he found no give there. No doubt about it. He either had to pack a bag or incapacitate her.

"I want you to untie that drawstring and let your pants fall to the floor."

"Interesting foreplay technique, sweetheart. New since last time we were together, isn't it? A little rough is one thing, but this…"

"Let the pants drop, Alex. And let the Glock go with them." She knew him well, but he knew her, too. Oh, she sounded cool enough, but he saw the flush on her neck. Saw her nipples harden under the light sweater.

And felt the hot rush of victory. Game over.

With slow, deliberate ease Alex pulled the ends of the drawstrings loose. *Wait for it.*

He ran his thumbs around the front of the waistband, loosening it, and the weight of the Glock drew the silk fabric low on his hips.

Grace's eyes slid down to his groin.

He dove, launching himself at her midsection. He heard the air whoosh from her lungs as he swept his arm up and sent the Sig clattering to the opposite side of the room.

He managed to slip his hand under her head before it bounced off the floor. Grace was pinned under his body, and he squeezed his thighs together just in time to block her jabbing knee.

The Glock had slipped down into the leg of the pajamas now bound uncomfortably around his thighs, but he didn't need it. Didn't want it. He'd shot her once, years ago, and she probably still hadn't forgiven him for it. He hoped never to have to do it again.

He grabbed Grace's wrists and raised them over her head, stretching her body beneath him.

"Tell me what this is about, Grace."

"Get off me," she growled.

Alex saw the muscles in her neck tighten, and barely managed to dodge what would have been a nose-breaking head butt.

"Enough, or I'll put your ass to sleep for a while."

Grace stilled. She'd known him for years—long enough to know he never made idle threats. Staring up at him with those blue eyes, she trembled under him.

"Talk to me," he said in a softer tone. He had never seen this woman desperate. But she was desperate now.

"I need you to come with me. Please don't ask me why. Please."

"I *will* go with you," he promised. This woman who owned a piece of his soul was on the edge, and he sure as hell wasn't going to let her go over alone. "I'll go with you, sweetheart. But you do need to tell me why. And why the gun?"

Her throat worked hard to swallow and her eyes flooded with tears. Against his own skin he felt her stomach muscles spasm.

"What the hell?" He lifted himself from her and she curled into a ball, sobs making her entire body shake. He swore viciously. "What's the matter with you?"

He stood, letting the Glock slip through his pant leg to the floor, and refastening the drawstring at his waist. Then he dragged her to her feet. "Grace, dammit, talk to me now!"

She collapsed against him, and fear pumped adrenaline through his body. He held her for a second, then grabbed her chin in his hands, forcing her to look up him.

Her teeth chattered, and her body shuddered hard. "They took my son, Alex."

Samhain Publishing, Ltd.

It's all about the story...

Action/Adventure
Fantasy
Historical
Horror
Mainstream
Mystery/Suspense
Non-Fiction
Paranormal
Red Hots!
Romance
Science Fiction
Western
Young Adult

http://www.samhainpublishing.com

Printed in the United States
65012LVS00005B/1-120